SEABORNE

BOOK 2 OF THE TERRAFOLK TRILOGY

FRANCESCA CRISPO

IBSN: 979-8-9885719-2-6

Cover illustration by Melissa Hudson - www.mhudson-illustration.com

Editing and proofreading by Three Fates Editing - www.threefatesediting.com

Formatting by Nezhda Seyfulova - www.nezhformatting.org

CONTENTS

CONTENT WARNING

This book contains explicit descriptions of sexual activities; mention of infertility; betrayal by family members; mentions of sexual assault (in a flashback); and active war, including death/burial

To old friends and new; to found family; and to Mother Earth, whose arms have always cradled me in unconditional love.

SUMMER

CHAPTER ONE

EARWYN

$\mathcal{W}$atching your best friend die is a unique type of hell… So is dragging his giant body across the beach and loading it into an overpriced sports car so that you can take it into the woods for disposal. You'd think one or the other would've been more than enough. We hauled Firth's body off only after my wife had emphasized that we couldn't leave a dead body on the shore, and we couldn't call the police – we couldn't exactly tell them there was a war going on between magickal races for the sake of humanity.

"How about a cairn? So his grave is covered…" I suggested to the group, trying to determine the best way to keep his final resting place safe.

Zara immediately shook her head. "That's too obvious." She sniffled, then wiped her face with the back of her hand. "What if someone gets curious and digs him up?" The look on her face suggested that she was imagining just that. I didn't know exactly where we were in relation to the city, but the idea of a lost hiker – or worse, the authorities – stumbling upon the cairn was unsettling.

"A pyre then," Mycel said, not meeting my gaze. Instead, she looked down at Firth's lifeless body in the dirt. It probably felt strange to her to suggest fire when firefolk had caused so much trouble for us and because Firth and I hailed from the ocean, but it was the most logical choice. A pyre would ensure Firth's body was never found by nosy humans. It was fitting, in a way. In Ulmos, the dead are treated differently depending on their rank in the society. Someone like Firth, who was viewed as existing solely to serve the upper classes, would've been discarded carelessly, his body allowed to sink to the bottom of the ocean where sea life would feast on his flesh. With a pyre, we would leave nothing behind to serve anyone else; he had done more than enough while he was alive.

When no one objected, we got to work.

Rhodes and I scoured the woods for fallen logs and branches, then dragged them back to the clearing where Mycel and Zara moved brush and debris to give us our pyre a solid foundation. They spoke amongst themselves while they worked, but every time I approached them, their conversation died down. By the end of it, my fingers were raw with splinters, and sweat poured into my eyes as Rhodes helped me hoist Firth's body atop the mound of lumber, and we set the structure ablaze. I stood vigilant by Firth until every last bit of his body – from his short, dark hair, to his giant boots – and the pyre itself had burned to ash.

The finality of the situation hung over all of us, hung heavily over the earth as we watched the embers flicker in the dim evening air. Firth… he was supposed to live for much, much longer. And now, would it only be a matter of time before another one of our group was gone, cut down for our disobedience? Was it worth it?

I tried to swallow but found my mouth dry and painful from the heat. My lips threatened to crack. I was momentarily grateful that my hair had been forcibly shaved from my head; otherwise it would have been plastered to my face with sweat. As I stood there, I reflected on the centuries I'd spent with Firth as my best friend. Our adventures could've filled tomes. Firth had seen the tender, tortured sides of me I had hardly shown anyone. Selfishly, I wondered if I would ever know someone so dearly as I had known Firth. I couldn't compare it to my relationship with Mycel… It was just different, the type of friendship that societal expectations and stereotypes tend to stop most men from having. I told myself I should say something in his memory, but the words were hard for me to formulate, let alone force from my scorched mouth. "Firth was—"

"Don't say his name!" Rhodes growled, his voice so gravelly that it sounded like he'd never spoken before. He gave me no time to react before he swung a beefy fist at my face and knocked me to the ground. He had been silent as we scrambled to hoist his brother into the car, stoic as we'd built the pyre and put Firth onto it. He had even lit the match that set his brother ablaze, but now it seemed his tone had changed. He was moving through stages of grief quickly, and it was clear that he had no filter for expressing them.

My head rang, and my vision blurred as I looked up at my best friend's twin in bleary-eyed surprise. Pivoting from his burning twin to the very much alive version of the two had my brain feeling even more scrambled. I couldn't blame him, so I didn't bother trying to stand or fight back; in fact, I felt I was exactly where I was meant to be. There wasn't much fight left in me anyway. My tongue explored the inside of my mouth where I could taste the metallic tang of my own blood. I was still getting used to how easily I could be injured in my practically human state. My family had, of course, tested out my limits plenty prior to my escape, but it still took me by surprise after centuries of being almost immortal. I had not expected to be further injured at this point in our escape, and yet it made sense: in Rhodes's mind, someone had to pay for Firth's death. I would be paying for it for a long time to come.

Rhodes crouched next to me and grabbed the collar of my wetsuit, which had long since dried and stuck uncomfortably to my skin.

"There's nothing stopping me from kicking your ass now, *Your Highness*. Try saying his name again, and you won't get past the first letter." His eyes were glazed with angry, unshed tears, glistening with the reddish reflection of the fire's embers. Who could blame him? I'd kick my own ass if I could. He shoved me back down onto the ground, where my head hit the dirt hard and bounced off it with a crack. I groaned.

Then there was Mycel. She appeared in my line of sight like an angel, backlit by the dying fire, and reached out to offer me a hand in a perfect reminiscence of the night we'd met. Time and time again, she put herself out there, put herself on the line for me. She was beautiful, warm, loving… I offered her as much of a smile as I could muster and took her hand to get to my feet. When she met my gaze with a questioning look, I tried to reassure her. "I'm alright," I said, giving her fingers a squeeze.

"You're alright?" Rhodes asked, whirling on me again. Well, damn, wrong word choice again. "Of course you are. You've gotten everything you wanted." His nostrils flared, and it took everything in me not to flinch at the thought of being punched again. I braced myself instead, and anger coursed through me at my new softness. I'd been reduced to a wincing pile of human meat.

I glanced at Mycel and cocked my head toward her roommate, who was sitting on the ground near the pyre in tears. I told myself that Zara needed her more than I did. That was probably a lie, but how much could I expect one person to carry? She had already rescued me, all while pregnant with our child. I couldn't put my grief on her as well, even if I knew she would gladly carry it with me. When I looked back at Rhodes, my hands balled into fists at my side. Despite thinking I had some fight in me, I knew I had no chance against the other man if it came down to physicality; he had both magick and his size to use against me. "You think I wanted this? He was my best friend, Rhodes," I told him, though my voice was drained and passionless.

"Don't make me laugh." Rhodes scoffed. "He was a tool for you... nothing more."

"I can't help where he landed, what his status was in a kingdom full of monsters. I had next to no power there, and you know that." It was a pathetic admission. Perhaps I should've said it more quietly. Now everyone could add it to my list of soft human traits: flinching, meat bag, powerless. *Check, check, check.*

My words did nothing to convince Rhodes. "Do I? Maybe you had all the power in the world and just loved watching us slave away for your family. Was that your way of getting a little bit of control in Ulmos? Couldn't stand being ordered around, but at least you weren't the lowest on the food chain."

I didn't dignify his accusation with a response. To think that I allowed myself to be manipulated and abused by my own family for fun was outrageous. He was grasping at straws; Rhodes knew as well as anyone that the structure of the Ulmosi kingdom had very little to do with choice and everything to do with where you were fortunate enough to be born. Fuck the right people, be born to the right couple, kill the right competition, and maybe you can move up if you don't get killed instead. But if you keep your head down, you're stuck where you're at. I was the perfect example of that, and so were the twins. If anyone could have fought their way out of their circumstances, it would've been them, and yet they hadn't.

Instead, I kept talking. "Firth was the closest thing to a brother I'll ever have, and you know that. You can blame me all you want, but I would've done anything to keep him safe." My heart pounded painfully against my chest as I struggled to continue facing the other man. Why had I thought it appropriate to use the word brother? Was I looking for a fight? Not only that, but in the end, it felt like I had done nothing to keep him safe. All I did was hold him while the light left his eyes.

Rage flashed across Rhodes's broad face. I'd never seen such disdain in his twin's mirror image. "Yeah, well, he was my actual brother… and he's dead thanks to you and your…" He looked over at Mycel and Zara, who were now sitting together. The expression on his face was pure disgust, not that I'd ever seen this man exhibit a wide array of emotions before. My wife held her friend in her arms as she alternated between sobbing and attempting to blame her, just as Rhodes was me. Thankfully, they couldn't hear much of our conversation.

"Choose your next words wisely." I gritted my teeth, vowing not to let him lash out at Mycel and Zara when they were hurting too. I knew that Mycel was likely blaming herself already. It seemed a cruel joke that we'd all be punished so harshly just for trying to live our lives, for trying to do the right thing. Zara, on the other hand, was probably reeling from all the information she'd received since our wedding, let alone the fact that she'd just lost someone dear to her.

"Why? You can't do anything to me that would be worse than this clusterfuck." Before I could say anything more, he stormed off. There was no point in following him. There wasn't anywhere for him to go, especially not as an Ulmosi entirely new to land. I just hoped he wouldn't draw too much attention to himself. I glanced back at the girls again, and Mycel caught my eye with a look that said she was torturing herself more than anyone else ever could. Tears rolled down her cheeks as she held her friend and stroked her hair. When she looked away from me, my heart sank. We'd worked so hard, and for what? For loss, after loss, after loss. I thought of our unborn child. Would this child always remind me of Firth, who was taken from us as punishment for attempting to exist? Would they live in his shadow, a life traded for another life – that is if they even got the chance to live, at the end of this war? It seemed a cruel fate.

We sat in silence until the pyre had completely burned out. When all that was left was a pile of ashes, I asked Mycel for her blade. She cast me a questioning glance before tossing it to me and returning to her friend. The knife sliced through the sleeve of my wetsuit with little effort, exposing my forearm easily. Thankfully, my wife was distracted when I used it to cut a thin line around my wrist. I grabbed a handful of Firth's ashes, taking one last thing from him, and smeared the makeshift tattoo until the lines were black with ashen blood, then pulled my sleeve down over it as much as I could before we looked for Rhodes. It burned. It stung. It was nothing compared to the other sensations coursing through my body, but this new mortal pain almost served as a reminder of the fact that I was still alive.

When I finally stood and dusted off the legs of my wetsuit, I looked at Zara and Mycel.

"Let's go home," my wife said softly, taking Zara's hand in hers as they both got to their feet. I, too, longed for the comfort of somewhere familiar and safe.

"We have a lot to do," I told her, not wanting to limit the time we had to grieve and recover, but fearing for everyone's safety. Mycel gave me a look that said she'd stay up all night to plan if that was necessary, but I had to walk the line between wanting to take action and needing to care for my loved ones. "But it will still be there tomorrow," I said. "Let's rest. Let's find Rhodes and get everyone home."

CHAPTER TWO

EARWYN

The next day, I returned to the Odyssey building alone to gather my belongings because Mycel wanted to stay with Zara at the apartment. I agreed that leaving her alone with Rhodes was probably a bad idea and that they would both benefit from some time together; I knew how valuable friendship was and wanted to make sure that they had space to heal theirs, even if I would've rather been with Mycel. Being apart from them, however, led me to obsess about the details of our precarious situation. For example, we didn't know if we were being hunted. There had not been any blatant signs of my people coming after us, but their relentless pursuit of Firth in order to send a message was difficult to take as a one-time thing. If our group had been willing to risk our lives repeatedly, including one of us breaking into Ulmos, they couldn't possibly believe that we'd back down, even when they hit us hard.

We stayed away from the ocean, but knowing that Anala had been conspiring with them meant that they likely had other earth-dwelling terrafolk who could keep an eye on us: maybe firefolk, maybe other undercover Ulmosi, maybe even some of Mycel's people. It was hard to know just how deep it all ran. Every time someone looked at us for too long or a bird cocked its head to the side, my paranoia spiked. I wondered how many of the Salt and Earth Alliance's faithful employees knew where to find me. Firth had been the only one who knew where Mycel's apartment was, but most of them knew we'd been staying at the Odyssey. They knew my car; they knew my hangouts. Many of them had been humans truly invested in the mock cause we'd created, but others had been my people, sent to keep a close eye on me and build close relationships with people earthside.

It felt like we were holding our breath until they closed in on us. How long would we be peering over our shoulders? It's difficult to say with terrafolk; an abnormally long lifespan comes with a long memory. We could be careful for months, years even, then lose the game when we finally thought we were safe.

Acting before they could was our only option, but it was difficult to imagine that we could gather enough allies to effectively protect ourselves against Ulmos alone. They were so powerful, it was likely other terrafolk kingdoms would side with them. We were also unsure of Mycel's ability to return to her throne and people. The Yannavi had suffered, but it hadn't been through any fault of her own. Even so, they were clearly at risk of further harm now. When I thought about the challenges she had faced in guiding them, I couldn't imagine the immense pressure of having an entire group so reliant on you. I had been only in mock power in Ulmos. I was a puppet, a face for the ruling family, rather than someone actually making decisions. I truly believed that Mycel was now equipped to be the best leader for her people. The commitment she'd already shown to justice and doing what was right was more than I'd seen from most "good" people. If it came down to a fight, where would we stand? And would it come to that? If I was ready to die protecting my wife and unborn child, would that be enough to make a difference? The thought of my own death leaving them vulnerable to attack was troubling.

I slipped into the apartment as quietly as possible, trying not to draw attention to the fact that it had gone uninhabited for over a month. It was a shock to me that everything was just how we left it. No one had come looking for us here, at least not yet. Firth's bedroom door was closed. I stared at it for a few seconds, imagining he'd come out like nothing had ever gone wrong, but then I passed it without opening the door. I would need to go in eventually, but I wasn't ready. There just wasn't time for me to dwell on our losses. Instead, I grabbed a suitcase out of my closet and tossed some of my clothing into it haphazardly. Everything else could stay. After all, I didn't know where we were headed next or how light we'd have to travel. There'd be no place for fine suits, soft sweaters, or shiny loafers where we were headed, regardless. There was a time when they were a part of my identity in the human world; back then, I despised all the showiness, but now I wanted nothing more than to fall into that charade again. It would be so easy to have the right cologne choice be my biggest problem again.

When I noticed that the card I'd left for Mycel was gone, I stood and stared at my bedroom for a few seconds, remembering the last night we'd spent there. Even with the loss of our magick and not knowing what exactly that meant for us, those moments felt so much simpler. Facing the consequences of my decisions, looking into the future, it all seemed so far away… and the present had been delicious enough to savor. I could've stayed there forever, in my bed, with Mycel, and blocked the rest of the world out…

"Got your vows ready, wonder?" my fiancée had asked me, propped up on her elbow next to me in bed.

"Vows? I thought that was just a human thing." The horrified look on her face in response had made me laugh, and I failed to maintain the facade that I'd actually forgotten. In truth, I'd put a great deal of thought into them. "I'm joking!" I told her when I couldn't stand to see her panic any longer.

"You better be!" Mycel scowled, placing a hand on her chest as if to feel her racing heart. This made me chuckle a little more.

I couldn't help but wonder, though. "Why? What would happen if I didn't have any?"

She chewed her lip in thought. "Probably nothing. I'd still say mine… and then you'd probably feel pretty silly when your turn rolled around."

"Well, not to fear, I have mine memorized. Sorry for scaring you." I winked.

Mycel tapped her chin in thought, a mischievous twinkle in her eye. "How sorry?"

Mere moments later we were in the master bathroom, with Mycel bent over the sink in front of me. I reveled in her expression as I pounded into her – her parted lips, the way her eyes fluttered closed in ecstasy, her sweat-slicked neck and collarbones… My ability to put that expression on her face filled me with pride.

"Yes, yes, yes…" she panted, punctuating each of my thrusts with a cry of pleasure. "Mmph, I've wanted to do this for a long time…" She gripped the edge of the counter with one hand while the other kneaded one of her breasts. In the mirror, her gaze was now locked on to mine.

I wiped my brow with a hasty swipe. "Why?"

"So I can see your face – ah, God – so I can see your whole body," Mycel confessed, biting her lip as she raked me over in the mirror.

"Why would you want—"

"Turn to the side," she directed me, brushing her hair out of her face so we could pivot without missing a beat. She rested a hand on the counter still to steady herself, and we watched our reflections come together passionately, electrically.

Seeing myself plunge in and out of her like that sent a surge of heat through my entire body. It was raw. Carnal. I felt outside of my own body, as if I were a voyeur peeking in on my own intense sexual encounter. I almost couldn't watch for too long. Instead, I let my head fall back as I thrusted into her, willing myself not to slow down a little and catch my breath. My goddess was demanding, and I wanted to meet each and every one of her needs.

She caught me, though. "Don't close your eyes, wonder. Look at us. Look at you..."

"I don't see what you see, Mycel," I confessed, not able to meet her gaze in the mirror.

"No?" she asked curiously, reaching between her thighs to touch herself as she watched me. "That's a shame," she whimpered, "because I see your deliciously strong, solid chest... each chiseled muscle of your arms – God – look at your forearms when you grab my hip, when you thrust into me... I see..."

MYCEL HAD ALWAYS BEEN ONE TO BUILD ME UP, BUT THEN AGAIN, PART OF her wonder was that she truly saw the beauty in everyone and wasn't afraid to acknowledge it. I loved that about her. I glanced at my wedding ring and then back at the bed again with a sigh. How foolish it had been of me to think that I could live whatever life I wanted without consequence. The idea of heading back to Mycel and Zara's apartment was daunting, so I fished one of the pay-as-you-go phones we'd gotten out of my pocket and sent Mycel a message. The device vibrated with each letter I typed. After weeks without technology, I felt foolish typing away.

TEXT MESSAGE

Going to shower and change here so I don't look suspicious on the way out. Be back soon. Need me to get anything on my way back?

I gathered an outfit and headed into the en suite bathroom. By the time I'd stripped down and started the water running, Mycel still hadn't replied. There was no way that Rhodes would respond to me; in fact, I was pretty sure he had no clue how to operate the phone I'd given him. He found the sound of the ringer annoying and struggled to operate it with his massive hands. So, I messaged Zara next.

TEXT MESSAGE

I don't want to bother you, but can you tell me if Mycel is okay? She's not answering my messages.

TEXT FROM ZARA

She's OK. Asleep.

I couldn't even think of sleep, but Mycel, who had traveled the farthest on her own to rescue me and all while pregnant, certainly needed to rest. The image of her resting in her bed with Maz nearby gave me a momentary sense of peace. I thanked Zara and put my phone down on the marble bathroom counter. The person I saw staring back at me in the mirror was alarming: the short hair, the sunken cheeks, the bruises. I cringed as I took in my naked form and recalled all that it had been exposed to. How I wished my appearance had been a side effect of something more valiant, like war, and not just being treated like garbage by my own family. In Ulmos, I avoided looking at myself; I couldn't stand to see my face in the mirror or in the reflections of other people's eyes. I learned to look above them or past them when they spoke to me; the tone of everyone who addressed me there was enough to impart shame without having to face the judgment in their expressions as well.

The sound of the rushing water snapped me out of my daze, and I forced myself away and into the shower. I didn't want to linger. Gone were the days where I took my time enjoying the hot water or bougie pine-scented soaps; wooing Mycel couldn't be a priority when I hardly knew if we could keep ourselves alive. When my hands brushed over my prick – a part of me I'd hated for so long until Mycel came into my life – my head spun, and my heart began to race. Not in a positive way. Not in a pleasant way, but rather in a way that made Maren's cruel face flash before my eyes. I withdrew my hands quickly and rinsed off. Sure, my reunion with Mycel was passionate, and the sheer joy of seeing her alive and well had overridden the trauma of my time back at home, but now that we were earthside again, it lingered in my mind.

I dressed with efficiency, grabbed my bags, and went to leave. I had my hand on the doorknob to the front door when I glanced back at Firth's room. I needed to go in, but secretly hoped to skip it. It took a lot of convincing for me to turn and enter, and I held my breath as I did so, almost as if it would make me move faster. I rushed. Instead of taking a stroll down memory lane, I grabbed the small bottle of Firth's favorite cologne off the top of his dresser, wrapped it in one of his shirts, and stuffed it into my suitcase before pushing his heavy bed frame aside. Behind it was a safe that we'd built into the wall. Firth insisted on having it in his room so that I wasn't tasked with protecting our valuables; his need to be a protector showed in every aspect of his life. I emptied it quickly, stuffing neatly bound stacks of cash into my suitcase. Before slipping out of the apartment, I forced myself to grab a couple more articles of Firth's clothing; Rhodes had next to nothing to wear, and getting his twin's clothes was an easy fix, even if I wasn't in the mood to do anything nice for him. If we were going to leave the city and attempt to be untraceable, especially by my people, we'd need resources.

A bubbly voice called down the hall after me. "Mr. Ulman?"

I continued to walk toward one of the building's exits.

It came again. "Er, Mr. Ulman!"

When I realized that I was indeed Mr. Ulman – a last name I'd made up for work – I froze in my tracks. Mycel had laughed at the unimaginative last name. *"Ulman? Like Ulmos? That's about as creative as Michelle, I guess."*

"Yes?" I asked.

The chirp of the woman's voice grated on me. I didn't recall it having that effect on me before. "Oh, good, I'm so glad it's you! We haven't seen you or your—"

When I turned to face the building manager, a busty blonde middle-aged woman in a pencil skirt, she gasped. It appeared that my shower and change of clothing had done little to mask my exhaustion and weight loss. Was it the circles under my eyes? The hollowed cheeks? Or perhaps the change in hairstyle? Maybe she could sense the cloud of dread hanging over me. Well, at least it would stop her from flirting with me like she had every other time we'd run into each other.

"We've been out of town," I told her matter-of-factly, hoping that she'd let me on my way without any further small talk. It wasn't a complete lie. "I got married. Long honeymoon, you know." The last part could not have been further from the truth. It probably left the building manager wondering if my honeymoon had taken place in a prison.

"Oh… that's, that's great, Mr. Ulman. I just came to check in because…" She lowered her voice to a whisper, clearly trying to save me from some shame I didn't have. "Your rent is due, and we haven't seen it come through like it normally does."

"Strange." It wasn't.

"Yes, w-well, would you like me to contact Salt and Earth? Perhaps they can send the payment manually themselves." She straightened her skirt, smoothing out the front to avert her attention from what was likely a very awkward conversation for her. This wasn't the type of building where people missed rent. "They could send a check or use the portal… You know, some people find that easiest—"

"Perhaps they can," I agreed, keeping my tone neutral. "I'll let them know to expect your call." I wouldn't. I had no clue what kind of portal she was talking about. When I turned to leave, she didn't call after me again. As long as I could get back to Mycel, it didn't matter what happened to the apartment. We wouldn't be returning; I'd come to terms with that.

I pulled out my phone once more to request a rideshare on my way out of the building, and when it arrived, I slid in with my suitcase. In a city like Seattle, it didn't matter if you couldn't drive, and the Seattle freeze made it so that I never felt pressured into small talk while taking an Uber. The ride was blissfully silent, and I spent the majority of it checking my phone to see if Mycel had texted me back.

I arrived at Mycel and Zara's place to find Zara on the couch, staring into a bowl of what looked like had been cereal at some point. By the time I got there, it was a bowl of sludge with a few questionable bits floating in it. I wondered whether Mycel had convinced her to prepare food for herself or maybe she'd set that in front of her before lying down for a nap. Zara still had her dirty, bloodied clothes on from the previous evening on the beach. I said nothing, just nodded at her, as I entered.

Rhodes was nowhere to be found. That should've concerned me, considering he wasn't a very discreet person. He could've been lying naked on the beach or terrorizing small children for all I knew. If that was the case, we'd never see him again; he didn't know the girls' address to tell a police officer, nor did I think he'd let them arrest him without a fight. Still, I couldn't bring myself to give a damn.

My wife was asleep in her bedroom with her familiar, Mazus, perched on her windowsill and watching over her. He was puffed up and nestled into his own round little body, but his beady eyes remained trained on his person. In front of him remained the spread of collected odds-and-ends that had always been there; only, this time I noticed a new button. It was difficult to know what he was thinking since Mycel lost her magick. After putting the suitcase in her room, I ventured back out into the living room to hand Firth's shirt and cologne to his abandoned lover.

"Thought you'd want those," I signed to Zara when she looked up at me. It was no surprise that our paths to healing from the loss of Firth would look wildly different, but I knew that if I'd had a piece of Mycel with me during my imprisonment in Ulmos, I would've felt some comfort. Instead, I'd been left without her, without my wedding ring, without any trace of her touch or scent. It felt like she'd been completely wiped from my world. I wouldn't let Zara suffer in that way, especially not when Firth had felt so fondly about her…

"She's loud, Earwyn. Way too outgoing, the total opposite of me," Firth had told me after our first night hanging out with Mycel and Zara. "She practically hopped into my lap the moment we walked into their apartment!"

I'd straightened my tie while looking into the mirror. Firth stood in the doorway of my room as he often did while we talked. Even though his tone was critical, I could see the reflection of his face in front of me, so his grin wasn't as discreet as he assumed it was. "Uh huh," I nodded, hoping he would keep talking while I finished getting ready for a work meeting.

"Did you see how pushy she was? She pretty much dragged me inside!"

"So… when are you seeing her again?" I signed once the tie was secured.

"Tonight." He had laughed, unable to hide the pure joy in his expression at the thought of seeing Zara again. His happiness was infectious. "I left my number in her phone."

CHAPTER THREE

MYCEL

*E*arwyn woke me with a gentle touch and brushed away the stray hairs that had stuck to my face during my nap. Waking up to his face was a privilege I thought I'd lost forever, so I couldn't help but smile. "You're back."

He nodded. "Of course. How did you sleep?"

"I've had better naps," I told him with a wry laugh. "You know, when everything isn't falling apart in the real world. Besides, I probably should've been keeping an eye on these two." I gestured to Maz, who sat at his post on my windowsill, watching us as if he was trying to understand our conversation. Ember, the tiny red newt that had once belonged to Anala, had hitched a ride earthside when we'd left Ulmos and had spent her time since hiding in my clothing. Sometime during my nap, however, she had ventured out onto the windowsill next to Maz and was soaking up some sun through the glass. I hoped that Maz wouldn't get too curious about the taste of lizard.

Earwyn sat down on the edge of my bed, and I couldn't help but close my eyes to breathe him in. He smelled different from when we had dated. Somehow the absence of his cologne allowed layers of saltwater and the faint musk of his sweat to come through... scents that were at once comforting and foreign. I was uncertain about how they made me feel. I repositioned myself so that my head was on his lap, and he ran his fingers through my hair as he told me everything he'd gathered from the apartment. Discussing money and clothing was an obvious excuse for us to avoid the actual topic of our next steps, but Earwyn eventually broached it. "You mentioned Aolan a long time ago, before we were separated. Do you still have contacts there?"

"Contacts, sure, but that's it. I don't know if they'll be willing to help."

"I can't think of anywhere else to start," Earwyn said with a sigh, and it was clear that he'd been stewing over our options all day.

I nodded, thankful that he'd taken the time to think of our next steps at all. "Aolan it is. I'll start packing."

"I have to step out again for more support if we want to leave soon... and you have to talk to Zara."

"What are you doing, sprout?" Later in the afternoon, Zara appeared at the doorway to my bedroom as I sorted through my clothing, setting aside and folding up just a couple of outfits. I decided I'd take only what would fit in a backpack because our transportation was likely to change during this voyage, and I was certain it wouldn't involve a lot of cargo space. The thought was bittersweet. I'd never been one to collect much "stuff," but I also was not a minimalist; I enjoyed pretty things, and so did Maz. My heart crumbled a little at the thought of breaking his collection apart and having no way to explain why. I would bring it along, of course, but part of his collection was the importance of having the perfect spot to arrange and display his treasures.

When I looked from my task over to my roommate, I recognized the shirt she was wearing. It looked massive on her; it was Firth's. I bit my lip to choke back an involuntary sob and got back to work.

I held up a dress, the green, lacy gown that I had worn to Earwyn's winter solstice dinner, and sighed before tossing it into my "leave" pile. I wanted to do more than just sigh, to lash out, to burn the damned thing as if to say "I won't let you take this from me, I'd rather destroy it myself," but I simply didn't have the energy for such rallying.

"Packing. We have to leave Seattle, and it doesn't make sense for me to bring more than I can carry. You can sell most of this stuff if you have ti—"

"When are we leaving?" Zara asked, her gaze on the pile of clothing as if she were avoiding my own.

I didn't stop sorting through clothing, but silence hung between us for longer than was comfortable. I couldn't tell if she knew just how off her assumption was or if she was oblivious to the reality of our situation. We were leaving. She was staying. There was no way that I would drag her further into danger after she'd been seconds away from being executed just the night before. "You're staying, Zara. You have a whole life to live here, safe from the chaos that's come with… well, us," I told her honestly as I shoved another shirt into my bag with more force than necessary. When I met her gaze, it was impossible to read. Juggling everyone's emotions had become too much for me when I could barely manage my own. "Look… Zara…" I sighed, dropping my hand to my side. "There will never be words to explain just how sorry I am for all of the… sadness I've brought into your life. I just can't risk doing that again. I can't put you in any more danger."

Zara's lips pressed into a firm line before she spoke again. "How am I supposed to go back to normal life after this? You guys owe me." Her tone was clipped. I'd seen human movies like this, where people tried to abandon each other because it was "what was best for them." I hated those movies.

I hurried to get my thoughts out as quickly as possible. "I know we do, and this won't even begin to touch what I owe you, but we have enough cash to pay your rent for the rest of the year. You can take your time easing back into work and life and just let all of this settle. It won't ever be the same but—"

"Dude… I don't want your money." Zara scoffed. When I looked at her in confusion, she continued. "No amount of cash is going to make it possible for me to just… like, go back to normal life. You have to know how ridiculous that sounds…"

I tried to argue, even though it was pointless. "But, it's not—"

"Not what? Not safe?" Zara was starting to sound frantic. "Not safe, like living with the rogue heir to the throne of some mystical forest kingdom? Not safe, like falling in love with a man whose best friend is a traitor prince of… uh… another crazy ass realm? How about 'not safe' like helping you break into a freaking oceanic palace to rescue him? Or do you not remember how we basically had to drown you in the bathtub for that to happen? Tell me, Mich— Mycel" – she bit out my real name, clearly betrayed that she hadn't known it for so much of our friendship – "what has been safe about our friendship, about our lives together, so far? Aside from things like working in a restaurant together and eating Chinese food on the couch, which we can never do again." Her chest heaved as she argued with my silence. "If you think you're going to leave me here to – to… I don't know… to mourn Firth in an empty apartment until I can't take it anymore, then you've lost it. You think I'm gonna go back to slinging cupcakes after the shit you've put me through?"

"Zara…" What could I possibly say to that? I shook my head in defeat.

"I'm coming with you… and you're gonna fix this shit and make me your co-queen or something, okay?" For once, her humor wasn't really lightening the mood.

Before I could respond, Rhodes passed by us in the hallway behind

Zara and laughed to himself. I had secretly hoped for him to walk off into the woods and never return, but he continued to appear around my apartment without warning. He bit a piece of beef jerky he had likely found in our kitchen and grunted. "I'd say you owe her." He did nothing but eat since we'd gotten to the apartment; I shouldn't have been surprised at the amount of calories it took to keep a half-shark half-man running, but I was a little concerned about how we would afford to keep feeding him if he became a permanent part of our group.

I shook my head in frustration as I zipped my bag shut and flung it over my shoulder to take to the doorway. "Fine." There was no use arguing, though the prospect of having yet another person to try to keep safe was daunting. It was starting to feel like I already had a flock of fragile, vulnerable children depending on me. This was how rag-tag groups of friends were assembled for adventures. What a cliché. *Mycel, the Forest Princess! Earwyn, Prince of the Ocean! Rhodes, the shark-man! Zara, fierce human baker! Along with their crow and otter, they'll save the world!*

"Great, so when are we leaving?" Zara asked, following me out to the living room. "I bet I could pack up pretty quick. I need my makeup, though. Can't leave that behind… and my phone charger. Oh man, what do I tell my mom if she calls?"

"Earwyn is getting some last-minute supplies," I told her, not bothering to acknowledge her other comments. "Then it's up to Rhodes."

The giant had followed us out, thoughtfully chewing on his dried meat still, but his eyebrows shot up at the sound of his name. "What the hell are you talking about?"

I turned to Rhodes and rolled my eyes. "How else do you think we're gonna get to Aolan? Submarine? You think we're gonna take a leisurely swim?"

"Good one." He laughed, deep and throaty, before taking another bite and chewing it without bothering to close his lips. Gross. Firth would never. "I don't think your human friend is up for an under-water excursion. I mean, if you want her to stay alive." Rhodes looked my roommate up and down, then shrugged, before turning back to me. "Besides, I never agreed to drag your asses through the ocean again. You think I'm fast enough to outswim the Ulmosi army? The second we get in the water they'll be on us. Don't be an idiot."

"How else do you propose we get there?" I asked in annoyance. I would've also rather refrained from being pulled through the ocean at warp speed, especially given my last experience with it. But we needed to move fast, and I had proven to myself that I'd do whatever it took, even if it felt like I was going to drown in my own puke.

"I might have an idea. There's a boat I could get us on… It'll take us most of the way, but that hook-up is gonna cost you," he offered, eyeing me as if he were waiting for a reaction.

My eyes narrowed as I stared at the hulking heap of a man, feeling thankful that he was a jackass so he wouldn't remind me of our sweet, lost Firth. What more could I owe this man? How could I possibly be more in debt at this point? But I didn't feel like groveling or even negotiating. I groaned. "Talk to Earwyn about it."

Then, Zara piped up again. "Hi, member of the team here. Um, what's Aolan?"

"It's an island," I told her with a sigh as I plopped my bag down near the door. As I turned to head back to my room and scan it for any last items, as well as find a way to communicate to Maz that we were leaving, I added, "It's the only place I can think of to find allies right now."

"Oh, so they're friends of yours. Hell yeah!" Zara chirped, running after me down the hallway. Her giant shirt practically billowed behind her. While it was nice to see her in a mood other than absolute agony, I couldn't bring myself to share her excitement. The road ahead was daunting. "That means they'll be able to help us then."

"No," I told her sharply, turning around to face her once I reached my doorway. "They're not friends. Acquaintances at best."

"Well, are they nice at least? Because I'm pretty good at making strangers into friends."

"Absolutely not nice." I grunted, glancing around my room to see if there was anything else I simply couldn't leave behind. "I know you're good at making friends, but even you couldn't crack these people. They're only helping us as an apology for Anala."

"Anala, like… game night Anala? The one you used to hook up with?" Zara asked, clearly confused about how the woman played into all of this.

"Long story…" I crawled onto my bed so that I could hold a hand out to Maz, who was sitting on the windowsill in the sun. He had to know that everything was about to change. I wanted more than anything to collapse into my bed and wake up to find this was all a dream, to hear him greet me when I opened my eyes. That wouldn't be the same. When I brought Maz up to my face, he nuzzled my cheek, causing his little head feathers to fluff up. "We have to go," I told him. He tilted his head, his beady black eyes boring into mine. I couldn't tell if he understood me, but when I gestured to the hood of the sweater I was wearing, he hopped into it faithfully and without complaint. At least this was easy; at least there was one creature who wasn't hellbent on arguing with me. Once he was settled, I leaned over to the windowsill and swept all of his treasures into my hand, then dug a sock out of my "leave" pile, deposited the treasure, and put it in my pocket.

When I looked back at Zara, I continued. "She wasn't human… and she…" I trailed off, not sure how much to tell Zara when it could bring her to tears again. After all, Anala was at least mostly to blame for Firth's death. "She definitely contributed to this mess. I'll tell you the full story one day."

Zara looked at me curiously. "Um, lots of past tense there… what happened to her?"

The laugh that left my lips was cold and harsh. I couldn't think of a more eloquent way to put it, so I simply said, "Rhodes ate her."

Her dark eyes went wide, but then she shrugged. Perhaps being inundated with information about the existence of a magical race of people living right under her nose had desensitized her a bit. When she spoke, she seemed silly and optimistic again. "So… this dude ate a whole person, and he still can't stop snacking? Sheesh."

CHAPTER FOUR

EARWYN

The next day, we loaded ourselves, our familiars, and our earthly possessions onto a boat in the Elliott Bay Marina. I wasn't completely sold on the viability of Rhodes's "hook-up," but we didn't have any other options. Despite the frequent innovation of humans, boats always looked old to me. The particular ship that we managed to hitch a ride on was even more decrepit than some others: it was an old fishing boat that ran out of a bay in Seattle and was manned by a group of younger men who frequently made trips to and from Alaska for work. They were quiet, grumpy, and spent most of their time setting the boat up to take sail. They also spit and grunted a lot and all dressed the same. With how efficiently and interchangeably they worked, I honestly couldn't tell them apart. No one questioned our presence, nor did they ask why we were bringing several free-range exotic animals with us; one of them even shrugged at the sight of Genny, my otter familiar, in my backpack. She rubbed her scruffy face with her paws and then buried herself between my shirts again. I knew that she was itching to go into the water and swim, but with my magick gone just like Mycel's, I wasn't able to explain why she couldn't. Instead, I hoped that she could piece it together herself; Genny had always been bright.

"How did you manage this, Rhodes?" Zara mused aloud as I brought a few of our bags aboard. Aside from Mycel's roommate's haul, the rest of our luggage was sparse; Mycel and I each had a bag, and Rhodes had nothing, given his abrupt departure from Ulmos. I'd grabbed him a bit of his twin's clothing to tide him over, but that hadn't gone over well. Though, neither had me telling him that he wouldn't be able to walk around naked like he did in Ulmos. I held on to the clothing anyway. Zara, meanwhile, insisted that allowing her to bring her full makeup collection was the least we could do given the trouble we'd caused her. There wasn't much I could say to argue with that. In fact, I'd tested out a few lines in my head, and they'd all been big failures. For example, "I know your man is dead because of me, but I can't allow you the small comfort of your lipstick" and "That's right, I expect you to bring nothing but your deceased partner's t-shirt for clothing." Not great, so I let it go.

"Okay, so," Rhodes began, chewing a piece of salted, dried fish he'd snatched from somewhere on the ship. He chewed with his mouth open, the sinewy bits of flesh sloshing around as he spoke. "Basically, we have an understanding. I don't eat their fishermen when they're in the water messing with the nets and stuff… and they owe me one." Prior to hearing his explanation, I expected something much more creative.

"You made a deal… as a shark? Like, how did they know you weren't just… you know, a shark? How did you talk to them? Were they afraid of you?" Once she got over the horrific murder and the potential annihilation of humankind, Zara seemed genuinely enamored with magick and our way of life.

Rhodes didn't have a chance to reply.

"Never mind that. Since he's got arms right now instead of fins, maybe he can help move some of these bags instead of eating the crew's food store," Mycel commented as she stepped onto the boat. She looked as exhausted as we all felt and was toting her overstuffed backpack aboard with her while Maz rode atop it. He cocked his head and shrieked at Rhodes as if to say "You heard her!" I liked that little bird. I always imagined him as ready to talk crap or fight.

"Sheesh." Rhodes chuckled, jerking a thumb in Mycel's direction. "Miss Rogue Heir over here thinks she's in charge of us." He looked toward Mycel, leaning on the edge of the ship as he watched her load bag after bag onto the deck without helping. "Let's see if you actually make it to the throne before you start ordering people around, huh?" When no one joined in picking on Mycel with him, his expression fell, but he still didn't bother helping. He simply relocated to another side of the fishing boat, where he looked over the edge as he continued chewing his stolen snack. He eventually went silent as he surveyed the water, and we were forced to carry on without his help.

Meanwhile, Zara had dutifully taken a bag from Mycel's hands and was being led below deck to her sleeping quarters for the duration of the trip. The hostility on board told me this trip would either be very silent or very violent. And though the sea beneath us was bright and clear, the sun shining off of it as if to indicate a new beginning, I avoided looking directly into it as I crossed the walkway onto the boat. It felt too much like I might come face-to-face with my parents. The thought alone sent a chill down my spine.

* * *

WE GOT SITUATED AS WELL AS WE COULD, GIVEN THAT WE DIDN'T KNOW anyone else on the boat and had no clue how we would be received on Aolan. The day passed in a blur, and when the boat became quiet with people retiring to their beds for the night, Mycel and I attempted to do the same. We got ready for bed in strained silence, gracelessly dodging each other in the tiny quarters as we brushed our teeth and shed some of our clothing. My wife was brave enough to lie down in the tiny bed first, scooting herself to one side against a wall, and I hesitantly lay next to her after there was nothing left to busy myself with. I'd never felt hesitant about anything with Mycel before, but now everything was delicate. I wanted to pull her into my arms and hold her close. Wordlessly, we lay together, our breathing eventually synchronizing. I turned to look at her in the dim like of the cabin and smiled a little. She put her head on my shoulder, and I let myself relax for the first time in a long time.

THAT EVENING I WOKE TO SHOUTING UP ON DECK AND THE SPACE NEXT TO me in our shared cot, empty. Mycel was gone. I scrambled to put a shirt on and leave the sleeping quarters only to find Mycel going head-to-head with Rhodes, who was not only bigger and stronger than her, but probably more rested and definitely retaining more magick. How he managed to hold on to his, I still wasn't sure, but I wasn't going to take that advantage lightly. "What's going on here?" I asked aloud as I stepped onto the deck, moving quickly to put myself between both parties. I glanced between them through tired eyes and found a mocking expression on Rhodes's face, not to my surprise, whereas Mycel looked positively furious. The rage in her eyes alone made me flinch; I prayed I'd never be on the receiving end of her anger. It was a bold move for the man to be taunting her, especially knowing how much fury she was ready to unleash at any moment. Perhaps if he had been present for all of her speech in the throne room, Rhodes would approach her a bit differently.

"Nothing!" Rhodes laughed, pushing me aside with a meaty hand so that he could close the gap between himself and my wife again. He was chewing on something else now, and the smell of his breath caused me to stifle a gag. "Just asking Little Miss Mushroom here how she thinks she's going to get back into Yannava, ya know, without magick, with no allies, and oh, I don't know… after practically being exiled from her homeland. Minor details to you all, I guess, but they might cause some problems, don'tcha think?" He pointed a bulky finger at her.

Mycel's nostrils flared, and I saw fire in her expression that I'd never seen before; this differed from the ferocity I'd seen in her gaze in Ulmos. Then she'd been defending me, fighting for our child, and arguing with people who she disagreed with fundamentally. This felt more personal, somehow. "Yes," she agreed. "I came on deck to deal with my morning… er, night… sickness. It doesn't really matter. But Rhodes followed me up here to have a little chat, apparently." She snipped out the last few words in irritation. "A chat that involves a lot of questions that are none. Of. His. Damn. Business."

Despite their difference in height and power, Mycel didn't hesitate to get her face mere inches from his. The fact that Rhodes seemed unfazed made me nervous; ever since she'd confronted my family in Ulmos, I had a new respect for the lengths Mycel would to go in order to get her point across. Would she punch him? Try to poke his eyes out? Bring personal insults into this? I wasn't sure. Either way, it was bad news for at least one of them, if not all of us. One of the crew cast a sidelong glance in our direction before returning to his duties, the threat of becoming a shark snack enough to keep him minding his own business.

Rhodes rolled his eyes, and I felt anger rise within me. Who the hell did he think he was? The circumstances only earned him so many passes.

"Yeah, well, it kind of became my business when you and Prince Charming made your love story everyone else's problem," Rhodes said.

"That's enough, Rhodes," I commanded, stepping between the two again before Mycel could respond. It was a tricky line to walk, knowing that Mycel was one to fend for herself, and not really knowing where I stood with her since our return to Seattle. I figured that defending my pregnant wife was a safe bet either way. Who could blame me? "Leave her alone."

"Why should I?" He was glowering now.

"First of all, you're drunk," I said through gritted teeth once I was close enough to smell the liquor on his breath besides whatever else was knocking around in his foul mouth. Perhaps an allotment of rum had also been part of his bargaining. "And not that I need another reason, but she's pregnant. The last thing she needs is—"

Rhodes stood up taller and looked down at me, dwarfing my six feet three inches easily. I forced myself to keep my chin high and meet his gaze without fear. "What she needs isn't my problem, man," he growled, glaring. I couldn't believe this man was related to Firth, and his twin, no less! Firth would never, could never speak to us in such a cold, crass manner; not because of the difference in our status, but because he respected everyone, especially people he cared about. I doubted he could even think such a heartless thought to begin with. "Why should I care if you knocked up some—"

Before he could bite out the rest of his insult, which sounded painfully like something Maren would've said to us, he was soaring over the side of the ship. His huge body hit the water with a splash, and I looked over to see Mycel standing in his spot, breathing heavily; she'd run at him and used the height of the gunwale to knock him off balance and send him into the inky blackness below. The way her chest heaved and the way her windswept auburn hair stuck to her face made her look nothing less than feral, and boy, was I proud… and yet, I had no clue how to tell her that or anything at all, for that matter. My cock stirred at the sight of her fiery warrior energy.

When I peered over the edge of the boat, the fin of a whitetip shark pierced the surface of the water and swam alongside the ship. Rhodes was fine… probably pissed, but alive. I was undecided on whether that was the best-case scenario.

"I wouldn't bother with that," I told a shipmate who was propping a roll-up ladder onto the side of the boat. The act seemed almost mechanical. Someone had gone overboard, and he'd dutifully fetched a ladder, no questions asked. Apparently, it didn't matter that the "someone" could turn into a shark. "Maybe give him some more time to cool off. He can meet us at Aolan."

"No can do, not if ya want him to get there alive." The man grunted as he threw the end of the ladder overboard and it unrolled loudly, clapping against the side of the ship. "There are horrors in these waters." *Worse than Rhodes, and so close to the surface? There couldn't be.*

CHAPTER FIVE

MYCEL

*R*hodes left me alone after I pushed him off the boat. He didn't say what he saw under the water near Aolan, but I also didn't bother asking. Instead, he pulled his sopping wet ass up by the ladder and stormed off below deck, his fins still reabsorbing into his body as his naked figure disappeared into the darkness. Still, none of the crewmates seemed fazed by his outburst or his brusque nudity.

"Please, just come to bed," Earwyn begged me once the shark was out of sight. "You really should rest."

"I'll be okay."

"Mycel." His voice was firm now.

"I'm okay," I told him again. "I'll come down soon, I just need to… let my mind settle after all that."

I stayed on deck long after he'd gone back to bed, and I'd somehow convinced Earwyn to go back to sleep as well. I stood on the side of the deck and stared at the waves, black and foreboding as they'd always been to me, as the boat continued its voyage toward the island in the distance. I couldn't see it. In fact, I couldn't see much as I stared out into the night. It felt impossible to conquer the vast endlessness of the sea and those who ruled it. What right did I have to try? I felt tired, lost, worn down – and while the rocking of the ship amplified my body's fatigue, I knew that I couldn't rest if I tried. Instead, I attempted to brace myself and stay.

Maz chittered on the ledge of the boat before looking longingly at the water. Perhaps he wanted to try his hand at catching a fish or even just peering into the water for a change of scenery, but we both knew better than to risk it. Genny, Earwyn's familiar, was likely below deck with him, asleep in his cot. I wondered how it felt for her to be so dry and so far away from the environment that she was used to. But then again, like Maz, she was more than just an animal.

I reached out to scratch the bluish-black feathers on Maz's head with a single finger before leaning forward on the gunwale of the boat.

That was when I saw him.

Just there, beneath the inky surface of the waves, a young boy swam effortlessly. He looked so comfortable in those endless sooty depths, much like I'd imagined Earwyn when he was younger, or when he'd still spent a lot of time in the water. It occurred to me then that in the entirety of our relationship, I'd only seen Earwyn – who had spent most of his life underwater – swim once, and that had been during our escape from Ulmos. As the little boy skimmed the surface of the sea, the light from one of the porthole windows below reflected off of his shimmering gills, iridescent and glowing. Beautiful. I was mesmerized.

Maz cocked his head to the side as if he were trying to follow my gaze.

Before I could wonder whether I was dreaming, the young boy floated on his back in the water, looking up at the night sky with a look of pure wonder on his angelic face. He could not have been older than four. His strawberry blond locks floated around his face like a halo of fire, and he laughed, so loud and warm that I could feel it in my chest, as he said, "Hi, Mama!"

Next to me, Maz looked startled. Could he hear him, too? Perhaps I wasn't just imagining things. Either way, I didn't care. I would happily spiral into this madness for a bit of relief.

"Sweet boy," I breathed, barely above a whisper. I spoke to him as if we'd known each other forever. After all, how else would the term of endearment come about so easily, as if I'd been saying it daily for years? "Come out of the water; it's not safe." I felt as though he was just out of reach, but so in danger as the depths stared blankly up at me. I could only imagine the horrors beneath the surface.

He giggled again, his eyes sparkling with the reflection of the light and moon above him. "Oh, Mama," he said, almost as if my words had been preposterous. His laugh was so joyful, so bold, that it almost transferred to me. "That's not true! You always keep me safe."

Before I could reply to him again, Maz was suddenly pulling the sleeve of my shirt with his beak. His intensity amplified, and he let go only to squawk loudly at me before pulling again. His beak tore at the fabric of my sleeve.

"Maz, what is—" I was about to shoo him off of me when the vision in the water changed, and below the little boy swam a looming, dark figure of colossal proportions. Its glittering eye looked up at us through the mirage, and I knew that this creature was real even if the child wasn't. I gasped. This was what my nightmares about the ocean were made of and… it could see us clearly. It was hunting us.

Maz pulled me again until I stumbled backward across the deck of the boat, caught off guard by the loss of Maz's guidance and the rocking of the ocean, which I still hadn't become acclimated to. Earwyn caught me right before I landed on the wood of the deck, and Maz was immediately on my chest, staring intently at me as if he wasn't sure I was right in the head. I was also unsure.

I wanted to protest and tell them both to leave me alone, but I didn't have the energy. Instead, it felt good to let myself collapse into Earwyn's arms and to hand off some of the weight I'd been carrying, even if it was only literally.

"What happened? What's going on?" My husband looked down at me, and in his gaze, I saw the mirror image of the young boy from the water: sharp, intense features that had been softened by the boy's age; deep, turquoise eyes; and a thoughtfulness that I could see even in the face of the little one, despite his lack of experience with the world. I reached out and touched his cheek, and I was certain he thought me crazy, but I couldn't help myself. The looming darkness deep in the water had been concerning, but all I could focus on right then was what was before me.

"I saw something in the water," I finally answered as Earwyn helped me to my feet. My own voice felt foreign to me, far away and entranced.

Maz, ever stressed by our communication barrier, remained on my shoulder until my husband reached out to him. "Let's give her a little room." The bird dutifully hopped over to Earwyn's shoulder, where he still kept his gaze trained on me. How I wished I could hear his thoughts again and know if I was completely hallucinating. He had heard the boy's laugh too, hadn't he?

As much as I wanted to rush to the edge of the ship again and peer into the water in hopes of seeing the boy again, I complied when Earwyn suggested I try to sleep. I knew he wasn't real, so he wasn't in real danger, but still my heart longed to see him again. At the same time, I didn't want Earwyn to be even more worried about me than he already was. I had to be stable, had to be a functioning member of our group, and I couldn't do that if I was hallucinating.

Our cabin below deck was small – a vacant crew cabin with bunk beds, a small bathroom, and a small desk. It had a single porthole window, through which we could see nothing when it was so dark out. The dark blue carpet of the room was scratchy against my bare feet; everything about being in or on the ocean felt foreign and uncomfortable to me. In comparison to Earwyn's old place, or even Zara's and my Seattle apartment, the room was microscopic. To think that people went for months on end holed up on a boat made me question the sanity of mankind.

Zara was asleep on the top bunk in the room, so we didn't bother turning the lights on as we entered the room and squeezed into the slightly larger bottom bunk. I wasn't sure where Rhodes had ended up sleeping. Probably with another member of the crew who shared his affinity for alcohol and vulgarity. I couldn't imagine him fitting into one of the bunk beds, so he was probably passed out on a table somewhere. Hopefully he'd put on some clothing for the sake of everyone else on the boat. Either that, or the crew would come down for breakfast tomorrow to a very unpleasant surprise.

Maz perched himself on the back of the chair at the desk, and once his panic subsided, I knew he would find a way to nestle onto my pillow next to me or sleep in the sink of the tiny bathroom. I left one of my shirts in the sink for him to lie in and put the sock with all of his treasures on the tiny counter next to it as a temporary spot for his collection. I hadn't seen him collect any treasures since he left his windowsill back in Seattle. I'd promised myself, because I couldn't promise him yet, that we would find a spot for a new one once we were somewhere safe… What else did he have that was really his?

I slid under the thin covers, almost as scratchy as the carpet, without protest. Earwyn tucked me in, but when I realized he didn't intend to join me, I grabbed him by the sleeve and pulled him down next to me. We threw the covers over both of us, even our heads, and whispered in the dark like small children staying up past their bedtime. The act alone made me feel some small sense of home and comfort again. It had been such a long time since I'd indulged my childish side. I loved that Earwyn let me get there without worry or fear; he was both my playmate and protector, indulging me and shielding me at the same time. He would be that for our child, too. I knew it.

"It's a boy," I told him suddenly, stifling a yawn. I could still see his sweet, soft face in my mind. Its resemblance to my husband sent a pang of longing through my heart: longing for safety, longing for resolution and reconnection. "I think."

"Who is?" Earwyn asked through the dark, whispering along with me.

"Our baby. I saw him."

My husband didn't question the soundness of my statement and instead, asked, "What was he like?"

I thought for a moment of how to describe him. "Lovely. Happy. He knows we love him." But had I known, until that moment? He'd shown me that, despite the unexpectedness of his existence, despite my fear for his safety, he already had a home in my heart.

Earwyn leaned forward to press his forehead to mine. He didn't ask how I knew or what that meant for us; instead, he just closed his eyes with a smile. Their sex didn't matter, but it was nice to know more about this person waiting for us… nice to know that he felt protected, that he had faith in us despite knowing nothing of the world he was coming into. My husband placed a hand on my belly, his rough fingertips snagging the fabric of my top as he flexed them against my body. We slept, and for once, I didn't dream. Instead, I fell into silent, soft sleep. That encounter, however brief and unimaginable, with my son had given me some peace. Not only that, but it reminded me that we had to carry on. Perhaps we wouldn't be quite as fearless as our sweet son, but we could try.

CHAPTER SIX

EARWYN

Our journey by sea lasted three days, and by the time Aolan was in the distance, we were itching to get off of the ship.

The island of Aolan rivaled my homeland, not necessarily in extravagance but in sheer beauty. The land was staggering, with rolling hills and a massive, looming volcano in the distance. Built into the mountainside and scattered along the shore were stunning villas, sleek and modern with floor-to-ceiling glass windows that faced the sea. Sunlight reflected off the water and back toward the glass, making the whole island look like a beacon of shimmering light. The isle was littered with fire-fueled technology in the form of lighting, entertainment, and more. This technology, along with the decor of each villa, meant that the island was a balance of both modern and natural features. With how luminous it was, it was a wonder that more humans didn't stumble upon it. Then again, I wasn't familiar with navigating the sea by boat and had no clue what it would take to find the island while sailing.

Because the ship was manned by humans, the fishing boat dropped us miles from shore, and we were forced to row ourselves there in a smaller dinghy that hadn't seen use in years. Whether this was a rule created by the humans or an understanding they had with the Aolani was not clear. By "we were forced to row ourselves there" I mean I had to row us there because Rhodes refused to do anything but kick back and relax, my wife was still fighting nausea, and we decided to keep our non-magickal passenger near the middle of the group in case we needed to protect her. I wasn't sure how Zara made it past what seemed to be a force field of magic, but we all held breath as our tiny boat moved through it. Zara was oblivious and simply marveled at the ocean beneath us, which was so clear we could see small critters on the sand of the ocean's floor. When I spared it a glance, my heart ached, but getting any closer than we were seemed dangerous, what with the sailors' mention of horrors and my own fears about the Ulmosi finding me if I got into the water.

When I looked up, Mycel was watching me. She offered me a sad smile as if to say she felt my pain too. Who could understand home-sickness, longing to be part of something that violently pushed you away, more than Mycel? But then the way the ocean breeze brushed her hair out of her face filled me with warmth, and I resumed my rowing without complaint. If I couldn't find home in the ocean, I was being reminded that it sat right before me in the form of a woman so soft and sweet that she radiated her own sunlight. I let myself soak it up.

Zara eventually broke the silence of our lengthy trip, probably bored of the creaking wood beneath us and the stifling silence. "So, uh… is there anything I should know about these… people?" I looked over in time to see her squinting at the island in the distance, her hand over her eyes in a makeshift visor. None of us had considered what it might be like for a human to walk onto an island full of magickal people. We'd spent so much time doing the opposite.

"Like what?" Rhodes snorted, then resumed picking something out of his teeth before flicking it into the water. The urge to push him off the boat like Mycel nearly overtook me, but I told myself that it might cause the boat to flip and then we'd really be in trouble. Did Zara even know how to swim?

"I don't know, like, customs? Do they have a king or… a president? Do I need to bow? Are they going to try to kill me because I'm human?" Zara looked between us to gauge our reactions. "You know, just minor details… that I would… like to know beforehand…"

Rhodes sucked another piece of food off his finger after picking it from his teeth. He opened his mouth to speak. "Well—"

Mycel shot Rhodes a look that told him to shut his trap before she shut it for him, and he grumbled before crossing his arms over his chest; it was clear he had been planning to set Zara up with some sort of prank, but the state of things was too tender for any sort of foolishness. "No," Mycel told her calmly, closing her eyes and breathing deeply to steady herself. "You don't need to bow. They have a king and queen. They won't kill you." When her eyes opened again, she caught my gaze. I wondered if she was about to make Zara a promise about keeping her safe, just like I learned she had made Firth… "As for customs," she continued, clearing her throat a little, "just follow our lead, though it's mostly common sense: take what they offer you, be gracious, don't make a mess, don't be weird about the way they do things. You'll be fine."

"We want them to like us as much as possible," I added, fatigue starting to set into my back and arms. "If there are allies for us here, we need them… As of right now, Aolan has stayed out of dealings between humans and terrafolk. So far it's served them well, so—"

"So they might not want to get in the middle of it," Zara finished for me, sounding downtrodden by the realization that allies would be harder to find than we had expected. In fact, it would be much easier for the rest of the terrafolk to pull back to let Ulmos and Yannava settle the score once and for all; most terrafolk didn't have much of a stake in the human world, nor did they want to.

"It'd be smart of them not to," Rhodes said with a grunt. "If they really care about their people."

Our pitiful human rowboat scraped the shore of the beach less than an hour later, bringing noise into our painfully silent trip. I helped everyone but Rhodes – who carelessly shook the boat, stomped onto shore, and left us all drenched in the wake of his size sixteen boots – out before turning toward the island only to be met by a row of Aolan's soldiers. They didn't bother with manual weapons and instead were manifesting another force field of magick around us. I could feel the heat radiating off of it and put a hand out to stop Zara from walking any farther while my other arm shot out protectively in front of Mycel and landed on her belly. A fly buzzed by and fried itself on the force field immediately as if to prove my point. Ah, nature. How every insect on the island hadn't been zapped to death by these invisible force fields, I wasn't sure.

"Thanks," Zara muttered, swallowing hard as her gaze followed the dead fly into the sand where its crispy little body settled.

Mycel placed a soft hand over mine.

Before any of us could protest being held hostage by their bubble of flames, a stern *tsk-tsk* broke through the force field. "Is that any way to treat guests of Aolan?" a full, hearty voice came. The soldiers split in half, creating a makeshift path for the king of the island to walk down. He was short, perhaps half a foot shorter than myself, and stocky, with a barrel chest and thick, muscular arms. When we were finally face-to-face, it was easy to see that his lighthearted demeanor did not reach his dark, serious eyes. "Down," he instructed the guards, causing the hot buzz of magick to vanish immediately. The soldiers of Aolan were a well-oiled machine, withdrawing their magick in effortless synchrony and resuming their at-ease positions until further notice. All men, they wore nothing but leather pants. They looked almost identical; with shaved heads and muscular, defined bodies.

They stood barefoot in the sand, but seemed to be on top of it as they left no imprint in the granules.

"Ossian," I addressed him, inclining my head a little without taking my eyes off of him and his guards.

Ossian regarded me with a curious gaze. "Earwyn. Mycel. And..."

"Rhodes," the tallest man grunted, not bothering to extend a hand. His ability to give absolutely zero shits about his appearance was truly enviable, as little as it did to further our cause. Instead, he was eyeing a few of the local Aolani women who were climbing trees to gather coconuts. He had no shame.

"And this is Zara," Mycel added. I could appreciate that she didn't bother adding any additional details about who Zara was or why she was with us. Besides, introducing her as "Zara the human roommate" didn't seem quite right.

Zara's lips pressed into a line in response, discomfort radiating off of her in waves. What a gracious bunch we were: squirming, ogling, or grimacing as we met the royalty.

"We don't mean to intrude," I began, unsure of exactly how this interaction was supposed to go. It seemed obvious to me to jump into the details. "You know that Ulmos is—"

"There will be plenty of time to talk politics tomorrow, Earwyn of Ulmos," Ossian said suddenly, cutting me off in a way that made me feel effectively quashed. The title made my skin crawl. Again, his judging gaze betrayed his true feelings. "For now, get settled in. Eat. Rest. Tana and I will see you in the morning." When he turned away, he put up a hand to gesture to his small army, and the soldiers turned and retreated with him, moving so gracefully that they hardly left prints in the sand. The ocean, so vast and powerful, felt like a prison to all it surrounded. We lived on the same sand, ate the same fish, and yet, we were divided by our alliances. I couldn't think of a single group of people who would've welcomed us with open arms at that point.

* * *

THAT NIGHT, WE STAYED IN WHAT APPEARED TO BE A GUEST VILLA. IT WAS built like a cabin or dormitory with multiple small rooms that all led out into a common area. Rhodes's and Zara's rooms were across from ours. The common area consisted of an open, outdoor seating arrangement surrounding a crackling fire pit, as well as an outdoor kitchen with as much food as we could've dreamed of. All of it appeared freshly sourced, from the bowls of various fruits, to dried pork, and filets of different seafood that lined the fridge. In addition, there were a variety of glass bottles in the fridge and on the counter, varying in size, color, and opacity. Firth and I had hardly cooked during our time in the apartment, despite its extensive variety of cookware and appliances, but this lineup made even me want to give it a shot.

"Blaze… brandy? Oh, I gotta try this," Rhodes muttered to himself as he read the handwritten labels on each bottle. His complete disregard for safety was alarming. Before I could comment, however, he grabbed a bowl of nuts and an entire platter of food from the fridge, stuck another bottle under his arm, and made his way back to his quarters. The only thing that was missing for him was the company of a woman, I thought.

Zara watched in amusement.

"Maybe wait and see if you hear him choking to death in there before you try anything," I told her, only half joking.

I had turned to haul our bags into the other room when I heard her call, "Wait, what?"

"If he dies," I called back, "just avoid whatever he was eating!"

Mycel and I retired to our room in silence, and she undressed without a word, slipping beneath the cotton sheets of our bed in just her underwear. I could see the tension radiating from her body and wanted desperately to soothe it, but we felt miles apart. We were keeping our relationship barely afloat with a passing touch here and a whispered sentiment there, but the toils of our relationship so far would've been enough to drive any other union apart. I longed for the days where Ulmosi turmoil was a thought in the back of my mind and I could distract myself with galas or hikes with Mycel, rather than facing them head on.

A fire flickered at the foot of the bed, this one buzzing with magick unlike the appliance in my apartment. Those had been simpler times, and the facade had made them comfortable; I was learning that living in reality, aligning with truth, was a painful fight. Authenticity did not come without consequence. The flames illuminated the bare flesh of my wife's back as I slid into bed next to her, hesitant to crowd her. I reached out and traced the sparse freckles on her skin, connecting them like constellations in the night sky, and felt her melt a little under the tips of my fingers. When she leaned back into my touch, I introduced my other hand and kneaded her tired back until she was clearly asleep.

"I love you," I told her quietly, pressing a kiss to her wild mane. "More than all of the stars in the sky."

CHAPTER SEVEN

MYCEL

"We can offer you a place to stay, for now. Food, clothing, resources while you're here," Tana told me the next morning as she sat cross-legged on her throne, barely acknowledging me before jumping into her boundaries and limitations when I walked in. She had the same high-class air as Maren, but none of the stuck-up attitude. In fact, Tana was one of the more approachable leaders I'd ever dealt with; it was clear she could be hot-headed, sure, but she didn't mince words. Although, Maren could've been the nicest person ever to my face, and I still would've wanted her to rot at the bottom of the ocean. Tana toyed with the end of her long, wavy mane, and she delivered the information, her nonchalance at our life-or-death situation rubbing me the wrong way. There wasn't anything I could do about it.

"For now?" I asked, slightly surprised. I couldn't expect anyone to offer us endless, unconditional refuge, but having limitations put on our stay from the start did not bode well. Hospitality seemed in short supply as of late, so I told myself to get used to taking what we could get and then moving on.

Tana nodded, not taking her attention off of the ends of her hair, as if she were inspecting them. "The moment you bring danger to Aolan, you'll be asked to leave." In this context, I knew that "asked" meant "forcefully removed if necessary." Again, I couldn't blame them, but I found myself disappointed in the finality of her wording.

War was inherently dangerous, and many leaders would not be willing to put their people in the way of that danger. I knew what this meant. "There's no chance for allyship between Aolan and our family," I commented. "You'll take the side of Ulmos over ours?"

"We will take Aolan's side, as we always have. You may look down on neutrality, but when your entire world is surrounded by the ocean, it's best not to make enemies with those who inhabit it." My expression must have betrayed my feelings, because she then added in a softer tone, "You know we have no dealings with the humans, Mycel. Their existence means nothing to us. To fight a war for the purpose of protecting them when they won't even know it, won't even change their ways because of it… It would be foolish to risk the safety of our people for such a thing. We wouldn't even get as involved as much as we are if not for Anala's egregious missteps."

I scoffed. "Missteps? Certainly, that's one way to describe attempting to overthrow multiple kingdoms at once all for the sake of self-advancement. Did you know what she was planning all along?"

"No." Tana's jaw clenched, and she turned her attention to her hand, where she pretended to be preoccupied with inspecting her nails rather than conversing with me. "And nothing I say is going to change what she did."

"No, but what you do can change the impact it's had," I insisted. If I couldn't pull it together to speak up now, I would never be able to.

"Enough!" Tana snapped, the flickering torches at either side of her throne bursting with light momentarily. I stood strong and made sure not to flinch, knowing that it was all just a show of her power and her short temper. It pained me that we wouldn't be able to harness this energy when it came down to it. For a moment I pictured Tana breaking a nail and setting an entire army on fire in her irritation. Like Anala had said, we needed fire.

"It's not just about the humans," I argued, annoyance bubbling deep within me. What use were connections if they wouldn't come to your aid? Like I had told Zara, though, these weren't our friends. Not even close.

Tana shrugged. "There isn't a single cause that will convince me to risk the lives of my people for the humans. Not revenge… not even bringing you back to your throne."

I threw my hands up in exasperation. "It's not about the throne, Tana!" I didn't care about the seat or the crown or the title. This was bigger than the formalities associated with being in charge. I didn't want to rule anyone; I just wanted to protect them.

"Not – a – single – cause," Tana snapped, gritting her teeth.

"Understood," I choked out finally, inadvertently cradling my belly as I spoke. We stood in silence for longer than was comfortable, until I finally dared to ask, "Where do you suggest I look for allies then?" When Tana raised an eyebrow at me, I continued. "Assuming I can even regain the loyalty of my people, that won't be enough if Ulmos decides to wage war. You know that. They could surround us, and we'd be helpless, even with Yannava's weaponry and magickal skill. We need more than just our kind."

"Maybe Barrow," Tana said with another shrug.

"Barrow? Barrow, Alaska? An island off the Pacific coast isn't close enough to care about humans, but you think terrafolk living in the middle-of-nowhere-frozen-tundra-land will?" I scoffed, my emotions running high. What could Barrow possibly give us? One lone lumberjack with an ax? A beluga whale with an attitude? Whatever it was, their population alone indicated it wouldn't be enough when it came down to numbers; an additional terrafolk or two, no matter how passionate, wouldn't make a dent in the Ulmosi army.

Tana laughed at my comparison. "They have the most varispirits of all of us," she noted. "Besides, they're living with the humans up there. Even if there aren't many of our kind in Alaska, they're closer to them than either you or I will ever be, with the exception of your little pet." The dark-haired queen jerked her chin toward the door as if she could see Zara's villa from her throne, and I rolled my eyes. Zara was not my pet.

"Speaking of pets," I muttered, reaching into the sleeve of my shirt. I pulled out Ember, the small red newt that had somehow managed to tag along on our adventure so far, and set her on the ground. Normally, I wouldn't dare call a familiar a pet, but it wasn't my familiar, and its connection with Anala made me feel less than friendly toward it. We'd saved the little critter; that was enough. Turning her over now meant that she would at least escape Maz's curious beak. Ember scurried across the floor in a panic and up to Tana, where she waited for a silent gesture that she was allowed to crawl up into her pocket. "Thought your people might want her back."

Tana glanced at her pocket and then back toward me. "I suppose it's not the fault of the familiar when one of our folk goes rogue, though I can't say what will happen to her without her person."

I decided then that I had to release my need to save everyone and everything. I could not worry about the fate of this stupid lizard.

I would probably worry about the fate of that stupid lizard.

CHAPTER EIGHT

EARWYN

Ossian and Tana eventually escorted us to our own private and presumably semi-permanent villas, as close to the shore as possible. They had a very structured system for how they shuffled and housed guests; I wouldn't have been surprised if they had a flowchart or housing map somewhere in their own lodging, which I hadn't seen yet. In fact, I wasn't sure where they slept. By keeping us near the shore, it seemed they wanted us easy to access if my people decided to come get us. No one in our group could blame them, but we weren't pleased with the possibility of being hauled off into the ocean by Ulmosi guards in the middle of the night. In fact, that thought alone made it difficult to rest; between us being doubly exposed and my still not having magick, it was all I could do to keep an eye on the shore while the people I loved rested. The ocean was in my nightmares frequently, which was an entirely new experience for me. To my dismay, they weren't balanced out by dreams of my son.

Despite the location, however, the villas were much like a resort. They were designed in a very modern manner, the likes of which I hadn't seen in any other native terrafolk land; it seemed our races favored older structures and classical buildings that echoed the structures found in nature. The Aolani, however, loved glass. I supposed it made sense considering glass was the byproduct of sand and heat, two things that they had a lot of. Each villa sported floor-to-ceiling windows that overlooked the ocean. Ours even had a small saltwater pool immediately off of the back patio where Genny was beyond pleased to take a dip. It had been challenging to keep her from the water with our inability to communicate, and I knew that she longed to swim, not only for the simple pleasure of it, but because her biology told her to. We unpacked while she spun through the pool, then floated on her back atop it in the first flicker of delight I'd seen since I originally left Ulmos. Maz watched her from the edge of the pool before daring to dip his beak into the water. Eventually, he hopped in and floated next to her.

Zara and Rhodes had been taken to their own quarters. While neither myself nor Mycel were concerned about Rhodes, I saw the worry in my wife's face when Zara was escorted to a building separate from ours. It wasn't clear if it was safe for her to be alone. Even so, we hoped that being away from the city and her apartment would help; what benefit was there to being in a society full of magickal people if you couldn't use it to take your mind off of things?

CHAPTER NINE

MYCEL

*L*ater that night we sat at the small dining table in our housing and made a list of all the allies we could think of. When it came down to it, there weren't many. We then mapped out the terrafolk communities that were close enough to make traveling to them worth it.

Washington State had other firefolk around Mt. Baker and the plethora of other inactive volcanoes in the area, but they were as spicy as Anala had been and were off limits because of their association with her. They would not be as willing to offer us resources or help in return for Anala's mistakes as the Aolani had been. It seemed fruitless to me to approach any other firefolk based on that knowledge and the Aolani approach of "neutrality," even if the others weren't on an island. Furthermore, disrupting volcano dwellers could quite possibly cause an eruption that would ultimately harm more humans and forests than it would help.

The Cascade Range mountain folk were widespread and far reaching due to the immensity of the range itself, but they were wild to say the least. They didn't live in big communities like many other terrafolk civilizations did and instead were more mostly nomadic along the mountain range, often living solo or with small groups of two to three families. To recruit them for the fight would take a great deal of convincing. For one, they were very high up, which meant that they would be pretty immune to most attacks from Ulmos unless the seafolk found a way to infiltrate water sources within the mountains. I couldn't see Ulmos thinking it was worth the effort to approach them. The Cascade Range folk were also skilled at foraging, hunting, building, and all-in-all were experts at caring for themselves with resources from the land and not much else. Finally, because they operated so independently, the likelihood of recruiting more than a couple of small groups would be slim. From what I knew about them, they didn't even communicate amongst groups and typically steered clear of each other while traveling; they used different methods to make it clear whose land was whose and avoided territories where other mountain folk had made their homes. Without even attempting to connect with them, I could guess that they had little interest in banding together with large groups of other terrafolk and even less interest in the humans, with whom they almost never interacted. It would've been unsurprising to me if the majority of the mountain folk had never encountered a human in their lives.

Last but not least, the water-dwellers of the lakes of the Pacific Northwest could have been an option, but Earwyn informed me that they had likely already been won over by Ulmos. Whether by actual convincing or by force and threats, it was hard to say. Earwyn and I had seen firsthand how they could infiltrate bodies of water like lakes and rivers and though it might cause them temporary discomfort to adjust to freshwater, it didn't seem to hinder their abilities in the slightest. We decided that if we came across any lake-dwellers, we would take the time to speak with them, especially because they likely did have interactions with the humans. Beyond that, we wouldn't seek them out. We were low on time as it was and needed to focus our efforts where we'd see the most results.

At the end of the night, our list looked bleak: Alaska, Aolan (crossed out), Yannava (with a question mark). As we reviewed our options for allies, I couldn't help but think how many hundreds of other terrafolk communities there must be out there. If the Pacific Northwest alone had this many, the continent had to be brimming. If we had more time, I could try to extend our reach. This also meant that if Ulmos won, if they made a dent in our team and had space to pursue the humans, the rest of the country's terrafolk would hear about it. We would divide. At that point, there would be no telling the fate of humankind. I laced my fingers around Earwyn's across the table, but couldn't find any words.

AUTUMN

CHAPTER TEN

EARWYN

We stayed in Aolan for as long as we were allowed because we needed time to figure out our plan of action. This ended up being almost a month. Unfortunately, plans of action were difficult to formulate, especially when all members of our team – Mycel and I included – felt divided. Zara and Rhodes, meanwhile, barely interacted with each other. Rhodes didn't really interact with anyone, actually. Zara occasionally connected with Mycel, who was trying to keep their friendship together in desperation.

The evening of one of our days on Aolan found me and Rhodes seated around a fire. Because the island was full of volcano dwellers, fire was everywhere: easy to come by, easily sparked if needed, and it fueled everything on the island. To magickal folk, this was fine. To a group of people who were all mortal or nearing mortality, it had us on edge; if you pissed off the wrong person, they might set you on fire.

On the bright side, sitting around the fire pits around the island was a nightly tradition for the people of Aolan, whether they spent that time talking, sharing legends and stories, or eating their dinner together. Rhodes fit in with the fierce, hot-headed inhabitants of the island. While they were wildly different from myself, Mycel also seemed to form a bond with them rather easily, even if it was just to keep the peace and keep us safe. Despite appearances, I had never been as good at schmoozing as Mycel was; it was almost like she could truly see into people's souls and understand their wants and needs. Zara, meanwhile, spent much of her time marveling at her new immersion into the world of magick and terrafolk. Both women, however, had long since retired to their quarters for the night when I found myself almost alone with Rhodes. I knew that Mycel simply couldn't stand Rhodes's vulgarity and the way he picked a fight at the drop of a hat, but Zara's absence was harder for me to dissect. She got along with the giant well enough, but sometimes I saw her face fall when speaking with him. Perhaps he reminded her of Firth just enough that it made her grief even harder to deal with. They were alike only in looks, which made it both easier and more difficult for those who loved Firth so dearly. Rhodes often seemed like an insult to his brother's memory, despite his vehement defense and passionate mourning of him.

I didn't wait long to start bargaining with him once the others cleared out. We were running out of time and felt less and less prepared as the days went on. If our current team was less than the number of people we had arrived on the island with, I had to know. I didn't know what I would do with that information, but it would certainly change things if we could no longer count on having a giant, magickal mercenary who turned into a massive, man-eating shark on our side. "I'm asking… no, honestly, I'm begging you to reconsider, Rhodes. We're going to need you with us when the time comes." We had already struck a deal for the boat to get us to the island, and I was ready to do whatever I needed to keep him with us, even if he was a pain in the ass. When it became a numbers game, we would need him.

"I have to stay," choked out Rhodes, his eyes red from exhaustion and taking too many liberties with the islanders' weed and booze. I'd lost track of how many days in a row I'd seen him with either a bottle or pipe in his hands. It was clear that he was attempting to drown his sorrows and even clearer that it wasn't working. I'd personally tried to steer clear of their libations, but had admittedly been drawn to the scent of one particular coconut-flavored liquor. When I was offered it for the millionth time that evening, I finally accepted and sipped it as we spoke. "I don't really have a choice, man."

"Rhodes, come on, it doesn't have to be like this," I told him. The young lady who had been sitting on the giant's lap, arms around his neck, eyed me warily. Her sleek black hair tumbled down her back, and her gaze, dark and deep, was among the most judgmental I'd encountered there. There was no doubt in my mind that he'd told her everything that had happened, including my role in all of it. Hell, she'd probably told every other person she knew all the gossip about our group. Why not? What other entertainment was there on an island in the middle of nowhere? But because I didn't feel like this conversation was any of her business regardless of what she knew, I gave her a curt nod and asked, "Would you mind giving us some space?"

Of course, she looked to Rhodes instead of me seemingly in an act of defiance. "I'll catch up with you soon, baby," he told her, then kissed her for longer than seemed appropriate given the circumstances. It almost looked like he was trying to fish something out of the depths of her throat while I waited. Gross. I thought of the way he was always eating and smelled like alcohol, then suppressed a look of distaste at their liplock. Maybe she really liked sharks. When the woman leaned in to whisper in his ear, he laughed in amusement and told her, "No, no, don't start without me. I'll be there soon." He watched her leave with a pleased grin on his drunken face, his gaze clearly following the swing of the woman's hips, before he finally returned to our conversation. "Listen..." He looked at me closely, bringing a bottle of ale up to his lips for a swig before he continued talking. "Earwyn, I don't hate you, okay? I don't, man. I think you tried… I think you tried to do what you could, and you tried to find happiness along the way, and you know, I get that, I do. Hell, I probably would've done the same in your position. I'm trying to find what happiness I can now, ya know?"

I breathed a sigh of relief, but it was clear he had more to say. Before even hearing it, I knew I wouldn't like it.

"But I'll never, ever forgive you." Ah, there it is. His voice was serious, steady, as if he hadn't been stumbling through words seconds before.

Silence hung in the space between us, heavy and oppressive and looming. The reality of hearing the words I'd assumed existed in Rhodes's mind, aloud, was staggering. I knew I made mistakes. Hell, if you're alive long enough, you're bound to. And while I couldn't bring myself to regret the actions that brought me and Mycel together, the actions that pulled me from the hellscape of Ulmos, it was difficult to hear that someone out there harbored such anger toward me… difficult to know that I failed my best friend so colossally to the point where people would be in pain because of his death for many, many years to come. I would, too, but I had taken that to just be part of my punishment. I nodded at Rhodes in somber acceptance.

Whether he didn't see my nod or he just had to drive the painful point home even further, I couldn't tell. But he continued. "I can't. No matter which way you look at it, you're the reason he's dead. I'll never see my brother again and… I just can't look at you anymore. Every time I do, I just wanna…" He made a gesture with his hands that symbolized strangling me. It was intense and lasted for far longer than necessary to get the point across. Then he raised a hand and slapped my imaginary face, the neck of which he was still fake choking. I was almost impressed. "There's no…" Rhodes shook his head as if he were searching for the right words, his voice wavering again. "This doesn't get resolved, man. That's just how it is now. I see you, I wanna knock your block off. I can't fight by your side, man."

"We need you, Rhodes," I told him, swallowing the pain I felt at his accusations. I swallowed my pride, too, and prepared to beg again. The validity of his words made them no less easy to face, but I needed to if I wanted any chance at resolution or at the very least, ensuring Rhodes was on our side when the time came... even if he was fantasizing about hitting me so hard that my head separated from my shoulders. "This isn't just about me and you. We have a chance to change things for our people... and you can choose what your role in that looks like." He didn't just have to be the varispirit that disposed of traitors or the muscle that intimidated others. He could pick his spot in the rebellion. "You can be the one to eat my parents if you want. I'll save that honor for you."

"Look at you, being all diplomatic. Your daddy would be proud of how easily you fall into the politician stereotype... And ya know, you are pretty darn convincing. But..." Rhodes laughed a harsh, cold laugh, and I felt the spray of his drink hit me in the face. I wiped it with the back of my hand as he continued. "I don't care about 'our people,' Earwyn, because they never cared about me. I don't owe those sick fucks anything, not even the gift of being the one to end their lives. And now that Firth is gone, I... I don't owe anyone anything, okay? So save the world on your own. I don't care if it goes up in flames. I'll be here, drinking and getting laid when it does."

I stared into fire for a few moments, appreciating the crackle of the palm wood inside of it, but still jarred by my new connection of fire to the loss of my best friend. Eventually, I finished my own drink and nodded at Rhodes, a solemn sign of understanding. Before I left, I dug into my pocket and pulled out the stack of cash I'd promised Rhodes for safe passage to Aolan and set it on my seat for him. As I got up to leave, he took another swig of his beverage and choked out what sounded like a sob mixed with cynical laughter. "They slit his fuckin' throat, Earwyn." I'd made it halfway back to the villa I was sharing with Mycel when I heard him call out again, "He never hurt anyone!"

I stumbled into the villa as quietly as my buzzed, fatigued, and heartbroken body would carry me. In our time on Aolan I'd regained the weight I'd lost during my imprisonment, all thanks to the generosity of our hosts. They missed no opportunity to provide us with fruit, roasted meat, and every fun bit of alcohol and weed we could possibly desire. Mycel hadn't partaken in any of the latter despite the reassurance of the islanders that "magickal babies can handle it"; as far as she knew, we weren't magickal anymore, so it wasn't worth the risk. The rapid weight gain also meant that I wasn't used to being at my normal size yet. I bumped into an intricately carved dresser as I made my way to the bed, where Mycel was sleeping soundly under the glow of a flickering flame on her night-stand. She looked soft and sweet and tired, a few stray strands of her auburn hair fluttered over her face with the cadence of her breathing.

When I turned away from the sight and sat on my side of the bed, I found that I was holding my breath. My shoulders trembled as I attempted to contain the onslaught of despair washing over me. When I finally sighed a heaving breath, it shook the bed, and as if on cue, I heard Mycel's sleepy voice behind me. "Wyn?" God, how long had it been since I'd heard that sweet nickname? When did I stop being Wyn and "wonder" to her? It seemed like forever.

I wanted to turn and drop all of my walls, to melt into her softness, but I couldn't face her. "Sorry to wake you, I just got in from talking with Rhodes. Go back to sleep." I was curt, even a bit cold. There was no mistaking that. I spent so long coping on my own, or coping with the help of someone who was now dead, that I didn't know how to let my wife in, to allow her to help me and me her. It wasn't her fault. This wasn't like me.

There was a moment of silence before the bed shifted with move-ment. Then, my wife placed a gentle hand on my shoulder, and it threatened to tear down any semblance of self-control I had. How could she do that so easily? And God, how long had it been since she'd been so close to me? Even in bed with each other we'd fall asleep together then settle on separate edges – ever since our return to earthside. Perhaps we were afraid of all that had filled the gap between us: pain, horror, suffering, death. I felt the outline of her wedding ring through the fabric of my shirt and recalled how she'd told me she never took it off. What had I done in my life to deserve such devotion? If I thought too hard about it, I'd convince myself I wasn't worthy of it and that I hadn't been worthy of rescuing; I avoided dwelling on it because it centered my own needs in a time when there was much, much more that needed attention.

"Will you tell me something?" Mycel asked me in perfect gentleness, the touch of her hand softening even more but not leaving me yet. Despite her intuition when it came to interacting with me, I didn't doubt that she was constantly walking the razor's edge in trying to figure out how to get close to me without pushing me away. It was an effort I didn't deserve and a strain I wished I wasn't putting on our relationship.

"What do you mean, Your Highness? What do you want to hear?" I asked.

"Anything. Everything. Tell me what's hurting your heart. Tell me what happened between the time I lost you and the time I got you back," she pleaded.

"There's nothing to say." A lie. There was so much we'd left unsaid because we knew that those discussions would be painful.

Silence again. "Perhaps without words then," she suggested finally, and soon she pressed snuggly against my back while letting her hands slide down my chest from behind. I grabbed one of her wrists and put my lips to it, savoring the feel of her pulse against my mouth. It was a sign that she was alive, that the world continued to be graced by her existence, and I needed that validation.

"Without words," I agreed, then replaced her hand on my chest and held it close, roughly, to my heart. Would she need words to understand me, to understand the agonizing ache within my earthly body? I was reeling, and still, despite the heaviness of our circumstances, I strained against the linen slacks I'd been gifted, ravenous with need for my wife. When I turned to look at her, she caught my lips with hers and kissed me softly. Her approach was hesitant at first, almost as if she feared I might break or become feral. I tangled my fingers in her tawny mane and wrapped an arm around her to pull her onto my lap, where I buried my face in her throat to hide the shame on my face.

The crash of waves echoed through the open windows of our villa, a rumble in the distance as a storm brewed. My agony felt reflected in the weather. When Mycel pulled my face up to meet her gaze, I held my breath again. The intensity of such a direct connection was too much for me.

"I miss you," she told me.

"I'm here."

"No," she said with a sigh, tracing my lower lip with her thumb. Her voice hovered barely above a whisper. "You're somewhere else. You're still in Ulmos. Come back to me, Wyn." Either I was that obvious in my detachment or she knew me too well, better than myself even.

"In Ulmos?" I mused aloud, wondering what assumptions had filled her mind when I was gone. Had she imagined my abuse? Seeing Maren, hearing her accusations, had surely done nothing for my image. I couldn't imagine what my wife thought of me following that shameful display. Perhaps now that the passion of our initial reunion was gone, Mycel would see me for who I truly was. I wondered how it felt to have a husband who had been overpowered, had been raped by another woman solely for the purpose of furthering a race of monsters. I shuddered, felt sick, and squeezed my eyes shut tight. I fought against the urge to pity myself, but it was hard to imagine what she saw in me.

"Come back," Mycel said again, a new fierceness in her gaze. She shifted in my lap, causing an involuntary groan to slip from my parted lips as she rubbed against my erection. When I forced myself to meet her gaze, she continued. "Stay with me. Here. Don't let your mind go back there."

I wanted to argue, to tell her what was happening in my brain, but the words seemed impossible to find. I feared that explaining myself would force me to relive all of it. "I—"

Again, she beat me there. "You don't have to explain anything. Just show me what you need."

I wasted no time in pulling her nightgown off and tossing it aside. When she was on my lap, naked except for her panties, I marveled at her body. Mycel of Yannava was soft and warm, her flesh supple and smooth. I kneaded one of her breasts, small but pert, while I leaned down to take the opposite nipple into my mouth. Her belly, only slightly rounder than it had been before we'd been separated, pressed against my chest when she arched her back. I reveled in the fact that it was me – my manhood – that had left her swollen with life, and that I'd given it to her passionately and enthusiastically. I throbbed and groaned as I hollowed my cheeks to suck her chest. Maybe I wasn't broken, maybe I wasn't the one at fault, even after the way Maren had emasculated me time and time again, Mycel helped me to feel triumphant and potent. Animalistic, even. Now she was telling me to show her what I needed, to follow whatever primal urges overtook me. I could do that.

"Goddess." My voice rasped when I pulled my lips off of her again. "Take my cock out."

I was shocked when she slid to her knees in front of me, not due to the gracefulness of her movement but the fact that it was promptly followed by her tearing the front of my slacks with ease. A button rolled across the floor. I chalked her unusual strength up to passion. Because I wore nothing underneath, Mycel had me in her hands within seconds and stroked me while looking me in the eye. Her gaze warmed me from the inside, and I panted as she worked me, understanding what each change in my breathing, each impassioned groan meant. I was about to surrender, to let my head fall back and enjoy myself, when I looked her in the eyes again. To my horror, for a split second I saw the cold cruelty of Maren's gaze flash in hers, and I panicked. "Stop!" I bit out, my panting now a byproduct of fear.

The way Mycel removed her hands from me as if I were on fire made my heart ache. "What is it? Did I hurt you?" she asked so softly, so tenderly, I may as well have been a child in her care and not a full-grown man.

My vision blurred, and I waited for the violent image to leave my mind, but it took its sweet time on the way out. "No, you didn't."

"I wouldn't, I didn't mean to," she told me, clearly mortified by my reaction and the suggestion that she'd ruined our first intimate moment in months. This was supposed to be our reunion.

"You wouldn't." My chest heaved as we sat there, face-to-face but miles apart still.

"I love you," she told me, her words sounding like a reminder to herself.

"You love me." I felt selfish. Bitter. Hollow. Angry that my past was ruining so much of my present and future. "I don't deserve your love."

"That isn't for you to decide, Wyn," she told me firmly. We sat in silence until Mycel's eyes raked down my body, where my erection lay heavily against my lap. The duality of the situation was stark. "Can I taste you?"

"No," I told her finally, swallowing hard. I was too raw, too vulnerable to give her access to me like that, to have her watching me as I unraveled. Whether she deserved it or not didn't even cross my mind.

I was supposed to show her what I needed, so I tried. "Get on the bed, goddess." When she complied, I choked out a surprised "good" and spun her around so that she faced away from me, her bare back pressed against my clothed chest. My cock, so hard it ached, pressed up against her ass. "Do you feel me? Hot and hard as stone for you?"

"For me?" she asked breathlessly, swiveling her hips so that her rear pushed back against me even more. I couldn't help but lean into the contact. My eyes fluttered shut.

"Only you," I told her, more confident in my love and devotion to her than I was in anything else.

"A gift, then," Mycel purred, transitioning effortlessly from comforting partner to seductive lover. Though with her, she was often both at the same time; our intimacy transcended just physicality and was drenched with emotional healing. "How will you give it to me?" She reached back to rake her nails along one of my bare thighs; what remained of my slacks had fallen to a puddle on the floor.

I pressed my lips to her bare shoulder, brushing her hair away as I kissed up her neck. "However I please," I told her with certainty. Then, I captured her lips in a scorching kiss, unable to control the groan that escaped from mine, and made quick work of her undergarments. They soon joined my pants on the floor, and I guided her onto her hands and knees in front of me. The position felt uniquely primal to me, almost vulgar, but it ensured she couldn't see me and that... That was what I needed. I needed her desperately, like water, like air, but I also needed her like this: with conditions and barriers to protect my fragile mind. I wasn't ready for her to have full reign over me. My hands explored the delicate curve of her hips, ran down the soft, sensitive flesh of her rear, until my fingers found their way between her thighs, where she was slick and warm for me. "Though perhaps I'm the one receiving the gift..." I mused aloud, running a finger down the damp slit of her cunt. Precome dripped liberally from my prick onto the floor beneath me.

Mycel leaned into my touch, impaling herself on my fingers as if she couldn't control her body. The resounding whimper caused my heart to race. "It's yours to do with what you wish, like I am," she said in breathless wonder. How could she submit to me so easily? She had only the faintest idea of what I'd been through, and that alone seemed dangerous, yet here she was, trusting me with her entire being. Did I deserve it? I withdrew my fingers. She must have sensed my hesitation, my fear in touching myself, because she reached between her legs to grab me and guide me lovingly into her without another word. I could see her toes curl as I stretched her and marveled at the way we fit together, perfectly but not without effort.

"Oh… God," I gasped, marveling at the sight of her taking me in, at the sensation of me filling her so exquisitely.

"That's goddess to you," Mycel purred again, stretching out so that her ass was right at hip level with me and she could look over her shoulder at me. Her fair skin was flushed, and the muscles of her back flexed as she pushed herself onto me even further before pulling off again. I took the hint and grabbed her hips roughly; she needed me like this. It was my duty to satisfy her.

We found our rhythm like we always did, and soon I was hammering into my wife as if I could find answers within her. I savored every sweet, sinful gasp that left her lips, every whimper, every "Wyn" and "wonder," and was relentless in staking my claim in her. I let my body take over because it meant that my brain would shut up, at least for a little bit.

"Wyn," my wife cried while panting again, glancing over her shoulder at me, her wild hair splayed across her cheek and back. "Earwyn!"

"Yes, goddess…" I was drenched in sweat then, droplets of it dripping down my chest, where my shirt had become unbuttoned, and decorating the curve of Mycel's ass. "Let the whole island hear it." I felt her clench around me as I angled myself to hit what felt like the perfect spot inside of her. When her first orgasm rolled through her body, I leaned forward to press myself close to her, kissing down her shoulder and back. "Just like that," I assured her. "I love how you squeeze me."

"Wyn! Ah, it's too good," she cried out, trembling. "Please…" We slowed, meeting each other with rolling thrusts until we'd caught our breath together. "Please," she pleaded once more, reaching between her thighs to grasp my balls and pull me deeper into her. "I need you to…"

"Not until you have at least once more, goddess… at least." The need to fuck, to pump her full of my come, was overwhelming and unrefined. It drove me forward without rational thought. But the way that I was reading her and pleasing her made me feel more masculine and in control than I'd ever felt. I brought her to the edge repeatedly, asking her to touch herself, then rubbing the sweet spot between her thighs myself until she came over and over again. When she was boneless and nearly delirious, I rolled her onto her side so that I could see her face.

"Wonder," Mycel pleaded again, her face flushed, her lips raw from her erratic breathing, and her hair plastered to her forehead. She was stunning. "Come for me."

"I need you with me," I told her, leaning forward to kiss her shoulder. I pulled her hand onto my bare, sweat-slicked chest. "Stay with me." The friction of her thighs squeezed shut on me made my head swim. "Squeeze me again, baby," I groaned. "Just like that, come on my cock like that." It felt vulgar for me to speak like that, to name things so ineloquently, but it felt necessary to combat the vulgarities I'd heard in Ulmos. I gripped my lover's hip tightly as I hammered into her, and when I came with a shuddering growl, I pressed my forehead into her shoulder and pumped every last drop of myself into her. When it felt like I had nothing to offer, I could at least give myself to her fully like this.

I collapsed on the bed next to my wife, my lover, the only person who had ever seen every side of me and still accepted my broken, tarnished self, and wiped the tears I couldn't stop from coming. What more could I have expected from her in that moment? Hell, in that century? Mycel of Yannava had given me all that she had and then more somehow. She surprised me by not missing a beat and pulling me onto her chest, where she stroked my hair and reassured me, "See how you please me?"

"How? How can you love me like this? You shouldn't. You can't." I wanted to argue, my mind unable to accept all that she gave me so freely.

"I can decide for myself if you deserve my love or not," Mycel told me sternly, pulling my face up so that we were looking at each other. The depth of her forest-green gaze captured me, as if pulling me into the foliage of an ancient wood. It was stunning and lustrous, too complex for me to fathom. She was calm, but firm as she declared, "And you don't need to understand it, you just need to accept it."

CHAPTER ELEVEN

MYCEL

Passionfruit, starfruit, Jackfruit… Why would they name a fruit Jack? Oh well, let's see how it tastes. Oh, wow, Jack, you're delicious! Okay, the star fruit is a star, that makes sense… kind of a boring name compared to Jack. I mean, that would be like naming me "Crow." Oh, could you imagine the embarrassment?

I hadn't heard the sound of Maz's small, ethereal voice in months, but when it floated into my mind that morning, I sat upright with a gasp. It took me a moment to brush my hair from my face and gather my wits. We were still in our villa in Aolan, yes, and the walls were crawling with vines that hadn't been there the night before. I'd have to figure those out later. Without stopping to examine them, I grabbed a robe and threw it on so I could explore what woke me. I spared my naked, sleeping prince one last glance as I flew out the door; I'd have to come back for more of that man later.

Will the passion fruit really make me feel passionate? Wow, alright, yep, I will admit it was named accurately. I mean, would it kill us to plant one of these trees in Yannava? Though I suppose the climate is—

"Maz?!" I rushed outside, not bothering to fully fasten my robe as I did so, and found my familiar standing on a plate of fruit that someone had gifted him. He pecked at each piece, tilting his head as he savored each flavor, then moved onto the next one. I had no clue how it was happening, but my heart was desperate for this connection, desperate to rediscover the part of me that had a relationship with my familiar. I stopped nearby and watched him with a hand on my hip. I couldn't help but grin. "Are you enjoying yourself, Mazus of Yannava?"

Completely startled, the little crow looked up from his spoils and tilted his head before letting out a sharp trill of elation. The way his dark eyes narrowed almost looked like he was smiling. *Mycel! I can hear you!*

"And I can hear you, you little fruit fiend!" I told him, putting out a hand. He hopped on, and I brought him up to my face where he nuzzled my cheek in contentment. My heart swelled as the fabric of our bond stitched itself back together, almost as if nothing had ever come between us; our friendship was so true that it couldn't be rattled by the passage of time or the presence of unexpected challenges. I smiled down at him before brushing a passionfruit seed from his small beak and setting him atop his plate once more. Despite the tension between us and the Aolani, Maz had obviously charmed some of the locals; I was glad to see him treated so kindly. Our catching up was cut short, however, when Earwyn's panicked voice sliced through the early morning air.

"Mycel!"

I looked from Maz, who I dearly wanted to connect to, back to the door of the villa where my husband's startled cries were coming from. "I'll be back, Maz."

It's okay! he chirped, hopping back onto his plate of spoils before distracting himself with them again. At his core, I supposed he was still an animal.

The sight inside the villa, however, was one I would not have imagined in my wildest dreams.

Well, maybe my wildest, most scandalous dreams.

In my brief time outside the building, the vines continued to spread until they crept onto our bed, where they bound Earwyn into quite a precarious position. I gasped as I surveyed the extent of their wandering, unable to do anything but gawk for the time being. He was still naked from the night before, only a sheet thrown haphazardly over his lap in his sleep, while his green captors had slowly moved to pin his wrists to the headboard above him. In a similar fashion, his ankles were restrained and pulled toward each corner of the end of the bed. He looked painfully beautiful as he struggled against his bonds, each muscle flexing with his resistance. Something about seeing him so on display caused me to stop in my tracks rather than rush to his aid; every event of that morning had me disoriented. In fact, it still felt a bit like I wasn't awake.

"Help me," he pleaded through gritted teeth as the vines continued their assault, meeting each of his attempts to break free with an even firmer restraint. Where were they coming from? What could I do? The last time I'd seen vines with this much energy, I'd been using them to knock Earwyn to the ground.

"Yes! Um, I… okay…" I scanned the walls, taking in the vines that were now decorating them and traced them back to Earwyn before realizing I wouldn't have to use my hands to pull them off. These were mine, duh. I shook my head, annoyed with myself, then crooked a finger at them. The vines stopped moving. It had been a long time since I'd been able to control plant life, and I'd gotten used to viewing them as their own wild beings with their own wild agenda. Slack returned to the tendrils holding Earwyn, and he breathed a sigh of relief. When I crawled up onto the bed to pull the vines from his wrists, I couldn't help but take a pause. If my subconscious had caused this, then… had I inadvertently tied my husband up? No, that couldn't be right. I knew enough about him to know that restraining a man with his history would be cruel, even with the best intentions. Perhaps the vines had just gone wild with the sudden return of my magick; if the return couldn't be explained, the abnormal plant activity was probably a fluke as well.

"I know that look." Earwyn studied my face as I knelt next to him and released one of the vines around his wrist.

I shook my head, trying to erase thoughts I'd had that aligned with his accusation. I continued working on the vines. "The look of confusion? You know, because I lost my magick and then we suddenly wake up and I can talk to Maz and you're covered in vines?"

"You can talk to Maz? Wait, no—" Earwyn shook one of his wrists free as I loosened the remaining greenery from it. "No, you know that's not what I'm talking about. That look of satisfaction… that look like you – you want me bound, you want me like this." His tone was defensive, accusatory.

"There's no look," I answered quickly, unable to meet his gaze as I worked to free him. The suggestion that I intentionally did this, was pushing his limits when we'd just reconnected, felt unfair. Not only that, but I had no clue where my resurgence of magick had come from, and its unruly arrival had me on edge. I was out of my element, literally. I struggled to undo a particularly stubborn vine, blood rushing in my ears, and threw my hands up in frustration. "I don't know what's happening! I wouldn't— There's no 'look,' Earwyn. I know better than anyone that tying you up would be a bad idea. The last thing I want to do is stir up memories of… ugh, you know what I mean!" I was frantic, rambling, but unable to stop myself. "I can't control what happened while I was asleep. I don't know if my mind got carried away or wh—"

"Wait." Earwyn grabbed my wrist with his free hand, effectively restraining me in the way he'd just been resistant to. I fought myself not to point out the hypocrisy. I bit my lip, unable to face him. My husband, of course, read me like a book.

"Look at me," he commanded, reclaiming some of the power that had been lost during our unplanned magickal interaction.

Then, we stared at each other in silence, any joy I'd felt with the return of my powers extinguished. I half expected him to reprimand me, though he'd never done so in the past. Then again, I'd never inadvertently subjected him to the horrors of his past in our own bedroom either, so we were experiencing an array of new things together that day. The vines had almost all since retreated when my husband looked at me and calmly stated, "Let's try it." I must have looked blown away by my shock, because he continued. "You're right. You've given me no reason not to trust you. You've helped me reclaim every dark, painful moment in my life so far… so if this is what it takes, if relinquishing control to you is what I need to do to prove to myself that you won't abuse it, then I'll try."

"Earwyn, you don't have to do this," I told him with a sigh, then rubbed my face in frustration after he let go of me. How many battles had he braved for me already, with so many more right around the corner? I always told myself that our bed would be a space of healing and reassurance. In my mind, that didn't involve the pushing of boundaries that had been created by trauma. It just wasn't necessary to add those hurdles when what we had was already working so well. "You can just know that I won't hurt you. It doesn't need to be a test… We've certainly had our fair share of gauntlets already. Why create one where it doesn't need to be?"

When he offered his wrists to me across the bed, my chest ached at his eagerness and the faith he so willingly placed in me. His expression was reminiscent of the day he had professed his love to me in my apartment. "I trust you." He lowered himself back onto the bed, as graceful as if he were in the water, and laid his arms down on either side of him. I marveled at his physique, thanked the gods for the rise and fall of his chest, and marveled at every dip and curve of his muscular body in the new light of the day. "Goddess?" he asked, when I'd been upright for far too long. He knew what I was doing because he added, "Admire me closer."

"Yes…" With a flick of my wrist, Earwyn's wrists were secured again, looser this time, and I was climbing on the bed to straddle him. I locked eyes with my husband, determined to be clear about how this was different from what he'd been through in the past. The safe, consensual exploration of his boundaries was a task I wouldn't take lightly. "I'd never hurt you."

He nodded. "I know."

I kissed him deep and slow, taking my time exploring his mouth with my tongue, soothing his racing heart as he lay there, bound to the headboard. The fact that he was hard and primed from just a kiss pleased me, made me feel like he was at least somewhat comfortable, and when I sat upright on his lap, I shed my robe. I, too, was laid bare before him and may as well have been restrained with the way his gaze held me captive. I told myself to lead with confidence and calmness, to guide him through these moments with the assuredness that it was safe and nothing would go wrong.

"Incredible," he said breathlessly, raking his blue-green gaze over my body.

Emotion surged through every fiber of my being as he admired me. What had I done to deserve the type of dutiful sacrifice that Earwyn so willingly laid down for me at every turn? I wasn't Maren, but neither were most of the people who could've loved him. What made me worth the effort? I bit back tears. "Kiss me," I told him.

"Where, goddess?" The slow smile that spread across his face caused my heart to race.

I didn't reply with words, just pivoted on top of him so that my thighs framed his face. Earwyn didn't miss a beat, buried his face between my legs the instant I was close enough, and he moaned deeply against my flesh when I swirled my tongue around the head of his cock. I wrapped a soft hand around his length while I sucked him hard and deep, slowing only to catch my breath when his tongue rendered me useless and trembling.

"Ah, God, just like that," Earwyn groaned and when he bucked into my mouth, I gripped his straining legs firmly to pin him down. I took him deep into my mouth, letting him hit the back of my throat, also working him with my hand so that none of his length went unattended, and savored each muffled groan that left his lips. When I pulled my mouth off of him, he hissed at the loss of contact, and I couldn't help but smirk a little. I turned to face him, straddling his muscled waist with my legs, and found his handsome face wet with his own spit and the dampness he'd caused in me. I kissed him hard while his cock pressed firmly against my ass. The way he throbbed against my flesh sent my heart racing; it made me feel powerful to have such an effect on him. "You taste like me."

"As I should, goddess. There's nothing sweeter."

I rocked back against him a little, savoring the breathless whimper it elicited. But nothing could compare to his reaction when I positioned myself over him, taking his cock's full length swiftly, as if my body craved it, as if I wanted to absorb him. Hadn't he wished to be consumed by my depths? I rode him with a tenacity that I didn't expect from my exhausted body, and he thrusted up to meet me in perfect rhythm. As his big muscles tensed and he strained against his bonds, I slowed my movements and savored the way his hair stuck to his sweat-sticked brow. I ran my tongue across the curve of his jaw, where more sweat gathered, and licked it clean. Every bit of him was delectable.

"Mycel…" he groaned, his biceps tensed as he pulled at the vines. All he had to do was ask to be let go, and I'd do so without question, without argument, without a moment's hesitation. He was probably more in control than I was. He was panting, watching me intently, but said nothing else. The way his blue-green gaze never left me felt so intimate it was almost intimidating.

"Yes, my love…" I rocked atop him lazily, savoring the way he filled me so completely, and kneaded my breasts as I looked down at him.

"You read me like a book." Our pace picked up, and again, I had him rapidly approaching the edge of a cliff when I pulled off of him without warning and leaned forward to capture his mouth in mine. He groaned into the kiss, his voice laced with delicious agony. "Does it make you happy, the way you can control me like this?" To my surprise, he didn't sound fearful or defensive.

"This is the only way I want to control you, my love," I admitted honestly, sucking on his lower lip. "Only when you're willing, only when it brings you pleasure."

"Only you," Earwyn told me as he panted, straining to get closer to me, and I saw the veins in his neck bulge as he fought against his leafy captors. The head of his cock brushed against me again, sliding smoothly between my slick folds, and my thighs trembled at the contact. "Please, goddess."

I knew I should be merciful during this, our first foray into a new and challenging domain together, so I reached back to grip him and slid him inside of me once more. I couldn't help the gasp of delight that escaped my lips as I did so, and when he groaned in response, I told him, "Come for me."

As if he had solely been waiting for permission, Earwyn's head pressed hard into the bed beneath us, and he let out a thundering moan. His cock twitched and pulsed as he emptied himself into me, my words alone enough to send him over the edge. "Ah, fuck…" he growled, "yes, goddess."

When all was said and done and my husband's come dripped down the inside of my thighs, I snapped my fingers and released him from the bed. I kissed his wrists tenderly and stroked his hair as we both came down from body-wracking orgasms together. This was only one facet of the complex gem that was our relationship; we could take each other back to our darkest places and shed light on them, bring pleasure and closeness and connection into them instead of harm. In fact, it was our duty as partners to do so instead of side-stepping every painful memory. Living for hundreds of years had, no doubt, given us many… but we couldn't allow them to dictate our time together.

When the bright midday sun shone into our villa, we mused at the unexpected reappearance of my magick via the aggressively spreading vines. "I don't know," I confessed, as flustered as he was. "Maybe I… dreamt it or imagined it somehow? I've never seen magick take from my subconscious and run with it. I mean, I've never seen magick this strong either… I almost forgot how to harness it, maybe because it's got a mind of its own." I couldn't help the wariness that came with its reemergence; after all we had been through and continued to face, suddenly getting my magick back felt too good to be true.

"*How* is it back?" Earwyn asked, leaning on his elbow as he looked over at me.

"Not sure," I murmured, then stood and chewed my ring fingernail. I wished Firth was with us for a plethora of reasons, but right then for his knowledge. He would understand why this was happening. Once we'd all come clean with who we were, Firth and I had spent a great deal of time discussing terrafolk lore and history. It was no surprise that he was beyond intelligent, but the fact that he'd read so many of the tomes lining the Ulmosi library walls came as a shock to me; with his interest in video games, beer, and food, he just didn't strike me as the researching type. Besides, he spent so much time protecting Earwyn, it was a wonder he fit in any reading at all.

When our magick started to fade, he was able to reference a similar account in a journal he'd pored over back home. This in-depth knowledge was also the only reason we figured out how to give me gills and break into the Ulmosi kingdom, though even that was a gamble based on one story he'd read in a very obscure publication. We lost so much when we lost Firth, and the twin he'd left behind was a pitiful looka-like with no similar qualities aside from his stature. Had Rhodes ever even read a book? Did he know how to read at all? Maybe that was why his magick was unaffected; the Ulmosi didn't think he was bright enough to use it for any big difference, so they left him to magickly steal snacks and woo women.

Back when we'd been safe and happy together, before Firth was even injured, we spent time bonding over his love of research and my love of our people. Fifth brought one of his books over to the apart-ment – a small, but bulky title bound in some sort of sea-leather – and let me borrow it without Zara knowing. We had to hide our identities from her for a good while because we assumed it was safest, so I kept the little book about ocean plant life under my pillow and read it before bed for weeks before returning it to Firth. With our departure, I had no idea where it ended up; it probably wouldn't have been trea-sured in Ulmos the way that he had loved it, but I didn't recall Earwyn having packed it when he went back to the apartment. It was a shame. Some apartment clean-up crew would likely find and donate it, thinking it was a book of fantastical, made-up plants, and not the invaluable tome of a magickal ocean dynasty.

"Neither of us have been back to Ulmos in a while," Firth had told me. "But I knew there was a reason I brought this with me, I just had a feeling it would be loved by someone on land." He held out the small book, which looked even tinier in his massive hands, and flipped it open. The parchment inside was perfectly preserved, and my mind couldn't comprehend how it stayed in such pristine condition while underwater. I bet Firth knew exactly how books were printed and bound and what they were made of so that they could survive the damp environment of an underwater library. Hell, maybe that infor-mation was in this very book.

"It's so pretty…" I mused, looking through the small pages, which were bursting with color illustrations of plants I'd never seen in my life. When I flipped to a page with a large, glittering plant that looked like holographic seaweed, I skimmed the words on the page. If I stared at the finely detailed drawing, I could almost see the shimmering purplish tendrils of the plant moving in the doodled water surrounding it. "Does this really exist?" I asked Firth, turning the book toward him. "It doesn't look real."

"Oh, Opanor? Yeah, it's real, but it's also really dangerous. It's practically kryptonite for seafolk. The pretty stuff is always dangerous though, huh?" Firth smirked.

When my insides rolled, a foreign sensation that made me feel like I swallowed the ocean, I couldn't help but yelp. It occurred to me then that Firth had never learned I was pregnant or he might've made the connection before I had.

"Mycel? What is it?" Earwyn asked when I went silent.

I placed a hand on my belly in wonder. "It's not my magick. It's theirs."

CHAPTER TWELVE

EARWYN

"Theirs? What do you mean by 'theirs'?" I repeated, unable to form a coherent question in response to Mycel's realization. The idea of one child alone had been a lot for me to wrap my head around, especially when I was so averse to the idea of procreation for so long. After all, that was my only purpose in Ulmos, and not only had I failed at fulfilling it, but the prospect of success horrified me to no end. Every time that Maren cornered and attempted to seduce me, every time she successfully took me to bed against my will, I imagined what those children might be like. In the horrors of my sleepless mind, they looked a lot like her. They were vain, cruel, and impolite. They were happy to carry out the bidding of their mother and grandparents. Not only that, but I imagined them killing me in my sleep. If my genetic donation had given them anything, it wasn't visible in the horrific imagery that my mind had cooked up. I had only recently talked myself through the ways that this child, this loved child, would be so different from everything I feared because of how his parents felt about him and each other. I shook off the thought that she might mean more than one baby and refocused. The theory that our baby could be the cause of Mycel's returning magick was one I hadn't considered.

Meanwhile, Mycel was wandering through her hypothesis aloud. "I mean, it would make sense, right? I can't imagine any kingdom can have say in a baby's magick… especially not one that hasn't even been born yet… and it's probably stronger than ours because, well, it's both of ours combined. I wonder if that means that I also have—" She must have noticed my hesitation, because she gave me a curious glance. "What is it?"

"If he's this mischievous while in your belly, what's he going to be like when he's earthside?" I asked.

Maz chittered nearby, as if he were joining in our conversation from afar.

Mycel looked at him and then back at me again with a confident smile, as if his commentary had included some sort of life altering advice. She gestured to the crow. "See? Maz says he's a perfect babysitter. He'll help us keep the little one from causing too much trouble."

The sound the bird made in response seemed oddly like laughter; great, my wife and her familiar were making fun of me. The bird's promise did little to ease my worries; after all, Maz was barely the size of a full diaper, so how much could he actually help with? I allowed myself a playful eye-roll, then tried to enjoy the fact that at least one of us had our magick back. That was worth celebrating!

We scrambled to get dressed to leave the villa and test out Mycel's newfound tricks on the land. It had been so long since either of us had been able to use any kind of magick unless it was carefully siphoned to us by other, more powerful terrafolk, that I was certain this was filling a huge hole in her heart. In fact, it felt like a win for both of us after such a long string of losses. Despite the impending end of the world, for a moment it felt like things might be okay.

I was still buttoning my shirt when Mycel blew past me to run out onto the beach, almost a blur in the air with how quickly she moved. The sun was high in the sky, and the island was warm and breezy despite the change in seasons; this was the exact weather that Earwyn of San Clemente, California would have loved. That life was long gone, but I could still appreciate the warmth of the summer sun on my flesh.

"Let's see what you've got, Your Highness," I told her with a laugh, leaning against a towering coconut tree as I watched my wife. I could almost forget everything we were up against if I focused hard enough on the present. Time even seemed to slow when she caught my eye then, with the sun shining behind her like a golden halo. A slow breeze took a few strands of her fiery hair around its nimble fingers, twisting them into the air. Daylight reflected perfectly in her gaze, dark and deep like a thicket of dewy moss. My heart hammered in my chest when her robe, barely tied at her waist, slipped a little from her shoulder and exposed her soft, freckled flesh; she looked like the ripest peach, smooth and supple, like I would be rewarded with a gush of sweetness if I put my lips on her. Mycel always radiated this beauty, but the fog of doubt had hung heavily over everything before me. I was grateful for a moment of clarity.

Maz watched her closely, too, curious about her newfound power. I couldn't imagine the relief he must have felt at their reconnection. Genny, meanwhile, kept an eye on us from a distance as she rolled in the sand. It was hard not being able to hear my own familiar, and it became more and more apparent to me that a life without magick was a life of isolation when you'd spent hundreds of years with that power. I think both the otter and I had to stifle our jealousy at Maz and Mycel's reconnection. If I looked too closely at Genny, I could see her gaze shifting into pure animal rather than the deeper bond we'd shared for so many decades. I hadn't heard of it happening before, but I couldn't help but wonder if familiars lost their connection forever if they were separated – physically or otherwise – from their person for too long. Would a bear familiar turn feral and kill its person if they were unable to communicate for long enough? I shuddered at the violent imagery my mind had whipped up. At least my familiar was relatively harmless.

I snapped from my thoughts when Mycel summoned our attention once more. "What if it's just a fluke?" Mycel chewed her lip as she looked up at another tree, skepticism apparent on her face.

I cleared my throat, amused by Mycel's suggestion. Hadn't her magick just had me bound and powerless? "At the risk of oversharing given our current company," I muttered, glancing at Maz momentarily, "I would hardly call your display of magick this morning a fluke. Come now, just give it a try."

The look Mycel gave me, dangerous and seductive as ever, nearly knocked me off my feet. Then she jerked her gaze over to Maz and spoke to him. "Yes, I can still hear you." She looked at me again, a hint of delicious teasing still in her forest-green stare. "You're right. I can do this."

A breeze blew past us again, and I felt a chill in my bones. The sea suddenly looked ominous – not as glistening and bright as it had been mere seconds ago – over Mycel's shoulder, as if it were keeping an eye on us to see what we were planning. She wrapped a hand around the base of another coconut tree and took a deep breath. Branches began to crack under the weight of what I soon realized to be rapidly growing coconuts. I looked up just in time to see one change from immature green to a husked brown, then snap and tumble to the ground. Before Mycel could withdraw her touch, several others followed. When they hit the base of the tree, some cracked open, spilling their sweet nectar onto the sand, while others rolled toward the edge of the water as if sprinting for freedom.

Nearby, Maz cocked his head at the onslaught of falling fruit.

"Watch out!" I reached out to grab a fruit midair, narrowly stopping it from landing on Mycel's head. The way she looked up at me between my arms caused my heart to skip a beat. The fruit fell from my fingers, landing in the sand with a dull thud, and I managed to confirm what we were all thinking with a breathless murmur. "You did it."

"I've never grown anything that quickly." Mycel sounded shocked and elated. "This is different." In the time I'd known her, I'd seen Mycel summon her fair share of living things from next to nothing: mushrooms, berries, other small plants. She had saved animals from the brink of death, like the rabbit during our hike. Back then, I didn't know that was the case, but once we revealed ourselves to each other it became obvious. Hell, now she was taking a small piece of me and creating an entire human from it. I was always impressed by her, but had to admit that I'd never seen anyone – even the most powerful terrafolk I'd encountered – cause something to grow so rapidly and in such a great quantity. She placed a hand on my chest and met my gaze again. "I really think it's him. I think he's doing this, which means…"

I must've looked confused, because she continued. "Which means there's part of *you* involved, so maybe I didn't just get *my* magick back."

My gaze wandered to the water, where Genny was once again rolling in the sand as close to the water as she could get without touching it. "That seems like a stretch, but stranger things have happened today alone. It's worth a try…" I mused, wondering what it would look like for Mycel to manipulate what had been up until that point my element. Perhaps this would open some doors we'd thought long closed; with Rhodes unwilling to help us, we had no allies with water magick. We had avoided the water for so long that I wasn't sure if it was safe, but I needed to know if we suddenly had some sort of advantage. I longed to reconnect with my home and took what small opportunity I had to do so. We walked closer to the edge of the shore, and when I turned Mycel toward the water, I ran my hands along her shoulders, then down her arms so I could help her position her hands toward the sea. Surely, water magick was a bit different from what she was used to, but even if she didn't need me, I needed this. "I don't think you should get too close," I told her. "But from here it should be safe. Just envision what you're hoping to do." I took a deep breath, and she copied me, then exhaled as she pushed her hands toward the water. "Now make it so."

To both of our shock, the tide rose, and the water in front of us ascended vertically before our eyes. As the tide pulled back into a sheer wall of water, colossal and majestic, it magnified the world inside of it. My breath hitched in my throat as I surveyed the depths of the ocean from the shore. I stared in wonder. Sparkling, crystalline blue filled with schools of shimmering fish and massive, coasting sea turtles encompassed the immediate space before us, and I felt transported deep into the sea. The ocean floor's soft, supple sands were littered with shells, seaweed, and scuttling critters all going about their day. How I longed to dip my feet in, to dig my toes into those blankets of grit. Nothing could compare to the sensation of gliding through the water nor the feeling of being so infinitely tiny in comparison to the life beneath the surface; it was humbling. No matter how much I hated the people who inhabited the ocean, it still screamed *home* to me. To see it so closely and be unable to run to it, to dive in, felt wrong. "Beautiful," I murmured on an exhale, still holding on to my wife's hands. It took everything in me not to sprint for the wall and let it envelope me.

Genny, on the other hand, was determined to admire up close. She zipped into the damp sand, merely feet away from the wall of water, and watched the fish swim by like a cat watching a bird.

"I get it, Wyn," Mycel said finally. "I get how it speaks to you." She looked away from her act of magick and back up at me to add, "Your son loves it, too." I wondered if he was rolling joyfully in her belly, and then I hoped, with all my heart, that it would be safe for me to take him into the water once he was born. Would he be a strong swimmer? For a moment the image of a little boy chasing fish and sharks through the water flashed in my mind. I wished I had seen Mycel's vision from the boat but knew that we'd be meeting that boy sooner than we could possibly imagine. Life has a way of happening to you, whether it aligns with your timeline or not. With the voracity that his mother possessed, I knew that this boy would arrive exactly when and how he wanted and not according to anyone else's plan.

Then, as if on cue, I was snapped from my homesick reverie.

"We're being watched," I told her, releasing her hands from mine to get a closer look at the water. At first, I was hesitant with my warning, basing it solely on a feeling in the pit of my stomach. Then, we both saw it. Fish scattered, and our portal of the ocean stilled momentarily before the gaping maw of a prehistoric monster, a liopleurodon, crept into view. Each tooth that lined its crocodilian mouth looked to be the length of my hand, at least, and as it came closer and closer to the edge of Mycel's oceanic wall, I saw one of its massive, empty eyes lock on to us. It was searching, seeking, hunting. Despite my bond with every living sea creature, I felt nothing familial when looking at this monster. Its gaze was soulless, as if it were being puppeteered by someone who was watching through its eyes from afar. It didn't take much to guess its intent; with a mouth like that, it could take our entire group out in one bite, and we'd no longer be an issue for the Ulmosi. The sight of the creature alone caused my stomach to drop. Had the sky darkened as well? It felt so. "Drop it, Mycel," I told her quietly at first before a sense of urgency hit me. "Let the water down before it gets any closer!"

"I can't! Genny's too close!" Mycel's hands shook with the effort of keeping the water upright, almost as if she were holding the whole ocean up with just her arms, while she stared at my completely frozen familiar who would be snapped up in an instant if she followed my instructions. She was my last connection to the ocean, and Mycel knew that we could not treat her as a casualty.

The maw moved closer.

I sprinted for Genny.

Maz squawked loudly overhead and dove for the otter, pulling her by the fur on her back until she complied and scrambled for the shore, where I hit the sand and pulled her into my body. "Now!"

The wall came down with a thundering crash, slapping the shore just in time for the creature to dive forward with it. Its massive head, as long as my entire body, crashed onto the sand next to me with a horrific snap of its jaw. The sound echoed through the air. I could only imagine how easily it would crush every bone in a person's body. Or perhaps it ate its prey whole. Its eye, colossal and vacant, locked on to me for a moment before it let out a wail the likes of which I'd never heard before. The piercing shriek shook the trees around us and vibrated the surface of the water so violently it almost looked to be boiling. I looked up in time to see a crowd of Aolani, led by their soldiers, pushing the creature back into the water with a field of fiery energy; it was being burned by staying too close and was shrieking in protest. As it retreated into the water with the returning tide, I imagined my parents watching us through its menacing gaze. Were they cheering it on as it closed in on us? Was there a single hint of remorse at their relentless pursuit of our demise? If anyone could summon a creature like this, it was my family. I had no doubt they were the ones behind its appearance.

Despite the sound of the waves lapping at the edges of the island, the air was still and silent. My chest heaved, and I held Genny close, gripping her tightly and digging my fingers into her dense fur. She had almost become a snack. I was clinging so acutely to my ties to the ocean that I hadn't even let myself imagine the rest of our group being devoured by that foul beast. What about Mycel? What about our child? Not only that, but what would this do to our relationship with the Aolani? Shit.

My wife, meanwhile, stood trembling, her hands hanging loosely at her sides as she stared at the water. Despite the joy of her renewed magick, I could tell she was rattled. All joy had faded from her fair face. Perhaps the realization that the safety of our group now sat on her shoulders was sinking in; without magick, the rest of us were useless against something as colossal and dangerous as the beasts being controlled by my family. Before I could check in with her, our audience broke the silence.

The Aolani guards turned to leave, and I had no doubt they were going to report to Ossian, who would probably delight in kicking us off his island. I could hear his stern voice in my head. We stared after them in silence, the sun shining off of their mostly bare shoulders as they pivoted away from us in unison. Again, they moved so swiftly that they seemed to barely touch the sand; I couldn't fathom having that level of grace. For a moment I considered running after them and begging them not to tell their king and queen what they'd seen, but it was pointless. Not only had we lost them as allies long ago, but we'd likely lost our temporary haven while in planning mode. Ulmos was closing in faster than expected, and there was no saying how quickly they would come for us now that they knew where we were.

I swallowed hard, staring at the space in the sand where the stalking beast had dragged its horrific body away in agony. I imagined being captured in its great maw, somehow kept unscathed until I was returned to Ulmos again, in some sort of sick, repetitive cycle where I got a little farther away each time before being returned to my captors. Despite Mycel's tender healing, I would never be able to shake the memories of my time there. A chill ran through my body as I remembered the day I'd been dragged into the water following our wedding... and all that followed it. Who knew what Maren could cook up if given more time to plan? As I stood there staring at the sand, I realized that I would rather be killed than forced to return, regardless of how weak that made me seem.

The voice that greeted me on the other side of my capture that day had been abrasive, shrill, and bubbling with faux enthusiasm…

"If it isn't my very own Prince Charming, come home to his fiancée at last!" Even the memory made my skin crawl. It was a surprise to no one that my parents had pushed our union so aggressively. Maren of Ulmos was the epitome of all that the kingdom embodied: greed, motivation, hunger for domination, and of course, vapid, one-dimensional beauty. It was hard to see the latter, even objectively, after all that I'd experienced at her hands.

"Maren." I'd coughed and sputtered as I was shoved onto the throne room floor, having been dragged through the ocean by my captor after months without so much as swimming. My lungs had burned, and the metallic tang of blood still coated my tongue. When I looked up to see my fiancée, Maren, through my dripping hair, I almost wished for death instead. It would've been easier. More peaceful. It was a stark contrast to where I'd been and how I'd felt brief moments before, with Mycel. That seemed to be my fate… if one moment was blissful, I would have to pay for it in the next. Where was my wife now? I hoped silently that she would get to Firth and Zara and keep herself safe. In my heart, though, I knew it was possible that others had closed in on her following my departure and that she was gone. The idea itself left me feeling devastated and hopeless, but I told myself to believe that they'd left her alone even if the purpose was ultimate malice. She had to be okay. Otherwise, what motivation did I have to persist?

The future queen of Ulmos stared down her pointed nose at me, careful not to incline her head too much lest she stoop to my level. "Looks like we interrupted something important, hmm?" She gestured to my clothing, my wedding attire, which was now sopping wet, stained, and torn. I knew by then that my ring was gone; I'd felt it slip from my finger in Mycel's last attempts to hold on to me. "Not to worry, though, we can fix that!" With a snap of her fingers, I was being hauled off again by another Ulmosi guard who couldn't give less of a damn that I was the prince of his kingdom and followed promptly by Maren's chambermaids.

Maren faded into the distance as I was carried off; the way she watched me, unblinking, made me fear for what I would face afterward. Her gaze was much like that of the liopleurodon. "Maren!" I called. "Don't do this! We can talk!" The shame I felt in having to beg for my own personhood in what was supposedly my own kingdom was immense and sickening; it was the same begging I'd heard from prisoners before they were publicly humiliated and ultimately executed. I tried to gain the attention of the maids that were flanking me, but they were dead-set on avoiding me as well. This had been planned down to the second. Maren had coached them, and in that coaching, I'm sure she'd stripped me of my humanity. Did they have no shame? What had Maren threatened them with? I found little sympathy for them as I was pulled into Maren's chambers and stripped bare, the guard using force whenever I fought back against the women who'd been sent to "prepare" me. He reminded me a lot of Rhodes: big, brutish, permanently scowling. He wasn't afraid to use any combination of muscle and magick that it took to keep me in place. When the group had gotten me fully naked, I was shoved into a bathroom where the chambermaids forced me to wash. The guard stood by the door, ready to intervene whenever I struggled, as they doused me with hot water and scrubbed my naked body ritualistically. I felt ill when they touched me with their washcloths and sponges, using soaps that reminded me distinctly of Ulmos and not the scents that I'd adopted earthside.

"Is that necessary?" I said with a growl when one of them sank to her knees and began lathering my pubic hair and genitals. I saw the guard shift out of the corner of my eye. It had taken me so long to allow anyone to touch me like that with my permission, and Mycel had worked so hard to gain that trust from me, only to have these people remind me exactly why I'd been hesitant to begin with.

"Yes, Your Highness," one of them replied, still not bothering to look me in the eye. "You must be exactly to Her Highness's liking."

The maids each used a towel to dry me; then I was escorted in front of the steamed-up mirror in Maren's bathroom. One of them brought a step stool and scissors and before I could argue began lopping off waves of my hair. I was in shock as I watched my locks float unceremoniously to the tiled floor and fan out, each thin golden strand going a different direction. I made a move for the exit despite the guard's presence, knowing that I'd hate myself even more if I didn't attempt to fight back.

"Guard!" one of the chambermaids screamed.

I barely slipped past him before he caught me, still naked, and tossed me back into the bathroom with little effort. When I got to my feet, I was rewarded with a fist that effectively split my lip and filled my mouth with blood. I hit the floor again seconds later.

It was the snipping sound of the heavy scissors that woke me from my stupor once again, but when I woke, I was sitting in a chair in front of the mirror. My hair was almost gone, aside from a few wavy inches, and when I realized that, I couldn't bring myself to continue looking at my reflection. This was not so that I would please Maren aesthetically, no, this was an assault to my pride. Despite my disconnect from the people of Ulmos, some of our rituals and beliefs still had value to me; like the others, my long hair was important to me. It was a symbol of my patience and connection to the earth. When I floated in the water, each strand splayed around me, I felt like I could reach every corner of the universe. That was gone, taken from me without my consent, and left me feeling violated and isolated. When the chambermaids dusted the cut fragments of my hair off my shoulders, I thought back to the way that Mycel had played with my mane to soothe me, had gripped my hair in the throes of passionate lovemaking, had brushed strands out of my face lovingly while we spoke… All of that had been taken from me.

"Alaina, look at me," I said as calmly as I could muster, flexing against the bonds the guard was placing on me as the chambermaid buttoned a fresh shirt against my chest. The way she'd dressed me in Maren's outfit of choice, not once looking me in the eye, made me feel like a perverted toy. "You don't have to go along with this. Please, you know me. This isn't right." I couldn't decide which made me feel more ill: the situation I was in or my fruitless attempts at bargaining.

The young woman averted her gaze again as she fastened the last button, then reached for a bottle of cologne she'd set on the bedside table. "You… you have to be ready for m'lady," she told me, staring at the bottle once she'd picked it up. She spoke as if this was normal, as if prepping a man to be assaulted by his arranged fiancée was common-place. Maybe it was a custom now in Ulmos, one that I'd help blaze the trail for against my will. "This is her favorite cologne of yours, you know."

When she attempted to dab a bit of the perfumed oil on my neck, I jerked myself away from her, rage coursing through my veins in an attempt to mask my fear. The scent made me retch. "I haven't worn that in years. This is sick," I told her through gritted teeth. "This is fucking sick!"

Soon, I was alone until I heard Maren's voice outside the room. "I'll call you in if I need your help," she said slyly to the guard who was, no doubt, stationed directly outside. She entered as if we were long-established lovers and I'd been impatiently waiting for her, salivating at the chance to be alone with her.

"Maren," I choked out, praying that I could appeal to some ounce of compassion that might still linger in her body. "I don't want to beg. I really… don't, but…"

"Hush now, you don't need to beg," she told me coolly, undoing her silver silk robe and letting it drop to the floor. She wore matching undergarments. As I said before, she was about as typically attractive as they came, but our relationship caused me to view her as the monster she really was. No thin, shapely body or luscious lips and wavy hair could mask my disgust. That was how I knew her comment about begging had a caveat. I didn't need to beg… why? Because I'd be unconscious if need be? Because she'd take what she wanted regardless? "Really, you don't need to do much of anything. I'll do all the work."

"Please, don't."

Sometime later, when she was straddling my waist and I was staring at the ceiling in misery, cursing my body and the way my appendage responded automatically despite my actual desires, she told me, "See? I don't even know why I need to tie you up. You're all ready to go for me." She squeezed my dick possessively through my slacks, and I cursed myself as it throbbed in response. I shut my eyes…

From somewhere in the crowd, I heard Rhodes's cynical laughter, and it snapped me from my memory. He'd heard of these creatures just like I had, and I was certain this attack had cemented his decision to stay as far from the fray as possible. Certainly, there was no greater assurance that he'd made the right choice than seeing his former travel companions almost become an appetizer for a monster the size of a boat. The sound of his muttering to what was likely one of his Aolani girlfriends said "yeah, I'm staying the fuck away from that" loud and clear.

Zara pushed through the crowd of locals and stood staring at the indentation in the sand from the monster's head before looking at Mycel. "Um, sprout… what the hell was that?"

CHAPTER THIRTEEN
MYCEL

*E*arwyn's distraction had been obvious, but deciding who to address first, following the dinosaur attack, was a challenge. I glanced from my best friend to my husband and back again. I didn't waste a look at Rhodes. To say something was wrong would've been a gross understatement and also beyond obvious; about thirty things were wrong, and there wasn't enough time to give each one the attention it deserved. The reality that was quickly sinking in was me being heavily pregnant and on a ticking clock to find allies before I either gave birth or we were attacked by Ulmos. I swallowed hard. "I need to leave… and you two need to stay away from the water. I'll talk to Ossian and Tana about finding you a place away from the shore." I was in problem-solving mode and needed to find solutions quickly, no matter how shocking they seemed to the rest of the group.

"What do you mean 'you two'?" Earwyn asked incredulously, as if the suggestion of us being separated again was outlandish. I understood the sentiment – the thought was nearly unbearable, but I also knew what needed to be done. There was no way he could look at that near-death experience and think it was safe to risk the lives of our magick-less group. In the back of my mind, I was concerned about whatever was going on with him and where he'd been during his period of distraction. But we had to act fast. I could only hope that we would have time to connect again soon…

I sighed, rubbing my face in frustration before I looked at him again. "You and Zara, Genny too, you'll have to stay here—"

They're not gonna like that, Maz muttered to me.

As if on cue, Earwyn began his protest. Still, the look in his eyes was distant. "No, that's not happening—"

Like I said.

"Yeah! We're not staying here without you, especially after that thing was just two seconds away from eating this entire island! You can't just go out there!" Zara added, the look on her face reminiscent of when I'd tried to leave her behind in Seattle; without using words, she was asking me where I got the balls to ditch them and run off on an adventure. A valid question of course, but not one I had an answer to. I never really understood the way humans equated testicles to bravery, but I'd adopted the phrasing anyway.

I chewed my lip as I looked at the two people I loved most. If everyone could just stop talking for a moment, I could think. That didn't seem likely, though. When I couldn't find the words to argue with them, Zara threw up her hands. "Fine, fine. You two duke it out, but I'm not letting my pregnant best friend out into the ocean with that… sea monster. Earwyn, don't let her leave!" As she walked over, she shouted over her shoulder, "Besides, you really think they're gonna let us stay after that? Guys… it's a sea monster! Following us! Come on! They're not gonna like that!"

"Listen." I turned to my husband with a sigh once Zara had gone, placing my hands gently on either side of my lover's face. I struggled to feel close to him, to feel connected, when I had to revert to logic in order to feel confident in my decision making. It was hard for me to toe the line, even harder when he was obviously struggling internally as well… It was unfair that this had to happen right after we had time to reconnect. It wasn't enough. Our relationship needed more closeness and connection, not more time apart. "This is different. You'll be safe here. Without your magick, as much as I want you with me, it's not—"

When Earwyn cringed at my touch, I couldn't help but wonder again where he'd gone during those seconds between the attack and our conversation. "If Ossian doesn't toss us all into the sea, I know *we'll* be safe, Mycel. It's not Zara and myself that I'm worried about."

We stood in silence, and I searched his gaze for some suggestion of a way that things could be different. This was our only option. How else could I gather allies if I was worried about the safety of my defenseless loved ones? I didn't see Earwyn and Zara faring well during a trek through the frozen Alaskan wilderness, and I couldn't imagine a way for us to reasonably bring enough resources to make the trip work. When I couldn't gather the words to defend my decision, Earwyn put his hands over mine and pulled them from his face onto his chest. "This is different, Mycel. I just… We just found each other again. I know in my core that you can keep yourself and our child safe. I know you are fine on your own, but…" He trailed off and broke our connected gaze, looking past me as if to avoid finishing his sentence.

I tried to meet him, to show that I understood. "I'd rather be by your side, too." When our eyes met again, Earwyn looked like he understood, but there was something still left unsaid. "What is it?"

"Nothing." Earwyn sighed, clearly deflated, and allowed my hands to be released from his chest. The metaphorical space between us grew, followed by the physical space as he stormed off toward our temporary housing. To top it all off, running in the sand, especially while pregnant, was a nightmare. Nevertheless, I ran after him.

CHAPTER FOURTEEN

EARWYN

"It's not nothing, Wyn!" Mycel shouted after me as I turned to return to our villa. Despite my hopes of us ceasing the conversation for the sake of our planning and overall safety, she followed close behind. She caught the door to our bedroom just before it swung shut. "Please, don't do this."

"Don't do what?" I sighed, suddenly feeling irritated at her constant prodding, at her need to get down to the bottom of everything, even when it wasn't the right time. Why did she have to fix everything? I'd never felt rage toward her like this before, never felt like we were on opposite teams, but now… I wanted her to let me stew, and in that moment, it made me feel crazy. "I'm letting you go, like you asked. We're doing what we have to do, like we always do. I get it."

When I turned to face her, my anger subsided momentarily. Something about her deep green gaze had the ability to disarm me, and that power seemed to take away from what I was feeling. The sensations of my most recent memory still fresh in my mind, I lashed out against my will and attempted to push my one true love further away, as if it would somehow protect my fragile feelings. "Our love has always been an uphill battle."

"I know, but it's always been worth it to me. The best things usually are." Her voice was soft and genuine. "But this isn't just about me or what I want," my wife said seriously. The way she looked at me suggested she could see right through me; she was able to make me vulnerable in a way that no one else could. She didn't need force nor coercion – she just saw me, and not only that, she accepted what she saw. "And I'm not going to leave like this."

"Why not?" I piled up the walls I wish I'd had around Maren, built them higher than I could see over, and still, Mycel attempted to scale them. Tired, overwhelmed, with the weight of the world on her shoulders, she carried on.

"Because I'm your wife. We're partners. I'm not going to leave without figuring out what's going on here," she stated, seemingly testing out each word as it slipped from her tongue. "I need this to be safe and solid before I go. You need that, too. That's the only way we'll get through being apart again."

I gritted my teeth at her assumption. I felt angry that it was correct.

"Just tell me what's going on, Wyn." Her voice softened, and I saw the warmth of the sun radiating from her as it had outside. God, she was trying so hard to get through to me, and I could give her absolutely nothing. "Please."

"We don't have time for this!" I growled finally, throwing my hands up in the air. "The fate of mankind is in limbo. We don't have time to talk about my feelings, okay?"

"If not now, then when? The world may fall apart, but we can't let our union go down with it." My wife approached me slowly, closing the gap between us with caution as if she were approaching a wild animal. When she was face-to-face with me again, she put a hand on my chest; it was as if she knew she had the power to tame me. My heart thudded painfully against her fingers.

I closed my eyes. "It's pathetic, Mycel."

She was quick to respond, not a hint of doubt in her voice. "It's not."

"I should be able to protect you," I admitted with a sigh, effectively melted under her touch and gaze. "You don't need me to, you never have, but I should be able to. The fact that I can't, that I have to stay here and hide away while you do all the work for us... I feel..." I opened my eyes again to meet hers. "Useless. Emasculated." It didn't matter that I knew masculinity had nothing to do with my magick. Maren had left me depleted, ineffectual, and weak. I had nothing to give to this beautiful woman in front of me nor my unborn child; I wasn't a provider, a protector, or a fighter.

"Wyn—"

"No, I know. It's ridiculous, and we have so many other, more important matters right now." I knew her. I knew she'd try to carefully address the situation, to reassure me, to patch things up before even thinking about anything else. I didn't want to feel like that type of tenderness was necessary for me, so I tried to dismiss things altogether. "Like I said, fate of mankind and all—"

"Not useless," Mycel said, running her hand up my chest to rest on the side of my neck. She pulled my face down to hers and kissed me, a move that never failed to disarm me. Her lips were sweet, like the honeyed nectar of the island fruits we'd been eating, and I dipped my tongue between them to explore her mouth. "Never useless. But I understand. I felt lost without my magick, too. It's okay that it's important to you, that it's valuable to you..." She kissed me again, and I felt the tension begin to melt, slowly, from my body. I felt grateful that she hadn't tried to convince me I could protect her without my magick; it would've been an insult. "As far as your masculinity..."

My breath hitched in my throat at the way she addressed things so bluntly. Mycel's approach had always been to face things head on, and I was still getting used to that being a positive trait.

"I wouldn't doubt it for a second," she told me.

"No?" My fingertips found her hip and automatically gripped her tightly. I couldn't help myself. I was torn with the way that intimacy had grown intertwined with pain and fear and needed to reclaim it in the right way with the person I loved. It felt like a battle that she shouldn't have to fight alongside me.

Mycel looked up at me with a delicious spark in her gaze. "You can't imagine the ways I need you, Wyn. I'll always need you."

"How do you need me right now?" God, I needed to know, needed to feel like I had value to her, more than anything else in the world. If she needed me, I needed to fulfill that need, whatever it was, whatever it took. Then the horrific sea monster could consume me, and I'd die happy and with purpose.

She kissed me again, this time deeper, and sucked on my lower lip. "I think you know."

"Goddess, we can't. You have to go, and I need to get the hell over whatever—" I paused. I didn't want her to leave, nor did I want to deny her, and I think she knew that. "What are you doing?"

Mycel looked up at me through hooded eyes, and when her blouse slid from her shoulders to the floor, I marveled at the new darkness of her flesh. Had she been lying on the beach naked? "Showing you how I need you," she purred, grabbing one of my hands and placing it on her bare chest. It shocked me how she could be direct and take what she wanted, and yet, it felt nothing like it did with Maren. If I pulled away, she'd stop. If I looked uncomfortable, she'd check in. But she knew none of those things would happen, so she confidently made a move, and I accepted it with absolute delight. The last thing I wanted was for her to treat me like I was fragile.

My cock twitched, and my fingers flexed impulsively against her skin. I kneaded her breast and leaned in for a kiss, but she didn't let it linger and instead pulled back to look me in the eye. She ran her hands up my arms, and when they reached my biceps, she squeezed them. "Mine."

"Of course," I told her.

"So strong, my wonder," she said, her voice silky and unhurried, as if we weren't in the midst of a crisis. Mycel's ability to focus on us and us alone when needed was a gift. Before I could respond to her compliment, however, she slid to her knees before me and snaked her hands beneath my shirt. Her fingers settled on the waistband of my slacks, and she nudged the edge of my shirt up so that she could explore my flesh with her lips. "Here, too," she mused, kissing a trail down my belly and then caressing the lines of my abdominal muscles. "You're just… made of muscle."

I laughed a little. "You flatter me, goddess." I reached down to twist a lock of her fiery mane between my fingers and stroked her cheek as she looked up at me. The sight of her never ceased to leave me speechless. And when she nuzzled her face into my lap, her nose and cheek pressing against my erection, I groaned.

"I love every part of you," she told me. The grace with which she slid down my pants and underwear, leaving me feeling very exposed, was astonishing. Thankfully, I didn't have much time to feel on display because before I could comment, Mycel had run her tongue up the underside of my cock, causing a wave of electricity to surge through my entire body. She gripped me firmly, then looked up at me to say, "Especially the way you taste. You satisfy all of my cravings."

Within seconds she had me in her plush mouth, working me methodically with her soft, skilled hands and lips. Whenever she pulled off of me, she continued stroking and swirled her tongue around the head of my cock.

"You spoil me," I told her while panting, stroking her cheek and swiping a drop of spit off her lower lip as she looked up at me. Her mouth glistened with my precome and her saliva. "Ugh, fuck."

"Not today, wonder. This is all about you."

Soon I was throbbing between her lips again, fighting the urge to thrust into her willing mouth. Her slender hands found my balls, where she caressed them and gave them a firm tug, bringing me to the edge as if it was second nature to her. Every muscle in my body tensed. and my quads trembled in anticipation.

"Give me all of it, wonder. Give me what I need."

"It's yours," I groaned, leaning into her touch as she jerked me expertly. She timed each stroke perfectly, and soon the wave of my orgasm was crashing through me. I jolted, emptying myself in thick spurts onto her lips. Mycel didn't miss a beat and licked my come up as if it were a treat, only closing her eyes when she swallowed, almost as if she were savoring it. Feeling fully unraveled, I reminded her, "I'm yours."

CHAPTER FIFTEEN

MYCEL

"I'll see who I can find here," Earwyn suggested as we emerged from the villa for the nth time that day. To both of our surprise, no one had knocked down the door in the time we'd been gone. We couldn't tell if that was good news or bad, but it had allowed us some much-needed reconnection. It likely meant that the soldiers had reported to Tana and Ossian and they were busy deciding if they should banish us or just kill us themselves. Well, at least we'd die satisfied. "Maybe I can talk to Ossian about weaponry if they're not willing to join us themselves."

I chewed my lip. "I think I should talk to him first, you know, after the sea monster situation…"

* * *

MOMENTS LATER FOUND ME ONCE AGAIN ARGUING OUR CASE TO OSSIAN and Tana, which had become quite the boring, monotonous pursuit for me. I had grown to hate standing at the edge of their throne room, groveling for resources and support. I could only hope that the

Alaskans would be less inclined to make me beg, because it was getting old and fast. "Look, they want Earwyn, but they want me more," I explained, annoyed that I had to rationalize everything so plainly for them. I shifted my stance a little, trying to ignore the ache between my thighs that my time with Earwyn had caused; I hadn't quite grown used to the increased sensations that came with being pregnant, and I still wanted him. *Focus, Mycel.*

Focus, Mycel, Maz echoed in my head as he tousled my hair with his beak. *I don't know what you're thinking about, but it better be the two angry firefolk in front of you! I don't feel like dealing with singed feathers…*

I took a deep breath to recenter myself; I needed to sound confident in what I was telling them. "The second I leave, anything that's been sent to follow us will come after me. They'll leave Aolan alone."

"Why should we believe that?" Ossian's tone was clipped as he looked me over. His light brown, almost golden, eyes were alight with irritation. The intensity of his stare reminded me of Anala; she hadn't minced words either, nor had she been particularly amicable. Despite his stature, he had an air about him that oozed power. I had no doubt that he was a force to be reckoned with, especially when it came to his wife and their people. I wondered if, perhaps, someone had talked back to him once long ago and had not lived to tell the tale. Maybe Ossian kept their skull in his home as a souvenir.

"Mycel, I told you… the second you dragged us into this, you'd have to leave," Tana reminded me, the look on her face one you'd give a petulant child. I hated it. In contrast to her husband, she seemed perfectly calm this time. They seemed to balance each other out.

"I don't think I dragged—" I caught myself and stopped, shaking my head as if to reset my approach. Despite my desire to remain calm and level-headed, I was starting to panic internally. Our options were running out, and my ability to keep the people I loved safe, even with the return of my magick, felt nonexistent. "What will it take?"

Ossian was first to voice his annoyance yet again, and I wanted to reach out and press a finger to his lips to shush him. "You can't bribe —"

"What will it take?" I asked again, each word sharp and irritated. "I'm not asking for permanent refuge, I'm not asking for allyship. I just need a safe place for Earwyn and Zara while I go see the Alaskans. What will it take for you to keep them here and away from the shore while I'm gone?"

The king folded his arms across his chest, and I stifled a colossal eye-roll. "Bold of you to think you have anything we'd want," he snipped.

"Not bold, Ossian. Realistic. Everyone has a price. We've established that you won't help us out of the goodness of your heart," I told him, fighting the urge to emphasize how little goodness they seemed to have, "so now it's just a matter of determining the cost of your assistance." It was one thing to be generous with the resources of their island, which they were, but I needed them to dig deep and give us more.

Tana crossed the room toward me, meeting my gaze despite our height difference. "It's our job to protect our people, Mycel, no matter the sacrifice to ourselves. You'd know that if you hadn't abandoned yours." She eyed me as if she were attempting to see how deep she'd cut me with her words. We'd never been friends, but I decided then that I'd never speak to anyone but a mortal enemy in the way she just had.

Steady, Mycel. It's not worth the fight. Maz eyed Tana from my shoulder.

"That you think you understand what happened proves how little you really know," I forced out through gritted teeth. I was trying to do right by my people, and yet, the constant shame and bombardment with memories of my failures had not made it easy thus far. I looked down and found that my anger was causing my magick to take action on its own, and vines from outside the hall were creeping their way in, past me, toward Ossian's and Tana's thrones. The couple ignored my creeping foliage, probably assuming their own magick could easily destroy them; they didn't know, however, that my newfound alliance with water made me a force to be reckoned with. While I hoped they wouldn't have to find out, a part of me was already imagining a monstrous wall of water crashing into the throne room and extinguishing every flame in sight.

"Then tell us what happened," Tana suggested with a shrug, then turned to walk back toward her husband. "Clear the air if you're so certain we shouldn't be judging you."

"No. I don't owe you – or anyone – that information. All you need to know is that now I will sacrifice everything for them and for this child, who is the rightful heir to whatever is left of Yannava and Ulmos when all is said and done. They deserve a world where we can coexist with the humans – and each other – peacefully. Wouldn't you want that for any child of yours?"

The silence that followed my question brought with it immense clarity; the bitterness, the defensiveness, the unwillingness to help, it all made sense now. The way the couple looked at each other briefly, as if this reminder of the missing piece in their legacy was too painful to even address with words, cut through me. I had never imagined myself to be one of those people who needed a child to find purpose and value in their lives. That didn't mean that I wasn't – or wouldn't be, once I had the time to actually process the weight of being responsible for yet another life – excited at the prospect of my own child, but I could only imagine how it was different for Tana and Ossian. "I can give you that," I blurted out, mostly believing my words. I had no proof to back up this claim aside from the fact that my new, child-fueled magick seemed to have given me more of an ability to create. I mused briefly over my experience with the coconuts, which were, in almost every way, different from growing an entire human from scratch. How hard could it be? "A child, the two of you. Someone to continue your legacy and protect your people once you're gone."

I hadn't expected the blast of flames that sent me sprinting from the hall out onto the island again, nor did I expect my eyebrows to be singed when I stumbled onto the sand. Hopefully they'd grow back.

Bold move, Mycel. Very bold, Maz commented as I picked myself up off the ground and dusted off my clothing. He hopped onto my shoulder to pick a twig from my hair. *Well, the tropical fruit was nice while it lasted.*

"Yeah, well, negotiation is apparently not my strong suit..." I muttered, looking back at the hall where the fire had gone out and been replaced by smoke and the sound of Ossian and Tana arguing. So much for showing them what I was made of. Where was my wall of ocean water when I needed it? "How are your feathers?"

I think your eyebrows took the brunt of the damage. Thanks.

Having heard the commotion, Earwyn appeared nearby seconds later. "What happened?" A flicker of rage passed over his expression as he looked from me to the hall and back again.

For a moment I feared our conversations about masculinity and protection would have him challenging Ossian with no possible way of coming out alive, so I put a gentle hand on his chest. "It didn't go as planned. That's all. Let's go back and... look at our other options. It's not worth the fight, Earwyn." I tried to stifle my own frustration as I looked at him, admiring the way his hair had almost grown back to the length it was when we first met. It probably wasn't the time or place, but I couldn't stop myself from tangling a lock around one of my fingers. I could imagine Tana's and Ossian's pain... Now that we had come so far together, the idea of the universe telling us there were things we couldn't have, like a family, felt devastating. I knew that I would do anything to continue my life with Earwyn and the brand-new life we'd created together, as separated as I felt from it just then.

We were halfway back to our villa, lingering in the silence of defeat, when Tana's voice called out across the beach. "Mycel!"

I stopped but didn't turn around. I hoped dearly that she hadn't come to lecture me about the insensitivity of my assumptions and offer because I just didn't have the strength to explain my shame to Earwyn. We'd already been brainstorming other plans.

Earwyn, meanwhile, was quick to put himself between the two of us. How he could doubt his ability to protect us when he would sacrifice his own safety in a heartbeat, was beyond me.

Before he could speak, Tana spoke again. "It's a deal."

CHAPTER SIXTEEN

EARWYN

Tana was out of sight in a flash, leaving us standing on the beach in confusion. Well, I was confused. They knew what was happening, and I didn't, which, of course, did not help the insecurity I'd recently expressed to my wife. "What's a deal, Mycel? What did you promise them?" I tried not to let my nerves show through in my questioning, but I wouldn't have put it past my wife to sacrifice something massive for the sake of protecting those she loved. I could only hope that it wouldn't be to her detriment; at the end of all of this, if it landed me without her, it wasn't worth it.

The way the setting sun reflected off of Mycel's tawny mane, tangled from her passionate reassurance of me earlier, left me in awe, but her expression was a stark contrast to the pure serenity of our surroundings. It was something big. It had to be. In fact, she'd almost seemed relieved when she met me on the beach, until Tana had spoken to us, even though that had meant that she believed her original plan was a failure. I waited and gave her space to reply, knowing that she would tell me eventually; ever since we'd dealt with the confusion of our identities – confusion that could have been resolved with directness and honesty – we'd vowed not to keep anything from each other. With each passing second, however, I doubted I'd like the answer even more. Tana was long gone by the time she replied to me seemingly due to Maz's incessant urging. "A baby."

We stood in silence, Mycel looking out on the water as if she couldn't face me, and I assumed the worst. "Whose baby?" Surely not the blond-haired, bright-eyed boy she'd seen swimming in the ocean alongside our boat.

She swallowed hard. "Theirs… they haven't been able to—"

"And how are you planning on getting a baby for them? I only know of one on this island, and it's not available."

Mycel turned to face me, her hands shooting to her belly. "What? No!"

"Then how?" I asked, waiting for some clarity… any second now.

When she started laughing, my relief must've shown in my face. "The only thing our baby has to do with this deal is… the fact that he is giving my magick an extra boost. That's all."

I swallowed hard, eyeing my wife. I looked down at her belly, where the life we had created together, despite the absolute madness of our love story, was nestled safely and completely unaware of the war raging around it. "I don't mean to doubt you, goddess, but do you really think you can do that? Hours ago there wasn't a speck of magick between us. Not that kind, at least."

"I believe it enough to bet on it, at least," she told me, her gaze softening as she closed the gap between us and placed a hesitant hand on my chest for the tenth time that day. My heart must've been hammering under her touch. "We won't know until I try… and that won't happen until I return, so…" She chewed her lip.

I sighed, then blew a gust of air upward to knock a rogue strand of hair from my face. "So we're safe for now… your goal, of course. What if it doesn't work?"

While she didn't move her hand, Mycel looked away, setting her jaw as she processed my suggestion. I hadn't meant to doubt her, but the thought of creating life from nothingness, especially when she hadn't done it before, had me worried. But then again, how many times had Mycel surprised me before? And hadn't she taken what little I'd given her and created a life from it right inside of her body? "Then we figure out another plan like we always do."

I gently put a hand under her chin and directed her gaze back to me. "Alright."

"Alright?" Her eyebrows shot up in surprise.

"Yes."

"You're not angry with me?" she asked.

"There's nothing to be angry about, goddess. Time and time again, you surprise me with your bravery and valiant heart. I just don't want all of your generosity to land you or our family… depleted." The word tumbled around in my mouth as I thought about its implications. I couldn't bring myself to suggest that she or our son would end up dead because she overpromised or miscalculated. If it didn't work, we'd come up with another plan, like we always did. There was something so reassuring about the way she'd said it, as if it was a given; I'd never known anything as safe and sure as the partnership she'd gifted me with.

"I didn't mean to frighten you. You know I'd never do anything to risk the safety of our son." Her gaze, sparkling like a field of dewy grass, bored into mine. In it I saw every passionate memory of our past and the potential for so many more moments in the future. All of them, no matter how heavy or serious, I felt ready to experience. I'd fight to the ends of the earth to make sure we had time for them. "You've been subject to so many horrors," she added. "Not with me."

"It's never been a worry with you." I was serious as I reminded her of that truth. Not once had I been afraid of Mycel being like those who had harmed me in the past; she'd never done anything to rattle my trust.

"God, I love you," Mycel said suddenly, almost as if she couldn't control the words bursting from her lips. "I love you and your tender heart."

When I kissed her, soft and deep, the smell of sea blowing through her hair, I savored our last moment together for the foreseeable future. The universe had bestowed upon me such a great gift, such a treasure, but it would continue to put me through hell to hold on to it. It was worth it. "I love you too," I told her. It occurred to me then that this was it; this was the masculinity I had feared was slipping from my grasp. In my tenderness, a part of me that only Mycel had seen, was my strength.

CHAPTER SEVENTEEN

MYCEL

There was no time to waste in leaving, unfortunately, and my reconnection with Earwyn made it even harder to leave. At the same time, however, I was glad to be leaving our union stronger than ever. I needed to know that what I was fighting for and would soon be returning to was solid.

Rhodes, who had been our muscle until our landing at Aolan, refused to help in any preparations, claiming that it would spiral into him being more involved in the impending war than he wanted to. Personally, I didn't believe that someone like Rhodes could "accidentally" stumble into being more generous than he wanted. We brushed him off, but I could see that Earwyn was worried about his stability; he had been drinking nonstop since our arrival. I wondered if, when I was gone, they'd reconnect somehow. Either that or they'd kill each other, it was hard to say. I didn't have it in me to have much of an opinion on Rhodes myself; his behavior angered me, but if I stopped to think about it, I understood every little bit. Sometimes it felt like he was just acting out each of our stifled innermost desires. He wanted to ease his pain, and I couldn't hate him for that.

Meanwhile, Zara couldn't stand the sight of Rhodes, even though he seemed to have initially brought her comfort. In fact, when we first arrived on the island, they spent much of their time talking through sign language. Even though she could've done the same with Earwyn, it was clear she resented him, too.

Before I left, I'd lain in Zara's bed with her and made promises about how I'd be back soon. That she wouldn't be alone for long. That we'd avenge Firth's death. That she would feel joy again when all of this was over. That she had to stay with us, here, earthside, to meet her nephew. He would need her. She'd promised to stay for me, but I hadn't seen her so tired and lost before. I wished I could take her on this small adventure with me and show her what the world was like outside of her grief, but it wasn't the same. It just wasn't safe enough.

She stroked my hair as I lay next to her, staring up at the open ceiling of her villa; it was one the many unique features of the homes on Aolan. I counted the stars in my mind to keep from dwelling on our farewell.

"He would've been a good uncle," Zara told me, her voice far off and distant, and I knew she was imagining Firth playing with my child.

"The best," I agreed, then turned my gaze toward her. My heart was heavy, fatigued, like the rest of me, but I unexpectedly burst into laughter. I tried to stifle it with no luck.

"What is it?" Zara looked concerned for my sanity.

I giggled again, trying to find the words to describe the image in my mind. "Can you imagine him giving my kid a ride on his shoulders?"

Zara was silent for a moment, clearly deep in thought. When she finally chuckled a little, I felt as though I had won the lottery. "He'd send that poor child through the roof, sprout."

We were quiet the rest of the night, and I didn't push conversation. There was so much power in our coregulation, our silent, synchronized breathing that I'd missed during the fray. If all we could do was lie there and listen to the sound of the waves in the distance, that would be more than enough. Before I left, I sat on the floor next to Zara's bed, my back between her legs as she sat on the mattress. She put a single thin braid in my hair, tucked into the tousled auburn foliage, and secured a small bead to the end of it. "So you don't forget your best friend while you're out adventuring."

I ran my fingers over the intricate braid and then turned to look up at her. "I could never. There isn't a word for what you are to me... a best-friend-soul-mate, basically. Hope you like that title." Zara smiled and leaned down to press her forehead to mine. "I'll be back soon, I promise," I told her.

* * *

Tana and Ossian, however, had become extensively helpful, thanks to my promise, and it took every ounce of focus for me not to dwell on whether I'd be able to fulfill my part of our bargain. I hoped that I would, but for now, I'd have to take the resources they were offering and ensure I was putting them to good use. One such resource was one of their people, a young man named Zahir. He looked young, even for terrafolk – probably the equivalent of late teens or early twenties in human years – and was thin, lanky, and of average height. His stark black hair fell over his eyes in a bit of a mop, but that didn't seem to stop him from dutifully hauling heavy cases of supplies on board. Instead, he kept his head down and worked tirelessly, seemingly without breaking a sweat. Maybe it paid to be a young Aolani... or maybe he was paying off some sort of debt he had with Tana and Ossian. It was hard to tell if they ruled the island with good-heartedness and respect or if their people had a healthy fear of them, but I didn't have time to muse over leadership styles.

The leadership and governing bodies of each terrafolk realm were as diverse and varied as those of the humans. Some had kings and queens, some had two kings or two queens. I'd heard of one group that had a president. And another where it was governed by all of the terrafolk in the group. Some realms, in stark contrast, did not have organized communities or leadership, like the Cascade Mountains folk.

Zahir helped load a ship with little conversation, equipping it with weaponry and clothing that I might need if I were to trek through the Alaskan wilderness. We had no clue what type of people or varispirits I'd find there, so our preparations had to be thorough. Tana and Ossian were generous with their provisions as they were determined they wouldn't be needing them for the upcoming war.

The ship itself appeared derelict from the exterior; anyone passing it would've just seen an old forgotten sailboat. Its once-cloud-white sails were dingy and grayish brown, fluttering in the breeze with little enthusiasm as it sat by the dock. Tana assured me that it was sturdier than it looked and the sailors accompanying us were skilled in their operation of the boat. The boat was lovingly named *The Spark*, but honestly, it looked more to me like the last dying embers of a flame Thankfully, *The Spark* only needed to get us to Nome, where Tana had arranged for a flight to Barrow. I had never been on an airplane before.

It wasn't until the ship had departed Aolan, leaving it in the distance with the setting sun, that I ran into Zahir below deck. Maz, who had been on my shoulder as I triple-checked our provisions – ensuring we'd packed enough fruit to tide him over during the trip – was just as startled as I was.

Why is he still here?

"Not sure… Zahir, I didn't realize you were still on board." I eyed him cautiously as I turned to head back on deck and find our captain. We'd have to turn around and bring him to shore unless he wanted to swim, but Tana and Ossian hadn't mentioned anything about him supporting us through the voyage. "Um, what's the captain's name again?"

Hell if I know.

"Er, captain um… captain! We need to turn around and—"

"Don't be mad!" Zahir's voice was panicked when he stood from his seat and waved his arms in front of me. "Wait, wait, wait – hold on, you don't need to do that!"

"Why would I be mad? Why are you here?" I glanced over his shoulder to a bag that I hadn't seen loaded onto the ship. He must've brought it himself. Well, at least this explained the excess of food; I was almost offended at how much they loaded us up with and wondered what they expected a pregnant woman to eat. Certainly, I couldn't put away that much, and even though Maz had proven to be quite the pack mule when food needed disposing of, the amount was still over-the-top.

"I want to go with you. I–I can help!" The young man looked frantic, almost as if he'd prepared a rousing speech that he was failing to deliver effectively. The jet-black curtain of his hair flopped in front of his face again, and he pushed it away with one hand.

"Maz, get their attention. I need to tell them to turn us around," I muttered to my familiar, watching as he soared across the below deck area toward the exit. We didn't have space – and I didn't have the energy – for a stowaway. It was enough that I'd have to convince complete strangers to join my cause.

Zahir watched Maz fly off, and his face fell even more. "No, please, really, I can help you. You see, my sister, she—"

"Who is your sister?" I asked, trying not to show my complete annoyance.

"Was."

"Anala." I sighed, surveying the young man's golden eyes. "I'm sorry."

"See, I knew you would get it. I can't stay on Aolan because they've associated me with a traitor." Not only that, but since the Ulmosi had disposed of his sister, I imagined he wouldn't mind putting some of them in their place either. As for why he thought I'd "get it," I didn't bother asking; I wasn't in the mood to discuss my knowledge of being outcast or labeled traitorous. I wasn't in the mood to discuss anything at all, so Zahir had really ruined my plans for the voyage. "It's not a safe place for me and my daughter."

"You have a daughter? Where is she? Why would you just hop onto a random ship and hope that you'd be allowed to stay? What makes you think that—"

"I want to fight!" he argued.

My eyes must've widened so much they nearly popped out of my head. I was on edge. Exhausted. Unprepared to entertain another person, terrafolk or otherwise. "What are you talking about? You won't be fighting. We aren't even fighting right now. That comes later, but you won't be part of it."

"Why not? I have every right to—"

"You have a child! Hell, you are a child!" I retorted, but immediately knew that my argument was useless. I threw my hands up before he could call me out on my misspeak. "Yeah, no, I heard myself. Point taken."

"Good, then it's settled."

"It's not settled, Zahir. Listen, if you fight alongside us and you die, I'll be responsible for your child being left an orphan. There's no way you're okay with that. I'm certainly not. A minute ago, I didn't even know there was another child I'd have to be responsible for!" It took me longer than I would've admitted, but I eventually took a breath to steady myself while Zahir watched me in half fear / half defiance. "It's safer for you to go back to Aolan and be with your daughter. When all of this blows over, you can look at relocating, but your best bet is being out of the line of fire, especially with a child relying on you."

The young man set his jaw, and I could tell this was a battle I was going to lose. "Safer, sure, for now. What if… what if Aolan gets pulled into the fight anyway? Then our hiding there will have been for nothing… and, and if I can help, then I should! I owe it to my family to get us some sort of redemption. You'll take care of her, you'll take care of Neeri if something happens to me, I know it. I'm strong. I can help."

"Where is she now?"

"She's… with your friends, um, and your husband. He said he wouldn't mind you having someone else with you and that… he could use the practice of taking care of a kid, so…"

I groaned. "You left my mourning friends and newly powerless husband in charge of a child?"

Soon Maz returned with one of the deckhands. He landed on my shoulder and chittered at the man, who looked at me in confusion. "What is it? Yer bird nearly ripped the hair off my head trying to get me over here."

* * *

On the first night of our trip, Maz and I resigned to sitting below deck with Zahir and chatting. He was part of our group now whether we liked it or not. Under any other circumstances, I probably would've thought him fine… charming, even. But his incessant enthusiasm and optimism was draining what little I had left. Still, I tried. The boat swayed as we talked, and Zahir, buzzing with nervous energy, somehow managed to stop our bowls of dinner from sliding off of the small table below deck. With every shift, he'd dart a hand out and grab the food just before it made it to the end of the table, then place it back in front of whoever it belonged to.

"She just… wasn't interested in motherhood, I guess. I mean, she wasn't interested in parenting with me. You see, she and I were kind of a one-time thing and then she ended up with someone else. She didn't want having a child to mess with her relationship," he explained, catching my bowl once more. I didn't want to pry, but when we ran out of topics to discuss, I figured it was fair game especially with Earwyn on babysitting duty. He slid the bowl in front of me without missing a beat and continued his story. "Once you meet Neeri you'll see, it's hard to imagine someone not wanting to be with her every day."

And yet, here you are, Maz mused.

I sighed and picked at the food in front of me, then let it slide across the table on its own again.

"Can I get you anything? Water?" Zahir asked.

I raised an eyebrow. "Let me guess… Earwyn's only watching Neeri on a very strict list of conditions."

Zahir shrugged, his expression sheepish. There was a softness in his gaze, an eagerness, that reminded me a lot of his sister. He lacked the air of an ulterior motive, however. I squeezed my eyes shut for a moment, the image of Anala's lifeless body being dragged through the water by Rhodes suddenly very hard for me to shake. Hopefully no one had told Zahir the details of his sister's demise.

Then, I responded. "Don't worry. I don't need to be doted on. I'm sure your daughter will be safe with him whether or not you insist on getting me a glass of water. I'm not fragile."

Zahir shook his head, intent on clearing the air. "He didn't suggest that you were, only that he wanted you kept safe." I knew that, though, and never doubted Earwyn's faith in me. Instead, I wanted to ensure that Zahir didn't think me incapable of securing allies on my own.

I was about to head farther below deck to find our lodging for the trip when I noticed Zahir rubbing one of his forearms. His expression was pained, but I imagined it was only so transparent because he thought I wasn't looking. "You alright?"

"Yeah, good."

* * *

MUCH LIKE OUR INITIAL JOURNEY TO AOLAN, WE WERE RELEGATED TO A small room below deck as our accommodations. Zahir didn't seem fazed by the fact that we'd be sharing a room, so I said a silent prayer that he also wouldn't complain when my pregnant snoring kept him up. Maz had long since gotten used to it.

"I get the top bunk," I told him pointedly as I threw my bag onto the bed above both of us. It would be a pain in the ass to climb up and down that ladder each day, but I needed to find some tiny way to be in charge here. I groaned internally at the precedence I'd set; it had already been such a long day.

"Yep!"

"And don't touch the passionfruit; it belongs to Maz," I added, stifling a yawn.

That's right! Maz chirped. He left my shoulder and hopped up to the top mattress, where he nestled into my pillow to wait for me. I still hadn't told him about my promise to find him a space for a new collection.

"Got it!" Zahir still seemed to have endless energy.

Before I crawled into the top bunk, I tossed Zahir a small plastic bag I'd found in the kitchen and filled with water, then froze using my newfound water magick. I figured it could act like an ice pack for whatever injury he was dealing with, and I hoped it was only soreness from helping me load up the boat. "For your arm," I told him.

"Oh. Thank you." He let out a sigh of relief as he pressed the ice to his wrist, and I felt like it might not be so bad to have another partner, even if he was a bit spunkier than I had the energy for on this trip.

* * *

THE TRIP TO NOME, EVEN WITH MAGICK, WAS TEDIOUS. THE OCEAN, cooling with the change of season, was oppressive in its frigidness. Not only that, but we couldn't actually get into the water, and travel by human watercraft, even if manned by magickal folk, was slow. It reminded me of our trip to Aolan, and the realization that our group this time was much smaller filled my heart with loneliness; without Maz, I probably would've started to lose it. Even with my renewed magick, I found that my body was not able to adjust to the changing temperatures; perhaps keeping our child growing was utilizing a lot of my energy resources. Again, I wished we had Firth's endless technical knowledge so that I might know what was normal and what was worrisome. How had other magickal pregnancies gone? How about pregnancies involving terrafolk from different kingdoms and elements? I missed him. Not just his brain, but him as a person, and wondered how Zara was faring with one less of her people on the island with her.

Maz spent much of the trip huddled inside my clothing, which we quickly learned was too thin for the upcoming climate. Since the boat trip took so long, we took advantage of the port stops along the way to acquire warmer clothing and any equipment that seemed useful; it was Earwyn's quick thinking with his Salt and Earth cash that allowed us this option. In several instances, Maz attempted to fly ahead then report back on his findings before the cold became too much for him.

When we transitioned from the ship to the plane, Maz admitted to me that he enjoyed being up in the air without the effort and coldness of having to fly. I found it nerve-wracking and much preferred being close to the ground. Because of this, I kept my gaze set on the seatback in front of me while my familiar looked out of the tiny plane window. It was when he found a polar bear and arctic fox tumbling playfully across the tundra that he knew we were headed the right way. He watched them for long enough to see them return to their folk forms, naked and laughing in the snow, narrating what he saw to me as he watched. I couldn't bring myself to look. He seemed less rattled by their naked human forms than the idea of a bear and fox fraternizing with one another and I had to remind him that varispirits were different from animals and familiars in their makeup and socialization habits. *There are at least two,* he told me. *The locals don't seem to think anything of their ways. Maybe there are more?*

The next time we saw the two varispirits in question, they were sitting in one of the few restaurants in Barrow. It was a dusky diner, with only a couple of windows that did nothing to lend light to space now that the days were getting shorter. Not just shorter, but practically nonexistent. Soon the sun would fully set for the winter here. The absence of sunlight for days on end was something I'd never experienced. The building was tiny and had a small seating area with a couple of tables and booths, as well as an old arcade game in the corner. The counter, where some patrons were eating while a waitress refilled their coffee and soda, was lined with barstools of all different shapes and sizes, no two matching. When we entered, no one looked up; instead, everyone seemed comfortable in their conversations. Some people looked like they were enjoying a hot meal by themselves after a very long day of work.

The couple sat at the counter which was cluttered with coffee mugs, menus, and the half-eaten meals of the others sitting there. Owen, the bear, was a man of average height with a big belly and a wild beard that was almost fully white. The top few buttons of his flannel shirt were undone, exposing equally snowy chest hair. Next to him sat his partner, Nora, the fox. Her own wild mane was graying, but she looked young in human years – maybe in her forties. They were both eating comfortably and seemed completely at peace within the diner, where other patrons regarded them in a friendly manner. The waitress knew them by name and kept their beverages – coffee for Nora and a big glass of soda for Owen – full without question. We watched them from a nearby table before approaching them to introduce ourselves. I was forthright about our intentions; we'd been gone long enough already and didn't have time to waste. This meant that I didn't have time to develop a relationship with these people before asking for their allegiance.

"That's why we're here, in Barrow," I finished, having explained to them as much about the history of our predicament as made sense. I didn't dwell on the losses we'd experienced, even though they fueled me, and instead focused on appealing to their relationship with the humans; their bond was noticeable even through what appeared to be menial, day-to-day interactions like socializing at the local diner.

"It's not Barrow anymore, ya know. It's Utqiagvik, that's its rightful Iñupiaq name," Nora explained, narrowing her eyes in suspicion for a moment before her comfortable demeanor returned. It had been a mistake, but one that probably made me seem careless. I wasn't.

While I immediately apologized and corrected myself, I couldn't help but smile inwardly; this automatic defense of the humans made clear just how close these varispirits were to them. They valued them. That was exactly what we needed; terrafolk who cared for their human counterparts enough to go to war for them and humans that might actually appreciate the sacrifice that entailed. We got our own snacks and sat with the couple, happily soaking up their tales of their time with the humans. Apparently, they weren't the first generation of terrafolk to live in the human village so openly, but their numbers in Utqiagvik had gone down significantly as many others relocated to other parts of Alaska.

"Why stay here when so many others have moved on?" Zahir asked as he sipped his own cup of coffee, clearly still undecided on whether he liked the beverages of humankind. He looked shocked at the bitterness of the drink, and I slid a few tiny plastic cups of creamer his way across the countertop. I stifled a giggle. I hadn't noticed him rubbing his arm in a while, but had made a mental note to keep an eye on him.

"Why wouldn't we? This is our home!" Nora insisted after finishing off her own cup of coffee. She looked at Owen with a sparkle in her eyes. "Food, shelter, good people, good land to live off of, and my best friend. What more could anyone ask for?"

Owen beamed in return, and it sent a pang of longing through my heart. I missed my husband so intensely, but I'd been stifling those feelings in order to focus on the task at hand. Hell, I hadn't even been able to focus on the thoughts of our child. I wondered if outsiders saw the little looks we gave each other and felt the same. Would we have the privilege of growing old together, becoming regulars at our local diner and recounting tales of our adventures? I hoped so.

Before I could comment, a small voice popped into my head. *Can I come out now?*

"Oh no, sorry Maz!" I muttered, unzipping my jacket without warning the others.

Maz flew out and landed on the counter and, surprisingly, no one batted an eye. In fact, the waitress glanced at him as if it were commonplace to have animals in the diner, then turned to me to ask, "With you?"

I nodded in response, and she returned a moment later with bowls of water and some fruit, which he placed in front of Maz on the counter. If not for the distraction, I likely would've gotten quite the earful from my familiar about keeping him in my stuffy jacket for hours. At least he didn't have to lie low anymore.

I wondered then if the rest of the world could be like this; perhaps we could find a way to live in harmony, without hiding and without fear. I thought back to my time at Peach & Port, and the way Anala had tried so eagerly to be part of that world without hiding her true self. It just hadn't been possible in Seattle. I wasn't sure it would ever be, but Nora and Owen gave me hope. Their relationship with Iñupiaq people was so unique to any cohabitation I'd seen between humans and terrafolk, but I hoped that once all was said and done, we could learn to replicate it.

"The people here are different from what we hear others are like," Nora mused aloud. She smiled a little at the waitress, who had just swung by to fill Maz's water once again. "They actually respect nature, and they respect us. They don't take advantage of our magick. It feels like a partnership here, you know?"

"I don't think the Ulmosi will differentiate between good humans and those who are ignorant, Nora… and I think the others have potential. But even if you don't, I'd ask you to fight on behalf of the humans you love. With enough backing force, the Ulmosi could drown the continent… as far as I can tell, we're the only shot at protecting the humans and those who associate with them." I tried not to sound forlorn or resort to threats, but the danger was real. Each of these people, who deserved life as much as any of us, could die, and they wouldn't even know why. The life that the Alaskans had here could be wiped from the face of the earth in an instant if they chose to lie idle. Even with these allies, however, we stood only a slim chance against them. What good was a handful of varispirits, familiars, and one rogue princess hanging on to her magick against an ocean full of predators? I tried not to dwell too long on the truth of the matter, but it was looking bleak even under the best of circumstances. "I can tell they're worth the fight to you," I said finally.

A silence hung between us while the rest of the room carried on. I wondered briefly if the waitress had heard anything in our conversation or if she ever found herself curious about the inner workings of terrafolk society. It was clear that Owen and Nora were part of this community, valued members that any human would defend as if they were the same species.

"What exactly… do we have… to offer your fight?" Owen asked between a sudden onslaught of hiccups, his repeated downing of carbonated drinks finally catching up to him. This time the gravity of the situation helped me stifle my instinctual laughter. His wife's commentary, however, threatened to break what was left of my walls.

"Owen," Nora scolded him, clearly shocked at his ignorance. "What do you mean 'what do we have to offer?' You're a fucking polar bear."

"And you're fucking a polar bear!" Owen's laugh was a booming, infectious noise that caused the rest of us to crack up immediately. It was clear that, despite how old this man must have been, he was just a giant child at heart. Hundreds of years on earth had done nothing to dull his sense of wonder and silliness. No one in the diner batted an eye at the noise, and it made me think that he probably spent a lot of time cracking jokes and consequently, laughing his big bear laugh, in that diner.

When a laugh escaped my own lips, I realized I hadn't so much as smiled in quite a long time. Seeing Owen and Nora interact warmed my heart and made me think of the playful jabs that Zara often threw my way. Even Earwyn and I, in the midst of our passion and healing, could delight in good-natured teasing. The way these two loved each other was inspiring. Could I ask them to risk it, to risk their lives for us? Yes. It wasn't just for us anymore. It was for them and those they loved.

"So is it, um, just you two out here then?" Zahir asked after the laughter subsided. He had the right idea and was making moves even though I was too fearful of breaking the bit of trust we'd built. Two wouldn't be enough. We'd take what we could get, but the odds seemed stacked against us, even with a few powerful terrafolk on our side.

* * *

WHEN OWEN HAD MENTIONED "FUCKING A POLAR BEAR," HE HADN'T been joking. Their family was proof that they had done plenty of that and then some. Nora and Owen lived on a large homestead in the Alaskan wilderness along with their seven – yes, seven – sons and one daughter. Somehow, by the grace of nature or survival or pure luck, all seven boys were varispirits whose alternate forms were also polar bears. When they introduced us to their group of sons, I marveled at them; all seven were big, tall men with barrel chests and frosty hair. Despite their obvious power and intimidating size, we felt relaxed in their presence. The fact that they even existed gave me a burst of hope.

They are beastly! Wow.

I nodded at Maz.

I wonder what Earwyn will think. I bet they could even give Rhodes a run for his money.

"These are my boys," Nora said, beaming, as she introduced them all to us. They towered over her, standing in a line like perfect gentlemen to be introduced to us. "Palmer, Sterling, Clark, Fox, Thatcher, Finn, and Forrest."

Zahir couldn't bite back his laughter. "Wait, your name is Fox?"

I jabbed him in the ribs.

"Well yeah!" one of the sons answered as Nora reached up – quite the distance for her – to pinch his rosy cheek. "I'm named after Ma!"

Once they'd been introduced, the facade melted away, and we learned that the young men were rowdy, goofy, and seemed to be constantly poking fun at their parents. Beyond that, they spent their time on their family's Alaskan homestead or in the town, where they assisted the village with repairs, hunting, fishing, and manual labor. When needed, the group had built houses for locals in a matter of days, lifting fully built walls and pallets of brick without breaking a sweat. They could take down bison, caribou, and moose with little effort, and often shared their wins with the humans they coexisted with. Because the boys were constantly alternating between human and bear forms, most folks around town had extra clothing stashed in their storefronts or homes in case they needed a quick change after morphing. In addition to the varispirit family, several humans lived with them on their homestead; two of the sons were married to indigenous Iñupiaq women. In return for their labor and protection, the people of the city offered them any necessities, and sometimes even non-essential indulgences, that they weren't able to gather themselves. One of the young men, Forrest, had an affinity for unique tea, for which he had a trade arrangement with a shopkeeper. Like me, several of them delighted in human culture.

As if their strength and skill weren't enough, when I learned that polar bears, by nature, were excellent swimmers and could stay steadily afloat for hours on end, I felt a burst of hope. If it came to flooding or Ulmos leveraging their element in some other way, we would have an unexpected leg up. These were the allies we needed. Not only would they bring precious resources to the fight, but they were also a prime example of how humans and terrafolk could coexist in a mutually beneficial manner. I knew they would fight for their people. They, like me and Earwyn, saw the value and potential in humans; they respected and appreciated them like they did any other part of nature.

If I dwelled on it too long, self-doubt began to set in. We had been the catalysts for this impending war, but someone had to be, right? Someone had to stand up for what was right, to put in the effort to gather terrafolk who believed the same and would fight to defend it. If not now, it would happen someday... perhaps still in our lifetime. I told myself that it was meant to be and that would have to be enough. Everyone who had joined us had done so voluntarily; I had to believe that they were sound of mind and able to make those decisions for themselves.

That evening we ate at the home of the Alaskans. We gathered around a huge table and enjoyed elk, pickled vegetables, and tea from dandelions I had gathered while walking to the property. The table was littered with scuffs and scratches and claw marks. I wondered how many arguments had happened around that dinner table... how many shared dreams and family meetings. I imagined the young bear boys gathered around this table learning to prepare meat, or weave baskets, or carve wood. I ran my fingers over the gouges in the wooden surface and looked at Owen. "Lots of passionate conversations around this table?" I asked.

"I'm not sure if you can imagine seven shape-shifting boys all going through puberty at around the same time, but uh... there was a lot of shifting happening mid-argument at this table at one point." The older man gave me a kindhearted chuckle.

I wondered if Earwyn and I would ever find our place like Owen and Nora had. It was clear that, with the new relationships in that home, there would be many more generations to gather around that table and share love like those before them had. I had just speared a piece of meat with my fork when someone pulled out the last empty chair and plopped down next to me. Before I could introduce myself, Nora spoke at the head of the table. "Let us give thanks for the earth that created this food and for the animal that gave its life so that ours may continue. May we use the strength it provides us with, for good."

"For good," the girl next to me agreed, grabbing a piece of meat with her bare hand before looking me over. In addition to their seven sons, Owen and Nora also had a daughter. "Name's Agnes. Who're you?" she asked as she chewed, looking from me to Maz, who was perched on the back of my seat. The girl addressed us with such casualness that we likely weren't the first strangers to gather for dinner with this family.

"Mycel and Maz," I told her, jerking a thumb at the crow behind me.

"Zahir!" my travel partner chimed in from across the table. I was pleased to see him so relaxed, as if he fit in better here than he had on Aolan.

Agnes grinned, food still between her teeth. "Welcome." She held out a shred of elk meat to Maz, who took it happily.

While not a varispirit, Agnes's magick related to the tundra was astonishing and more potent than any I'd seen before. After dinner we stood on the balcony of the family's cabin, which overlooked a frozen lake, as Agnes walked out onto it in bare feet. Her own white-blond mane flowed behind her in the breeze, and she looked up at us briefly, her ice-blue eyes so pale and stark that I could see them glimmering with the reflection of the moon from afar. Without warning, she struck a fist onto the ice, causing a tremendous fissure to crack through it in an instant. The sound – much like gunshots I'd heard in the city – echoed across the land surrounding us; it was so powerful that I feared it might cause an avalanche.

I gasped, but Nora put a hand on my shoulder as if to say "wait."

The ground shifted, and the entire earth seemed to move, but just as Agnes's legs began to drift apart on either side of now-floating pieces of ice, she plunged her hands into the open water. I couldn't imagine how frigid the lake was. Within seconds, the ice had regenerated, effectively sealing the crack. She looked up at me with a triumphant smile. In all my time on earth I'd never seen someone capable of such rapid destruction and repair, and all in such a short span of time. The family's ability to work with ice and consequently, water, would come in handy if the Ulmosi got too close. From what I knew about Earwyn's magick and my own, likely temporary, water magick, it didn't have much bearing on the frozen tundra.

Did you see that? Maz asked from within my hood, peeking over the fabric with fear in his eyes. It had been hard to miss, but I too wanted to ask everyone if we were all seeing the same thing.

Though she was only one person in contrast to her seven siblings, Agnes brought raw, undeniable power to our team. She did so without embellishment, without warning, and without apology; she was just herself and seemed not to care what that meant to anyone else. Additionally, she was often flanked by her own familiar, an American kestrel named Oona. Oona and Maz communicated easily and determined that their ability to travel long distances without being noticed, as well as pass messages between us, would be crucial in the coming war. Familiars were different from regular animals, but Maz still seemed to delight in chittering away with Oona as if they were regular birds. Later that evening, they'd leave to hunt together.

Following her impressive display of power, however, Agnes retired back into the house for the remainder of the night and was nowhere to be seen the following day. When I asked Nora if she was alright, she nodded with a soft smile. "It takes a lot out of her, that big magick," she told me. "Sometimes she's down for days afterward, you know? I know Aggie wants to fight, and we'll let her, but we'll need to be ready to step in and get her to safety if she does anything big like that when the time comes."

I assured Nora that I understood and that I would be prepared to shield her while she moved to safety if needed.

"Thank you, Mycel. The boys… they know, too, and they'll keep an eye out for her." Later I saw Nora bringing a tray with a bowl of soup, a hunk of crusty bread, and a cup of tea into Agnes's room. My heart warmed at the familial love that I was being welcomed into, and I found myself wondering if I'd be as good as a parent as these two… and also missing my own family. It had been so long since I'd seen my aunts or anyone I'd grown up with. Though I'd run from my shame when I suddenly left Yannava, I also ran from the first family and friends I'd ever known.

Zahir immediately bonded with the youngest of the bear family, Thatcher. Like his brothers, Thatcher was kind and welcoming to all of us, but he seemed to click with Zahir more than anyone else. We had only a couple more days in Alaska before we had to return to check on

Earwyn, Zara, and Neeri and continue our planning. The moment the two young men began conversing, however, I knew we'd be bringing Thatcher back with us.

"Take care of my boy, Mycel," Owen told me as we packed up to leave again, this time bringing additional clothing and food with us from the Alaskans. I had not planned to return to Aolan with so many additional people in tow, but it boded well for us to have made so many connections. The rest of them would join us when the time was right, but it didn't make sense to drag them back to Aolan before returning to the mainland.

"You have my word." I was starting to feel like I was giving my word a little too freely, not because I didn't want to keep it, but because I became responsible for more and more lives each day.

* * *

WE AGREED THAT THATCHER WOULD JOIN US NOW AND THE OTHERS would meet us later, when the time came, as it made little sense to break up the family any sooner than needed. Transporting a huge family of bears back to Aolan also didn't seem like it would be well-received, nor would we have the resources to sustain their massive appetites. Hell, I still didn't know under what terms we'd be leaving Aolan. Agnes had been raring to go and ready to join us, but we convinced her to stay back so that we'd have the familiars to communicate with each other if possible. The Alaskans also had the use of a phone, unsurprisingly, so I made a note that the easiest way for us to get ahold of them would be to get one as well. We'd only been away from Seattle for a couple of months, and already, I felt the urge to abandon the human technology that had sustained me for so long while there. I did miss the ease of texting, though, and still mourned the loss of my cell phone that had all of Earwyn's sweet voicemails on it. If we ever lost each other again, I'd have no way to hear his voice.

Our new troop crossed the frozen tundra leading from Utqiagvik to our plane's landing location with Thatcher and Zahir pulling a sled of supplies that the Alaskans had gifted us. We followed Thatcher, who convinced us to take a shortcut across the small inlet over the ice. Even with magick, it was all I could do to trek across the ice with my pregnant body weighing me down more. Zahir had also summoned a small glowing flame that floated between us, sharing some warmth in what was proven to be desolate coldness. I felt it in my bones. Maz was in my hood again, his feathers not enough to keep him warm against the chill of the open expanse. Wind blew over it as if to flush out any living creatures attempting to cross and it was so painful when it hit us, that it almost worked.

When the ice began to crack, however, we halted in our tracks.

"The fire," Thatcher blurted out, glancing at our heat source. It was floating several feet above the ice, but it was impressively hot. "Is it melting the ice?"

"No, I don't think so," Zahir countered, but he extinguished the flame with a snap of his fingers just in case. We looked around our feet at the rapidly splintering ice, and the air was once again, shattered by a loud crack that reminded me of Agnes's formidable magick. It echoed across the vast emptiness of the frozen water in a way that made it very clear how far out and very alone we were. If we went under the water now, there would be no scrambling to land.

"It's not the fire," I said softly as a colossal shadow shifted beneath the ice. No, we'd seen this shadow before, and it had nothing to do with fire. I swallowed hard and watched the shape pass under us before turning around again and returning toward us. It was taunting us. It had waited until we were in the middle of the ice to make itself known. Clever, awful beast.

Run, Maz muttered to me alone. Then, he screeched, and it pierced the air. *Run. Mycel! Tell them to run!*

The horrific form of the liopleurodon passed beneath us again, moving swiftly despite the frozen temperatures. As we watched it in horror, it slowed in time to slam its monstrous head up against the ice, which cracked again.

"RUN!" I finally managed, finding my voice.

The men, refusing to leave our supplies behind, pulled the sled at full force while I attempted to sprint across the ice toward solid ground. We slipped. We scrambled.

It's too heavy!

When I realized that my partners weren't directly behind me, I turned to double back and grab part of the sled's rope.

"Don't!" Zahir yelled, putting an arm out to stop me.

"Shut up!" I snaked past him and pulled on what I could grab. We couldn't afford to lose our provisions, nor did I want it to drag the rest of my group under the water if the ice broke.

The creature kept in pursuit, smashing at the ice as it followed our trail.

"Thatcher," I panted. "We aren't fast enough on the ice like this!"

There was a twinkle in his eye as he looked over at me, still running, and let go of his part of the rope knowing I'd hang on it. "I thought you'd never ask!"

"I didn't!" I told him, the thin rope burning a line into my palm that felt like it tore and healed repeatedly as we ran.

Thatcher let out as deep of a laugh as one could while in the midst of a chase. In a flash, the burly young man had changed into a tremendous white bear, leaving his clothing in ruins on the ice. It caused us to slow for a second, but Zahir got the message and helped me climb onto the bear's back along with him. As we clambered onto him, unfortunately using fistfuls of fur to move ourselves up, the creature once again closed in. "Sorry!" I yelled to Thatcher as the beast slowed, hovering beneath us, and banged its head against the ice in relentless rage. Just as the ice cracked and chipped, red spread beneath the surface; it was bludgeoning itself.

The ice broke, finally, and our sled began to dip into the water just as the monster's eye peeked through the hole in the surface. It was frantic and searching, trying to close in on its puppeteer's victims.

"Thatcher! Go! Zahir, we have to pull it out!" I was screaming then, breathless in frustration as all of our hard work threatened to be thwarted time and time again. The being inside of me kicked in mirrored rage and an attempt to cheer us on.

"Got it!" Zahir hollered, gripping the rope of the sled as Thatcher took off again, his huge paws pushing off the ice to launch us forward. We were so close. The sled dislodged itself from the hole in the ice, sopping wet and frozen as it clanged onto the surface again, and we were off.

Time seemed to slow as Thatcher bolted us toward solid ground, his speed impressively hitting twenty or twenty-five miles per hour. The sound of his huge paws beating against the ice filled my head with thudding that matched the rush of blood in my ears. Our breath fogged the air around us, and I watched the space where the monster had broken through the ice, tension building in my chest. With how quickly we were moving, it was hard to see if it was still following us beneath the ice or not.

When I finally caught sight of the shadow again, it was directly beneath us.

Solid ground was painfully close, close enough to see, and yet this beast threatened to ruin our plans again… and I had just promised his mother that I'd take care of Thatcher, too.

"Thatcher!" I yelled again.

He huffed in response.

"Turn, hard! Maz, settle in!"

I miss Aolan! Maz yelled at me, hunkering down in my hood. *I miss the beach! And fruit! And the warm sun!*

The bear did as he was told and just in time, too, because the ice where we had just been running exploded into a sea of red and white.

The dinosaur's head blasted through the surface, bloody and determined, and pitched forward, mouth open, toward where we had been running. It let out a deep, violent scream. It, too, echoed across the empty frozen wasteland.

We reached solid ground and yanked the sled onto it with us just in time for Thatcher to collapse, sending us all tumbling into the frosty dirt. I lay there panting for longer than expected, and when I lifted my head toward the ice, the dinosaur was retreating back into the water. Its scaled head had gash upon gash from its relentless ice-breaking and its eyes, still empty, caught mine as it slipped away beneath the surface again.

"No more ice," I panted, letting my head fall back against the ground once the thing was out of sight. "No more fucking ice." Maz squeezed out from behind my neck and let out a trill of agreement.

When our hearts had settled at least a little, we dug through the sled to find Thatcher some clothes that hadn't gotten wet since his original attire was lying in scraps on the frozen water. Then, we kept our heads down and moved toward our plane again and despite my distaste for flying, I was ready to be as far away from the water as possible. I'd have to get Thatcher a steak or five when we finally got where we were going.

CHAPTER EIGHTEEN

EARWYN

To be left alone on an island with the lover of my dead best friend seemed a cruel punishment for losing my magick. Each time we passed each other, working diligently to prepare for Mycel's return and our consequent departure from the island, the tension grew. Without my wife there as a buffer, a peacekeeper, I could feel hatred rolling off of Zara. When we weren't interacting with each other, I knew she was glaring at me. In the end, I couldn't blame her. I, too, was harboring pain from the loss of my best friend in addition to my worries about Mycel being gone without me. Thoughts of Firth's last moments, when he had fought so hard to protect me and my loved ones, plagued my mind whenever I attempted to rest. I often found myself picking at my makeshift tattoo, which I hadn't allowed to heal yet between my neurotic touching and constant sweating while on the island. But now that I had signed myself up for babysitting duty on top of everything else, I had to stifle any reaction to Zara's obvious disdain and focus on being positive. Everything was fine! We were all going to live! War happens, no big deal!

Eventually, when we'd gotten word that Mycel was returning with allies secured, we began to pack what little belongings we had. I left Neeri, who had been sleeping in the living room of our villa, to pack up the belongings that Zahir had brought over for her. Then, I knocked on the door of Zara's villa before entering so that I could grab her bag and secure it with the rest of our things, but found her standing with the shirt I'd given her back on the mainland. She trembled as she held it against her chest. When she turned to look at me, her sadness seemed rapidly replaced by rage. Admittedly, the number of people who looked at me that way was growing faster than I'd expected. She accused me immediately. "This is your faul—"

I caught her fist before it collided with my chest as it had so many times during Zara's somewhat justified fits of rage. I understood… or at least I tried to. I didn't have the same relationship that Zara had with Firth, but if I put myself in her place, if I imagined losing Mycel… I couldn't bear the thought. I probably would've hunted down anyone even remotely related to her death. I knew Zara must be suffering. I was suffering the loss of Firth, too, but this had to stop. "It's not, Zara," I said calmly, lowering her hand back down to her side before releasing it. At some point, I'd also have to release my self-hatred; maybe it could start by disagreeing with those who aimed to pin their own misplaced hatred on me. "It's not my fault."

"How can you say that when you know this happened because he was trying to protect you?" she hissed, her dark eyes boring into my soul. I hated this.

"Firth was a grown man who made his decisions for himself," I told her with a firmness I'd been avoiding since we'd arrived on the island. I set my jaw and looked Zara in the eyes. We needed to handle this before Mycel returned, before things escalated, before there were more urgent and serious matters at hand than our mutual grief and rage. "He chose to encourage me to stay earthside, chose to stay with you, with us. To suggest that I strong-armed the strongest person I've ever known into doing something that he didn't want to do would be a slight against him and his memory."

Zara looked beside herself. Her eyes widened as she stared at me, and her mouth gaped before she could formulate a retort. "Y-you think he knew he was going to be slaughtered for his choices and made them anyway? He wasn't stupid!"

I wanted to lash out in return, to air my frustrations just like she was, but she deserved more than that. After a deep breath, I tried to let my walls down for her sake or at least for Firth's. "Do you think I knew?" I asked her. "We both know what we were doing would be dangerous. I didn't know he'd be killed, Zara, least of all protecting me. I would have protected him better…" I struggled to find the words that I should've said much sooner. "I would've found a way if I had known it would end like this. I wish I could have."

The way Zara stared up at me, her small hands balled into fists at her sides, made my heart ache. "I know my people did this, and… I'm sorry, Zara," I told her, all of the fight draining from me as I humbled myself with an apology. "I'm not like them. They deserve your hatred, your anger. Not me. I can't carry it anymore. I have a family to protect and be present for; I can't keep holding on to the guilt that I've been putting on myself. That you are putting on me. It's not right."

Zara scoffed. "A family…"

"You're part of that family, Zara. Come on," I told her with a sigh. "You have to know that by now." Firth was part of our family, too, and he'd continue to be part of our history. In fact, I couldn't wait to tell my son all about the amazing things he had done in his tragically short life.

We stood in silence, the tension that had built up over the previous months making the air between us so thick it threatened to choke me. When it finally broke, I caught Zara as she let out a sob that had been trapped since Firth had been killed. "Hey, I—" There were no words, though. Instead, I lowered us both to the floor, where we sat until she seemed to have no more tears left to cry. It was the least I could do for her and for Firth. I had silently promised to protect his lover; she was one of our own now.

* * *

DESPITE THE CONSISTENTLY WARM TEMPERATURE ON THE ISLAND, THE nights became slightly cooler as autumn wore on, and so, the fires scattered around the island became a comfort to us while we waited for the rest of our team to return. Mycel's agreement with Ossian and Tana had led them not only to protect us, but apparently to encourage the rest of the Aolani to treat us more kindly. After all, the promise of an heir to the Aolani throne was a big one. Neither Mycel nor myself knew if it was common knowledge that Ossian and Tana had not been able to conceive on their own; if it wasn't, then Mycel's deal with them would be saving them in more ways than one. Prior to that point, they'd provided us with resources, but beyond that (and Rhodes's fraternization with the Aolani women) they'd simply tolerated us. That evening we sat around the fire again, this time near our new villas which were closer to the center of the island (and consequently, farther away from water-dwelling dinosaurs) after having eaten our fill with our temporary neighbors. Despite my lack of appetite, I forced myself to eat. Neeri sat with us and enjoyed her fill of roasted chicken, vegetables, and far more mango than I thought one small child could put away. The scent of the fruit was so strong that it permeated the air.

Zara and I, it seemed, were feeling the weight of our recent encounter and had been left silent from fatigue as we stared at the flames. I only hoped that we could recover in time for the fight, whenever that might be. The weight of the future had me in agony.

Much like they did other nights, the Aolani folk gathered around the fire and shared stories about their people's history. Some of it was common knowledge to any terrafolk; others were myths that clearly only the locals knew. All of it seemed to dazzle Zara, however. I couldn't help but think of how Firth would have enjoyed the tales as well. He had been a voracious reader and brimming with knowledge of everything from history to useful, but amusing facts. I had no doubt that he would've consumed the Aolani fireside stories with great amusement. I rubbed my face to stop from sinking into a spiral of longing yet again.

Genny sat against my bare feet, basking in the warmth of the flames; I could tell she felt depleted, too. She seemed comforted by Neeri, who had joined her in the sand after eating and was petting her broad, fuzzy head as she listened to the stories. I had long stopped listening to the story and was distracting myself by staring into the fire when Zara jabbed me roughly in the ribs with her elbow. "What?" I hissed, probably a little too loudly given our company. When I noticed my neighbors staring at me, I held a hand up in apology, then looked at Zara expectantly.

"Did you hear that?" Zara's voice was an excited whisper, and I could see some new hope sparkle in her dark eyes. I hadn't seen that look since she'd wished Mycel and I well on the morning of our wedding. Given the outcome of that venture, it no longer had a positive association.

I shook my head, then looked to the elder Aolani who was speaking to see what I had missed. Lalago of Aolan was, by my guess, nearing 900 years old. She was regal with long, straight locks of gray that felt over her shoulders like a waterfall. Her features were sharp, and her eyes, deep and soulful, had stories to tell even without words. She held her head up high as she spoke, and around her neck and wrists was an array of jewelry. They seemed to be fashioned from carved and polished molten lava rock and clacked with her animated gestures. Similar-aged elders in my homeland would've been growing algae and barnacles and melding into their surroundings, but Lalago was spry and animated.

Zara piped up when there was a pause in Lalago's story. "Sorry, I must have misheard you. What did you say?"

Neeri piped up, her small voice answering the question before Lalago could. "Rebirth."

Then the elder gave her an appreciative smile and continued. "Yes, in this case, it's like…"

I had heard this word before or perhaps read it in a book from the library of Ulmos. There were only so many things to do to pass the time while holed away in my old kingdom. Or maybe Firth himself had told me about this theory in an attempt to distract me back at home. "Resurrection," I replied.

Zara looked at me in confusion and mouthed, *"Like Jesus?"*

Lalago inclined her head in a slow nod. "For lack of a better translation, yes. It's not quite how you'd imagine, though. Would you like to hear more of the story, young one?"

Zara nodded with such enthusiasm that I immediately felt set on edge; these were just stories, and they didn't have much to ground them, so I hoped that she wasn't getting sucked in. Like many tales that were passed down through generations, it had likely changed greatly over time to be less and less of the truth. Nevertheless, I sat silently and listened in.

"It's said that one of the first Aolani queens, Moa, lost her lover, Hani, in battle; he died protecting their home and family. She was distraught and spent every night praying to the fire, to the earth, for just a few more moments with him. She wished, too, that her children could see their father one more time and hear that he was at peace. But how could it be so when the Aolani know that when we die, we return to the earth from which we came? Our people do not believe that our souls wander the earth after our passing."

I could feel the tension radiating from Zara next to me and shifted in my spot, hoping silently that she wouldn't put too much stock in these legends, whose truth had been manipulated over many centuries. Ulmos had stories like this, too; they were intertwined with lessons, sure, grains of truth, but they weren't actual accounts of real-life events.

Lalago continued, despite my hopes. "One night, after she had put her children to bed, she sat by the fire again. Her hope was beginning to fade, and in her anger and frustration, she threw a lock of Hani's hair – a gift of self that he'd given her when they'd exchanged vows and the last remaining piece of his earthly body that she'd held on to – in the flames."

The last word had barely left the elder's mouth when Zara asked, "Then what happened?"

I was certain the rest of the group had faded into the background for Zara as she sat there, leaned forward on her elbows, watching the elder intently.

Lalago, ever generous given the Aolani's newfound hospitality for us, chuckled warmly. Her dangling earrings clinked together as she laughed. Meanwhile, I held my breath. The fire before us crackled enthusiastically, as if it were in on the theatrics of the story.

"Patience, patience." For a race of terrafolk that were typically quick and hot-headed, the elder struck me as surprisingly calm. Perhaps time, like the beating of ocean waves, wore down the rough edges of the Aolani people. "Moa fell asleep by the fire, heartbroken and defeated, resigned to never see or hear from her lover again. When she woke, however… she found the form of Hani standing over her, brushing her hair from her face. It was him, flesh and bone, having emerged from the flames!"

Zara gasped. "He came back!"

Some of the young Aolani sitting at the fire seemed annoyed by Zara's interruptions, but she hadn't noticed. Neeri seemed just as fascinated as Zara, though she'd certainly heard this story before; it was easy to see the draw of its sentimentality. Meanwhile, I was getting cold chills; I could see what this story was doing to Zara's hope, and it wasn't good. I managed to catch the elder's eye and gesture for her to please wrap the story up as respectfully as I could.

"Oh, well… you might say that," she continued, eyeing my warily. Who was I to tell her to wrap up her own legends on her own island? "They embraced each other and shared stories of all that they had missed during their time apart. Then, they returned to their home together, where Hami kissed each of his children's foreheads as they slept and assured them that he was at peace. He told them how much he loved them, and their bodies immediately relaxed into rest after many months of fretful nightmares. Then, the lovers spent the rest of the night in each other's arms. By morning, Hami was gone again, but the agony of loss no longer plagued Moa's heart, and she was able to begin the path of healing. She carried his memory and the memory of those sacred moments together to the end of her days."

I closed my eyes as the elder spoke, soaking in the warmth of her voice and the reassurance in her words; to find peace even after such a great loss was all one could hope for. I hoped that Zara could do the same. When I opened my eyes again, the rest of the Aolani were leaving, likely heading back to their homes for rest. Lalago, too, was wiggling her bare toes in the sand as if working up the energy to rise from her seat and do the same.

Zara, however, was relentless in her questioning. She clearly hadn't found the same comfort in the story. "One more question, if I may, your… um, elderness… uh, ma'am?"

Lalago looked up from her feet, which kept wiggling away and digging themselves deeper into the sand. "Certainly, child."

"The fire that Moa threw the hair into… where was it?" The island of Aolan was scattered with fire pits, each one easily ignited by the peoples' magick.

"No one knows for certain, but I like to think it's the very one we sit around each evening to share stories," Lalago said with a smile that reached her twinkling, wrinkled eyes, gesturing to the flames before us. "I've always felt a special connection to this spot, but maybe that's because they say I was born from these flames." She snapped her fingers, and a small, flickering flame appeared in her palm. She held it in front of her as if to light the way. Moments later, she left us alone, just the sound of her molten jewelry clicking as she traversed the sand back to her home. I watched the small flame fade into the distance. I had heard of terrafolk being born from the elements before, but it was rare. In fact, there was only one Ulmosi with such a background and even he was just a legend; his name was Aegir, and our stories said he was born from a giant clam shell. If anyone had burst from the flames of Aolan as an infant, it was definitely Lalago.

It was only then that I realized Zara was trembling silently next to me. Every ounce of my tact long gone, I asked, "Why are you crying?" Genny looked up from her spot on the ground and tilted her head at Zara. I wished I knew what she was thinking. I reached down and scratched behind her ears while keeping my gaze on Zara. The bristles of her hide were comforting to me, but the interaction reminded me that Neeri was still with us. I hadn't gotten used to being responsible for another person, let alone one who needed my guidance and censorship. "Uh, Neeri… I think it's time for bed, I didn't realize how late it was." When she opened her mouth to protest, I looked from her to Zara and then back again, frantically needing to get her out of earshot before my wife's best friend combusted in front of us both. "You can take Genny with you!"

Having effectively bribed my young ward, I escorted her to the villa, tucked her in, and nearly ran back to the fire to check on Zara. Again, I found her spiraling into hysterics. "His shirt, I… I washed it, I held off as long as I could, but it got dirty, and it felt like an insult not to wash it and—"

"Zara!" I was exasperated by the emotional rollercoaster we'd boarded together. I was all for sentiment, but to be so distraught over washing a t-shirt especially since she'd been holding on to it for so long already... I was incredulous. "It's okay that you washed his shirt, really. What is going on?"

"It might've..." she mumbled between sniffles. "It might've had some hair on it or something, I don't... I don't know!"

It took a moment for me to piece things together. "Zara, it's a story. A legend, that's all. I know you want to hold on to hope that there's a way to get him back, but..." I trailed off, not wanting the finality of stating that he was really, truly gone for good. Magick was a wonderful, incredible resource, but I'd never heard of it bringing someone back from the dead. I couldn't imagine the implications of such a powerful magick. Even the story made it clear that any return, even in fables, was temporary and for the purpose of closure alone. There were no tales of terrafolk returning from the dead to live a full life; that wasn't how nature worked.

"What if it's not? What if there was a chance for me to get him back, even for a second, and I screwed it up because I washed his fucking shirt? That's some... cruel punishment, don't you think? What did I do to deserve that?" Zara was wailing now, gripping the collar of my shirt to unleash her fury on me once again. It brought us painfully close, and I found that I had very little energy left to fight with her.

I swallowed hard, then put my hand over one of Zara's to pry myself from her grip. The reality of the matter was that Firth was gone. As much as I wanted to find a way to put Zara's hopeful theory to rest, if she hadn't held on to part of him, then no one— I stopped my own thought with a single word: "Wait."

I pulled up the sleeve of my shirt to reveal my forearm, where my makeshift tattoo had half healed into a scarred black band.

"What is that?"

"It's sort of a, um… tattoo… with Firth's ashes. I wasn't sure how else to hold on to a bit of my best friend." For someone who had so many tattoos, Zara's face expressed an alarming amount of judgment at my decision making. "Come on, grief does weird things to people. Don't look at me like that." She was one to talk, considering how desperately she'd held on to a t-shirt.

Because Zara believed so deeply that this would work, she insisted on gathering Rhodes to join us, and the two fetched a sharp blade on their way back. I begged them to be silent if they dipped into our housing because getting Neeri back to sleep was not an easy task as I'd learned over the previous weeks. Rhodes was, of course, intoxicated and had probably become more so at the suggestion of resurrecting his dead twin brother, but he'd tagged along anyway. Bracing for disappointment had me on edge, and the consequent chills made it hard for me to focus on removing a bit of Firth from my flesh. The light of the fire reflected off the blade in my hand, which trembled as I held it up to my wrist.

"I'll do it!" Rhodes hollered, apparently having noticed my hesitation. He wasted no time in stumbling over to me and reaching for the blade. "Gimme that knife."

I scoffed. "Never in a million years will I give you a weapon when you're that drunk."

"Suit yourself, man, but I bet I can do a better job than you, even drunk." The man was ever combative, even when he could hardly stay upright: classic Rhodes.

I ignored him, trying to refocus myself and using the light of the fire as my guide.

Zara paced nearby.

The legend hadn't said how much hair Moa had used, so I had no basis for how much of my skin I needed to peel back. The whole thing seemed very unmeasured and difficult to replicate. I settled on removing an inch or so of the tattoo, leaving a puddle of blood in the sand, and held the dangling flap of skin up for Zara to see. "Do you think that's enough?" I asked, cringing at the sight of my flesh so far away from my body; the blood, too, was a bit alarming after so many hundreds of years not being injured. I avoided the sight of my arm, where the tendons and muscles shone clearly through the wound I had made.

Zara chewed her lip. "Yeah, I… I think so, oh man, you're bleeding a lot." She scrambled to take off the sash that had accented her pants and pressed it firmly to my arm in an attempt to stifle the bleeding. When she looked up at me again, and the deep, dark walnut of her eyes met mine, I could see that she was appreciative. What was a small bit of flesh when it came to making amends for something so tremendous?

Despite our moment of bonding, however, I wasn't sure how to handle the honors. "Feels a bit unceremonious to just chuck it in, but…" I chucked it into the flames. It cracked as it hit the fire, and the scent of burning flesh momentarily popped into the night air before dissipating in smoke.

"Mmm, bacon," snorted Rhodes.

We sat. We stared. We waited. I gripped the cloth tightly around my arm until it stuck to me, plastered by my blood alone. It dried like a makeshift cast.

"Well, we're out one brother and a hunk of your skin," Rhodes mused aloud. I could see right through his joking and into the fact that he'd had a bit of hope left in him until now. It was almost as if the last bit of light in his eyes had been extinguished. "One is slightly more disappointing than the other, I'd say."

Neither Zara nor myself had it in us to reply, but then a fourth, unexpected voice filled the night air. "Drinking again, big brother?"

I looked up in time to see the hulking figure of Firth step out of the fire, which had died down quite a bit and had only smoldering embers left. When his feet hit the sand, the flames sparked up again behind him, which left him a dark shadow surrounded by red and orange. There he was. In all reality, it hadn't been that long since I'd seen him last, just a few months, but it felt like my heart had been aching for decades. "Firth..." I managed on an exhale, but that was the only word I could make myself say. I couldn't even bring myself to look at Rhodes and Zara, but knew that they were likely just as shocked as I was.

My blood pounded in my ears, and dizziness overtook me, Firth's figure wavering in the heat of the fire in front of me. I found it in me to look at my companions and found that Firth and Rhodes were looking intently at each other across the gathering space. Eventually I noticed that Firth and his twin weren't speaking aloud, but instead were communicating as they had prior to Firth's loss of magick: telepathically. They looked at each other thoughtfully for some time, the other two of us careful not to interrupt, before Rhodes let out a drunken sob and stumbled over to his brother. They pressed their foreheads together, and I heard tiny bits of Firth's quiet reassurance. "It's okay. I'm alright, but I need you to pull it together, Rhodes. You're going to kill yourself like this."

I tore my gaze away, the intimacy of the situation feeling too much, and looked at Zara.

She caught my gaze immediately. "It worked." Her mouth was agape, and the t-shirt still hung from her limp fingers, the hem of the garment grazing the sand.

"Yeah..." I let go of my arm, where the fabric of Zara's shirt was now plastered with dry blood and rubbed my face as if to wipe away my confusion.

It's funny how all of your manners go out the window when you're faced with a scenario that's so beyond belief, so outlandish that your brain just doesn't know what to do with itself. I'd encountered so many bizarre and wonderful things in my long life, things that would cause any human's mind to struggle to process it, but this… this was new even for me. I found myself staring at Firth, taking in each little detail of his newly reincarnated physical existence. When I breathed deeply after reminding myself that I needed oxygen, I could even smell him in the air. Somehow, the fact that this had worked caused a part of me to panic more; I'd have to say goodbye to my best friend again. I hoped this would bring closure for Rhodes and Zara, but for me… hadn't my heart just started considering healing? I swallowed hard and looked back down at Genny, who was watching Firth closely. She looked uneasy, confused by his presence, but given how much she'd been through by my side I imagined she was used to confusion by now.

When it was my turn for one last moment with Firth, he leaned down to pull me up by my hand. We stared at each other for a moment before he crushed me into a hug, and I felt months of tension leave my body immediately. I held on tighter than I thought I would, and when we faced each other again, I couldn't stop the dampness creeping into my vision. I wiped my eyes with the back of my hand before signing to him, "I'm so sorry." No sign, no word, no act of apology could truly describe the remorse I felt for everything that had led us to losing Firth.

He furrowed his brow, and I braced for a much-deserved lashing out. In fact, I almost hoped for it. *Punish me,* I thought to myself. *Punish me so that I can stop punishing myself.* "Don't," he responded, shaking his head. "You didn't do this."

"I may as well ha—"

Firth covered my hands with one of his and pushed them down in the clearest "shut up" I'd ever gotten from him. The warmth of his hands, no doubt heated by the fire, surprised me in contrast to the last time I'd seen him. I remembered holding him as the blood drained from his body and his flesh went cold and limp. I remembered closing his eyes before we placed him on our makeshift pyre and sent him into the abyss. "You know that I'd still be fighting by your side if I could. I would have followed you to the ends of the earth."

"I know."

"But this is the way our cards were dealt. Since I can't be here with you, I need you to do me a favor." Firth's gaze was soft, as it always was when we spoke heart-to-heart, as if there could never be anything but love between us. It gave me hope that Rhodes's and Zara's accusations had been wrong and that I hadn't betrayed my best friend. At the same time, it reminded me that I had lost a type of relationship I'd likely never see again... how rare it was for another man to see the deepest, darkest sides of me and still stand behind me in confidence and without judgment.

"Anything."

After Firth and I had said our final goodbye, this time unrushed by the imminence of death and the dangers of being pursued by our people, he kissed my forehead and let me go. When he and Zara finally embraced, I pulled Rhodes away to leave them in peace. He struggled to leave his brother again. The morning light would be there before we knew it, and they deserved to spend their final moments together however they pleased. I only hoped it would give Zara some closure.

Silence hung in an oppressive thickness the next evening as we sat around the same fire pit, anxiously awaiting the return of the rest of our group and hungover from the emotional weight of the night before. We hadn't spoken all day, I assumed because we were all grieving the fact that we'd lost Firth again. Rhodes hadn't brought a drink to our gathering this time, but I didn't know how long that would last; I couldn't blame him for the way he was coping or had been trying to. I also didn't know what ghostly threats Firth had made to him last night. Maybe he'd threatened to haunt him if he kept drinking. I smiled a little at the thought.

"Did he ask you for a favor, too?" Zara piped up suddenly, casting me a sidelong glance before looking back at the flames. I hoped she wasn't getting any more ideas about cutting off more of my skin. There was no way that ritual would work more than once. What was left of my makeshift tattoo had also become an important part of me. Not only that, but the tenderness of healing a flesh wound had proven annoying and reminded me how badly I needed my magick back. How did humans endure battle when a single injury felt like this? Ridiculous.

"Yeah." I rubbed my eyes as I reflected on our encounter; it had been a long night after we'd left the couple, and I still found myself doubting its reality. With the outlandishness of what had happened, it could've easily been a dream fueled by Lalago's vivid storytelling. In fact, when I finally fell asleep as daylight piped into our villa, my dreams felt like a continuation of our encounter with Firth. There, I told him everything he had missed in the previous months. I told him about the way Mycel and Rhodes got us out of Ulmos, about our child on the way, about the things on Aolan that I thought he'd enjoy experiencing. When I woke, the tender ache in my heart matched my arm.

"What was it?"

"To look after Rhodes," I told her with a sigh. It seemed an impossible task. I stifled an eye-roll. "I guess I deserve to be stuck with that."

Rhodes let out a half-grunt, half-laugh.

"And yours?" Zara looked at him, not quite as amused as he was.

"To look after you," the hulking man replied, still staring into the fire. Rhodes didn't seem to think of that assignment as a joke, and I wondered what the implications of that favor might be. Did we have another ally? Or did Rhodes really have it in himself to deny his brother's last request?

"How about yours, Zara?" I couldn't help my curiosity.

"To keep an eye on you two idiots." Of all of the promises, Zara's seemed like the biggest commitment; Rhodes and I were undoubtedly, major pains in the ass.

"Hope you like a challenge," Rhodes told her.

CHAPTER NINETEEN

EARWYN

When Mycel and Zahir returned, additional companions in tow, I was on the beach waiting for their ship to approach. Since it was an Aolani ship, it brought them much closer than our original transport had, and I found myself holding my breath as they docked and let down the walkway. News of their return had been passed via written note from Maz to any other familiars that were close enough to complete the route between wherever they were and Aolan. I realized each time we got an update that I'd never received a handwritten note from Mycel before, and so, each curled scrap of paper with their approximate travel time lived in my pocket. What else could I cling to during our months apart? At least this time, I knew she was coming back to me. Gone were the days where we could call each other on the phone or send text messages, a component of human life that I sorely missed, but at least I wasn't trapped in Ulmos wondering if I'd ever see my wife again.

I waded into the water carelessly when I saw the ship on the horizon, digging my bare toes into the sopping sand. I forced myself to stay close to shore, knowing that just my presence in the sea was likely setting off some sort of alarm for my people, but anxious to see my person again. I trusted Maz and Zahir to keep her safe, sure, but I needed to see her myself. Hell, I needed to hold her, to feel her. I could only imagine how much she'd changed in a few short weeks, which had felt like years on the island.

They docked. I paced. The moment Mycel of Yannava's feet hit the sand of Aolan, I had her in my arms.

"Goddess," I greeted her, pressing my face to the warm, soft crook of her neck. I could've lived there, in the space between her ear and shoulder, nestled in the warmth of her flesh. She smelled like the sea, like whatever soap she'd used to wash her hair, and just like… her. I could've found her by scent alone in a crowd of others. That space was as much a home as any I'd ever had. I pulled away, though, and searched her gaze to make sure she was okay.

"Wonder. I missed you," Mycel told me, reaching up to stroke my cheek. Maz eyed me from her other shoulder, but for once I didn't bother wondering what he was telling her.

"You can't imagine."

Before we could talk any further, Neeri came splashing onto the shore next to me and leapt into her father's arms. I hadn't expected the sight to knock the wind out of me, but I found myself picturing our own child. Would we ever be separated from each other like that, for safety or otherwise? I watched them silently, still holding onto Mycel, and my heart pounded roughly inside my chest. Just like I had, Neeri nestled into her father's neck, her long black locks mingling with his.

"What is it, Wyn?"

I tore my gaze away from them and looked back down at my wife. "Nothing, I just don't want us to be apart again."

THAT EVENING, I TOLD HER ABOUT FIRTH. I TOLD HER ABOUT WHAT HAD happened between Zara, Rhodes, and myself. I even told her about my adventures in babysitting. In turn, she told me about her adventures with the Alaskans, who seemed like exactly the kind of passion and muscle we needed behind us. Thatcher, who had vanished after our introduction to help Zahir and Neeri pack, seemed bright and pleasant. Mycel also inquired about my time taking care of the child and seemed amused at my recounting of our time together; I could only hope that I'd painted myself as a caregiver in a positive light. When Mycel described the haunting figure of the dinosaur stalking them across a frozen lake, however, my heart nearly stopped. "Magick or not, I can't have you that far away again, Mycel."

"Since when do you call me Mycel?" she asked, raising a curious and too playful eyebrow at me.

I was serious, and I tried to show it in my tone, which I found exceptionally hard when I was around my forest goddess. "Since you trekked across the tundra and nearly got eaten by a prehistoric carnivore the size of this island." That carnivore had to go. I didn't know if I could stomach the anxiety of it following us all the way back to the mainland, especially when our group's last encounter had been so close.

"Well," she purred, leaning over the bed to kiss me. "I didn't get eaten, and I'm back." She kissed me again. "And now you're stuck with me until the end of your days, *Earwyn.*"

"It's Wyn," I corrected her. "And I'm holding you to that."

The next part of our plan involved sailing for the mainland and returning to Yannava. But first, Mycel had to fulfill her part of our agreement with Ossian and Tana; she had to give them a baby.

"I've been avoiding thinking about it," Mycel told me when I mentioned the pact. "There's no… preparation I could've done. Either I can make it happen or I can't… and we work with whatever the outcome is."

CHAPTER TWENTY

MYCEL

The next full moon was three nights away, so we were stuck. By the second night, the other members of our group were anxious, itching to depart and set sail for the mainland. After all, we still didn't know how soon we'd be face-to-face with the dinosaur again, nor did we know when the rest of the Ulmosi army would find us or if we'd have other allies by then. If it came down to our group of a handful of terrafolk which included one child, a human, and a powerless prince, we were probably screwed. More members of our group needed protection than I cared to admit. I instructed the group to triple-check our packing again and ensure that we'd tactfully acquired as many provisions as possible. They did so, then checked every inch of the sailboat again for soundness. Then, they waited.

By the night of the full moon, I'd acquired enough materials to make my attempt at a fertility ritual at least believable insofar as it was theatrical and visually convincing. Unlike the coconuts, I didn't think I could just place a hand on Tana's belly and bless her with a stable pregnancy, nor could we stick around to see it all the way through, so I had to compromise.

I met the couple in their villa, where they'd followed my instructions to the letter. Both of them wore loose, soft clothing; Tana had on a flowing linen dress while Ossian wore slacks of the same fabric and an unbuttoned white shirt. They'd arranged several vases of island flowers – birds of paradise, lilies, and lantana – in orange, the color of fertility, around their bedroom and had accented the room with what looked like hundreds of tiny candles. Upon further inspection, I realized that they weren't candles, but simply flames that they'd summoned and set levitating around the room. It glowed with warm light and energy. They reported that they'd eaten and slept, just like I'd told them, and had spent the day bathing and relaxing together. Again, I hoped that all of these things would contribute to their bodies' willingness to reproduce, both for their sake and mine.

I wore a sheer, floor-length white dress with a plunging neckline and a thin cord that cinched it shut at the front, right above my now very round belly. In the light of the moon and flickering flames, I felt like the embodiment of fertility. I plucked a flower from one of the vases and tucked it behind my ear, then took a steadying breath. This was a big ask: a big ask of me, of my body, my magick, and the temporary boost I was getting from our child's magick. But in the name of gathering as many allies as possible and keeping my husband and best friend safe while I was gone, I had to try.

The couple complied with every one of my instructions, lying down on their freshly made bed when I instructed them. We opened the roof of their home so that the full moon shone in on them, and I placed my hands, gentle but focused, on Tana's belly as she lay down, the moon illuminating her stern, beautiful face.

"Close your eyes and breathe," I instructed her. Then I did the same, and when I exhaled, I willed my own magick, the excess life-force I'd felt within me, into her flesh. I visualized openness and nurturing within her body, the same openness and nurturing that had led to my own pregnancy. My child tumbled and rolled within my body, as if to say he felt called upon, too. When it was Ossian's turn, I did the same, and willed vitality into him. I was motivated to help them for my own selfish reasons, yes, but also because I could see the love between them and felt their pain when I touched them. It seemed cruel that the universe, that nature, should deprive them of expressing their union in this way, so I had to try.

When all was said and done, it was my duty to leave them to each other. My body was depleted, tired, sore, and felt empty aside from the life I was harboring myself. I needed to leave and recuperate where I could before we set off again. "Wait," Ossian whispered harshly, grabbing my arm as I turned to leave. In our time on the island, I'd never detected such nervousness from him before. His dark eyes searched my face, the flickering light of his magickal fire reflecting off of them. I sensed fear; his self-worth was at stake here. "What if it doesn't work?"

I mustered as much confidence as I could and placed my hand over his, then looked him directly in the eyes. "It will. If it doesn't, you know where to find me; on the throne in Yannava." That was where I had to go next.

AND THAT WAS WHERE WE WENT. THE VOYAGE BACK TO THE MAINLAND was uneventful at first, all the members of our party passing the time with idle chit chat or card games. Neeri seemed to love the additional attention, and even Rhodes, who I was shocked to see board the ship along with us, had a soft spot for the young Aolani. She was quick and spry, and I often found her hiding up in the crow's nest or tucked away in the cabin, waiting for the giant to walk by so that she could ambush him.

We'd been on the water for a couple of days when the density of our group below deck had pushed me up onto the deck for a bit of reprieve. I loved all of them, but I needed to breathe and look at something less human than the close-up faces of our group.

Maz joined me and stood perched on the gunwale at my side, overlooking the water. *It's a lot...* he commented suddenly after a few moments of silence.

"What is, Maz?"

The little crow looked at me briefly before looking back to the water. *This, everything... it's a lot to carry.*

"Yes," I told him with a sigh, realizing that I'd never acknowledged it aloud myself. The wind off the surface of the water sent my hair flying around my face. I brushed it away and kept my gaze on the water as well. "I'm not carrying it alone, though."

No, of course not, but you must be tired.

We stood in silence, nothing but gusts of wind filling my ears, until I confessed. "I am tired." It felt like both defeat and freedom to say it aloud, to let myself be just a person with a body that had limits instead of the ever going, ever protecting, ever sacrificing leader of our troop. It meant nothing other than exactly what I'd said; I was tired, not giving up. But I needed to say those words. Maz said nothing, but I knew he heard me, and the value of that act alone was not lost on me.

"There!" a voice from the crow's nest came suddenly, loud enough to rattle me from my thoughts. "On the horizon!"

I looked up and followed the sailor's point back to the horizon, where the head of the liopleurodon once again made itself seen. How it was still going after the way it had abused its own body in Alaska was beyond me, but there that fucking beast was again, as if it had heard my confession and thought *I'll give her a reason to be tired*. It swam toward us with great speed, and as I saw it approach, I whirled around to alert the rest of our group,

Earwyn, however, was standing only a few paces away. Had he heard Maz and I? Well, not Maz, but I supposed he could fill in the blanks of our conversation.

"It's back," I told him. I didn't have a plan this time. "It's closing in fast. I don't even know how that thing is still living."

His voice was even, but severe when he responded. "We can't keep running from it." The look in his eyes was one I hadn't seen before, as if he'd been anticipating this moment for a long time. I couldn't place his intent, however. If we couldn't run, then what would we do? Even the entire Aolani army only had enough power combined to push it back into the water.

"Can you let the others know?" I asked him, knowing that I had to get into planning mode as soon as possible despite my exhaustion. Maybe I could rally again. "Maybe we can slow it down together."

He nodded and ducked below deck again, but when he returned a few seconds later he had only his sword and Rhodes with him. Before I could ask him where everyone else was, Earwyn pulled me into a kiss that took my breath away. He tangled his fingers in my hair and held me close, then looked me in the eye to say, "I love you, my goddess. More than anything."

And then, he and Rhodes approached the edge of the boat where they watched for the approaching monster as I stood speechless a few steps away.

Here it comes, Maz told me from his perch near them. *As quick as ever.*

"What are you—"

But then they were gone. Both men stepped up onto the gunwale, and, with Earwyn's sword drawn and Rhodes tossing his shirt back onto the deck behind him, they jumped.

"Wyn! Rhodes!" I screamed and ran to the edge of the boat, both terrified and desperate to see where they'd gone and what was happening. The others must have heard me or sensed that something was off when Earwyn and Rhodes went off together, because they were soon gathering on the deck around me. "What—what are they doing?" I asked no one in particular; I was convinced they hadn't told anyone what their plan was before coming on deck. I saw Rhodes's fin pierce the surface of the water, and then Earwyn climbed atop the shark, the two positioning themselves to face the approaching dinosaur head on.

I whirled on the group, rage bubbling inside me along with confusion. I had no clue what was going through my husband's mind, but for him to jump in after this monster with no magick and only Rhodes by his side had me panicked. I looked at Zahir, at Thatcher, and yelled at them in frantic confusion, "Did you know about this?! Did they tell you?" I looked at Neeri and Zara. "Please, just go back below deck. It's not safe." It wouldn't be safe below deck if the liopleurodon got hold of the boat, though.

Mycel, they need you!

I spun again to peer into the water, where Rhodes and Earwyn were pursuing the beast who appeared to be leading them in circles. It was narrowly avoiding whatever they were attempting to do – I still had no idea – despite its tremendous size. "How?" I asked Maz in my panic.

The others had gathered near me and were looking on in horror, including Zara who had her hands over Neeri's eyes. Neeri peered through them easily and looked up at her father, who seemed as confused as I was.

"Daddy?" she asked Zahir who was standing beside her. "What are they doing?"

"I wish I knew, baby."

Can't you trap it? Keep it in one spot so that they can get closer?

I shook my head more in frustration than denial, feeling crazy at the suggestion of trapping a prehistoric dinosaur next to my husband

and friend. Nevertheless, I put my hands out over the water and like Earwyn had taught me, envisioned what I wanted to happen. Seconds later the water around the group had created a whirling cage, in the midst of which the liopleurodon circled, snapping at the other two while they narrowly avoided its teeth.

Earwyn gave me one last look, and from where I stood, time slowed. He balanced himself on Rhodes's wide back, sopping wet but somehow managing to be steady despite the rapid movement of the water and his ride.

Then, he drew his sword.

When the liopleurodon swam alongside them once more, he moved to leap forward, and the beast knocked into Rhodes, sending Earwyn flying into the water, sword in hand.

I saw him dip beneath the crashing waves in my whirlpool, and then the shriek of the liopleurodon filled the air. When the water of the makeshift cage turned red in an instant, I dropped my hands.

The men were nowhere to be seen.

"Oh, fuck, Neeri, come with me." Zahir's voice echoed in my head as he led his daughter away.

I stared into the ocean, the deep, deep burgundy of blood dispersing into the open water and held my breath.

Mycel…

What felt like hours later, the surface of the water broke with the hilt of Earwyn's sword, then the looming, horrific body of the liopleurodon, the head of which had been speared fatally by the reddish-gold weapon. It was dead. Its wide, terrible eyes stared into the distance with nothing left to report to its masters.

And then, in the distance, the fin of a whitetip shark broke the surface, and Earwyn crawled atop it again to let out a courageous, earth-shattering yell.

How did they do that? And together no less?

"I haven't the slightest idea," I told Maz, barely able to join words together to make a thought.

When Rhodes swam the two of them back toward the ship, Earwyn leaned over to grab his sword and yank it free from the beast's body, sending another gush of crimson into the tide. He also closed the dinosaur's eyes, and I could sense his relief when the people of Ulmos no longer had a way to watch him from afar. I could sense his pride, his joy, and the overwhelming feeling of regained control and masculinity that he'd been longing for. I couldn't blame him. And God, was it alluring to see him feeling so powerful…

I pulled my husband aboard by his sopping wet shirt, and the others helped a now-naked Rhodes to join us. The group cheered and clapped so loudly that Neeri and Zahir soon returned on deck to see what had happened. As soon as someone had thrown Rhodes some pants, Neeri tackled her giant play partner again in celebration. Once Earwyn had dropped his sword and pushed his saltwater-soaked mane from his face, he grabbed me close to his body and looked at me again with the same smoldering intensity as before he'd risked his life for our group.

"Don't do that again," I told him, fighting back tears as I ran my hands over his damp cheeks. His eyes glistened with a ferocity I hadn't seen since our reunion.

"I'm sorry I didn't—"

"Earwyn, I'll kill you myself." We stared at each other for a long moment, Earwyn unable to stop smiling in his triumph and me torn by the rollercoaster of emotions he'd thrown me on. I wanted to shake him and tell him how badly he'd scared me, how he needed to save the antics for the actual fight, but I could imagine how much this had meant to him. How long had he felt like he was running from his family, being taunted by their ever-watchful eye? Now that was gone, and he'd been the one to do it… and without magick, nonetheless! He deserved his moment of triumph and then some. I wondered what this meant for his relationship with Rhodes, but I didn't dwell on it.

"I know. Kiss me, goddess," he told me. So I did. Then, I dragged him below deck to strip him of his wet and frozen clothing, and I kissed him again and again.

WINTER

CHAPTER TWENTY-ONE

MYCEL

The early winter air of the Olympic National Park was cold and damp. Droplets of fallen rain slid from leaf to leaf down the dense thicket of northwest woods. Each step we took farther into the forest was accompanied by the crunch of frozen leaves and brush. Mushrooms sprouted from beneath the brush, thanks to the increased humidity. I wished I could slow down and marvel at every species, knowing that this part of the state, this part of home, was host to so many different varieties. Instead, I regarded them in passing and told myself that one day, when things were calm and peaceful again, we would reconnect. I would teach my child how to spot those that were safe for eating and those that were safe for admiring from afar; he would know to appreciate every single type. With their complex networking systems, I wondered if they were communicating with each other, with the rest of the forest, about our return and how there would be a great deal of change in the very near future. If I stood still long enough, which I couldn't, I thought I might be able to tap into it and speak with them myself.

More than anything, though, the air was brimming with tension; it was hard to tell if we were on the cusp of eliciting change or if we were saying goodbye to the earth as we knew it. I was torn at my return to my birthplace and the place in which my soul used to feel most at peace; I had missed each little sound of nature, but knew that our relationship had changed significantly since our last visit. Did the forest still know me, still know my footsteps? Did it remember my birth and childhood? The forest was old and full of history, yes, but it was also constantly changing, and I wondered if traces of Mycel of Yannava had been washed away with the seasons as well. I prayed not.

It wouldn't dare forget you, Mycel, Maz told me, though I hadn't said anything to him. The way he understood me in a way that was unique to our relationship, like the uniqueness of my relationship with Zara or Earwyn, made me feel complete regardless of the circumstances. *You're as much a part of it as it is of you, just like you and I are one. When we couldn't talk, I felt like a piece of me was missing. But even if we have to face something like that again, I'll be by your side like I always am.* Warmth bloomed in my chest at his reassurance.

I was dressed in a combination of attire I'd been gifted from the Aolani as well as the terrafolk and human communities in Utqiagvik. It consisted of a parka and pants made of elk skin, fur-lined boots, and a new knife made of a metal that almost looked like it was still under the fire that forged it. I was grateful that the clothing had been tailored to my new body, which had felt caged in my old clothes as it expanded. It felt only fitting that my attire reflect the support and adoption of so many different groups. At the end of the day, though, if my newfound magick couldn't protect me, no amount of armor or fancy weaponry could either. Once again I found myself coming to terms with the potential for my demise; at least I would go down in the warm embrace of those who believed in my fight.

Unlike the last time I'd tried to return home, I was now flanked by an army in comparison. Earwyn walked proudly next to me again, still mortal by all accounts but wielding a hand-forged Aolani sword that was alight much like my own weapon, which he could swing almost as well as he could make love to me. We'd seen that firsthand on *The Spark*. He wore a thick green coat that laced up to his chin and had a wide hood. Genny rode along in his backpack and peeked her head out occasionally to take deep sniffs of the forest air. I wondered if she'd ever been in a forest before; she wasn't a typical familiar for the setting by any means, as forestfolk generally found that birds, rodents, and sometimes frogs were drawn to them. Frog familiars always gave me a chuckle. Under any other circumstances, I would've delighted in showing her around, but I would delight more when we could let her near the water again as I was sure her bones ached for the sea like mine did for dirt and trees.

Behind him was Zara, whom we'd outfitted in as much discreet armor as the Aolani could create; only the edge of their fire-blasted chainmail showed from beneath the collar of her shirt in a subtle glimmer of reddish-gold. We'd taken great care to equip her, knowing that even with all of our efforts, she still remained the most vulnerable and least skilled in the dealings we were about to enter into. I didn't know where we'd put Zara when the time came because I had no way of knowing when the Ulmosi would close in on us, nor could I imagine what sort of welcome we'd receive in Yannava. Rhodes walked dutifully by her side without a word, chin held high as if he dared any stupid forest fairie to challenge him. He was sober and focused, seemingly realigned with the group's mission after reveling for so long in his newfound freedom; I assumed his rebellion on Aolani had come from centuries of being controlled by others and needing to reclaim his own autonomy and identity. I didn't blame him for wanting to burn everything to the ground rather than submit to an organized team with a leader again. While I didn't care for his cockiness, his willingness to make good on his promise to his brother had redeemed him in my eyes, especially because it helped me keep my best friend safe. Not only that, but the way he'd selflessly risked everything to tackle the liopleurodon with Earwyn would never be forgotten; I wondered if it was as satisfying for him, another Ulmosi, as it had been for my husband. When it came down to it, I'd be willing to protect him like any of my own.

Zahir, vibrating with heat and energy, followed close behind, his daughter next to Zara so that we were all creating a protective huddle around them. It had been hard for me to come to terms with us bringing Neeri into the fray. She was just a child and knew nothing of the brutality of the world. I wished I could keep it that way forever, wished that she would never witness the horror of war firsthand. I knew that my people wouldn't harm her, but would the Ulmosi differentiate between us and the innocents? Whenever I was still, I panicked for both Zahir's child and ours; it was such a great risk to be pushing back when we had them to care for. One wrong move and they'd be parentless or dead; both situations were horrific and felt like they were out of our hands.

Owen and Nora in their varispirit forms were next; I could hear the persistent huff and snort of the polar bear as we walked along while Nora's small fox feet pattered lightly over a layer of fallen leaves. They had linked up with us upon our return to the mainland and had decided that feeling out Yannava before bringing Agnes or the other bears was their best move. There were bears and foxes in my forest, in Yannava, but they looked nothing like these two, who stuck out so obviously they may as well have had a target on them. Back in their home, Nora's fur would've changed with the seasons, but here the white that was meant for the snow made them flashing beacons.

Also unlike last time, Maz stayed perched on my shoulder rather than flying overhead. The further along my pregnancy got, the closer he seemed to remain. We'd need him to carry a message to the rest of the Alaskans when the time came – and whether that would be a message to summon them or inform them of our demise was yet to be seen – but for now, my constant companion stayed close. Unlike Anala and Ember, we'd go down together if the time came. No matter what happened here, I knew in my heart that we had truly rallied, and if we had any chance of changing the fate of our people, this was it. Thatcher brought up the rear of our group of misfits, as big and lumbering as his father, but a bit more spry. His gaze frequently shifted from his parents to Zahir and Neeri. Neeri often looked over her shoulder at him to smile and stifle a giggle. The creatures filled the cold air with their breath and caused the ground to tremble beneath us. Our presence filled me with pride and hope.

We returned, hesitantly, cautiously, to the place where I'd been threatened and turned away only months before. The immediate silence was heavy. Were they expecting us? We paused, and I closed my eyes, breathing deeply. It felt necessary to fill my lungs with every particle of earth floating in the dense forest air. Everything felt amplified; each rustle of leaves, each croak and chitter, they all buzzed in my mind. My breathing slowed, and I was able to sense the presence of each member of our party so acutely that I may as well have been viewing us from the outside. I felt their breath, their tension, their concern… felt the strength and bravery that they had gathered to so willingly venture into unknown territory. When my eyes opened again, I felt strangely attuned to the forest in a way that I hadn't in a long time. I flexed my toes against the inside of my boots and longed to dig into the dirt instead, but my feet had softened in their time away from the forest, and I wasn't nearly as quick as I had been before.

Maz must have sensed my hesitation because he thought curious, whispered questions into my mind. *Do they know we're here? I don't see anyone… Where are the guards, Mycel? Something seems off…*

By the time we'd made it into the city, we'd encountered practically no one. I heard the shifting of the trees above us, perhaps the sound of an arrow being drawn, but nothing had come of it. As we entered the clearing that indicated the transition into Yannava proper, I halted our group and looked around. Humans who had made it this far – there weren't any – could've just kept on walking without ever seeing one of my people. But for those of us who know the way, the clearing was a spot of great transition between worlds.

"Uhhh, sprout?" Zara piped up, and I could hear her shuffling behind me to get a better look past me. It must've been irritating to be surrounded by almost all people who were bigger than her, but it was a necessity. "Is this the mystical forest realm you've been going on about? The one with all of the ethereal beings and dreamy woodland homes? Just wondering…"

Rhodes chuckled a little, but the others didn't dare to speak.

I snorted. "Not much to look at, huh?" I was grateful for a tiny moment of levity when everything had felt so heavy for so long. Before we could get into any more banter, I raised my hands and bowed my head. Yannava was so heavily guarded, and having my magick back was so new that I wasn't sure I'd be able to get back in… and yet, when I squeezed my eyes shut and let my mind connect to the earth, I heard some members of my group gasp. I flexed my toes within the leather of my shoes, aching to feel the wet ground between them. I imagined the forest opening its arms to me, welcoming me back in, and when I opened my eyes once again, it had begun to do so.

The forest before us transformed, the facade peeling away as if a fog were being lifted. I couldn't marvel for too long, though, because I lifted my head to meet the gaze of a crowd of Yannavi, including the guards we had avoided on our way in. Their weapons weren't drawn yet, but I noted that each one had a hand on the hilt of their swords or their fingers primed to snatch an arrow from its quiver in an instant. In my moments of increased attunement, I heard the fingertips of a soldier brush against the fletching of an arrow, and it set the hair on my body on edge.

Everyone was silent, except for Maz who had no filter when communicating with me. *Well, that's just rude.*

"Not sure where to go from here," I muttered under my breath, realizing that I hadn't really thought we'd make it this far. I was impressed, yes, but also stumped.

Then, through the silent stares and speechlessness, came a voice – gravelly, harsh, and unmistakably familiar. "Well, go on… let 'er in."

I gasped. "Reed."

Maz squawked.

CHAPTER TWENTY-TWO

EARWYN

*ho the hell is Reed?* I thought as I wrapped my hand around the hilt of my sword.

CHAPTER TWENTY-THREE
MYCEL

"Come on, all," the voice continued. The Yannavi who'd been blocking his way moved and made a path; for a society that prioritized the voices of women, Reed had always been the exception. When he appeared before my group, I was taken aback by the fact that I hadn't thought of him in so long. How? Perhaps he was such a part of the woods, a part of my old life, that I had left my memories of him here; he had simply grown into the moss of the forests of my mind. But even in the most literal sense he was hard to miss. He towered over us and was built in a way that suggested he could pull a colossal tree from the earth without breaking a sweat. His hair, a brown so dark it was almost black aside from a few streaks of gray, was tousled as if he'd been doing just that before our arrival. He wore a loose linen tunic, the front of which was slightly torn and displayed the crux of his pectoral muscles: thick, tense, and furred. "That's no way to treat our rightful ruler, is it?" As his dark gaze – the richest brown I'd ever seen, framed by dense, dark lashes – met mine, he inclined his head in respect, which only put him at eye level with me. He winked. "Long live the queen."

I was speechless until Zara jabbed me from behind. I could hear her voice in my mind asking "Aren't you gonna say something to that hunk of beef?" She was right.

"Thank you," I sputtered.

We were escorted into the heart of the city without another word, Reed vouching for us apparently enough to convince the others that we should be allowed in without frisking or conversation. It seemed strange to me that I hadn't seen my aunts yet, and with each step we took, I could feel the tension in my group rise. Sure, we had one person vouch for me, but we were still in foreign territory and highly outnumbered if it came down to it. I was hopeful that it wouldn't. Maz stayed on my shoulder rather than flying off to explore the land in which he'd grown up, and he frequently pivoted to look around us as we walked. He didn't speak to me, almost as if he was worried someone else might hear.

Unlike Aolan and Ulmos, my homeland was less obviously a city in the sense that humans might think of one. Instead, you really had to look to find our presence as everything blended into its natural surroundings. Unlike many of the other domains, we couldn't have an obvious kingdom with throne rooms and villas. Instead, our royal rooms were halls within the forest that had grown in a way to accommodate each activity. There was a central gathering space with a gnarled, intertwined table of red cedar that had grown to accommodate the entire village during celebratory meals; whenever our numbers expanded, so too did the table and the consequent seating spaces. And the throne room, well, it was a treat for the eyes that I hadn't set foot in for what felt like ages. In fact, no one had, since Yannava didn't currently have a crowned leader.

We were led farther into the woods to where the tree cover became all-encompassing and all traces of humans, like hiking trails and campsites, were miles and miles away. The greenery was abundant, of course, as was the presence of life-sustaining plants that each Yannavi had the ability to magically summon from the earth. Animals – familiars and others alike – crossed our paths and regarded us without a second glance. It must have been a shock to Zara when a young black bear tumbled into our path and then scampered off, but I was so intently focused on the life I'd left behind that I didn't have a chance to check in with her.

Neeri giggled at the sight.

Some of our people lived up in the trees, in what looked perhaps like human tree houses but were much better camouflaged by moss and other natural growth. Other Yannavi had found their homes in the ground or on top of it; my people lived in the ways that spoke to them most and that varied greatly depending on the person, their skills, and needs. Those that lived in the trees, for example, were excellent climbers and likely to gather their resources from high branches. They might even have a familiar that found its home in a similar place. Many of them, in fact, were part of the Yannavi guard and spent their shifts perched in the trees with their weaponry elegantly balanced along with them. They blended in with the leaves and birds easily, some of them so committed to their role that they began to grow moss from their earlobes and overgrown beards.

Although I couldn't be sure what sort of treatment the rest of my group were receiving, I was saddened by just how deep it cut to have my people meet my gaze and look away in a hurry. While everything seemed to be operating normally, things felt wrong. It couldn't have been solely due to my presence. Reed, with his extensive knowledge, seemed welcoming as ever, like nothing had changed since my golden days in Yannava. Why was everyone else so somber? Not only that, but what would I have to do to regain the favor of the rest of my people?

And where were my aunts?

Our group was escorted to open housing at the edge of the community, much like we had been on Aolan. Again, I found myself surprised at their preparations; it was clear they'd known we were coming, but how had they known how many people to make space for? We were given four ground-level dwellings and opted to split ourselves up into groups that made the most sense: Zara with Rhodes; myself and Earwyn; the Alaskans together aside from Thatcher, who opted to stay with Zahir and Neeri for the sake of her safety. When Zahir insisted that he could stay with his family and that the father-daughter duo would be fine, Thatcher emphasized that nothing could be safer than having a polar bear bunking with you. Had it been under any other terms, I would've been alarmed, but I could appreciate everyone's skepticism toward this hospitality.

"Go on then... Acker'll show you where to get food and water and other resources," I heard Reed inform my group as I hesitantly entered one of the dwellings and set my bag down. Acker... that name was so familiar, like an old relic being unearthed.

"I'll wait for Mycel," Earwyn told him. His voice was laced with tension, and I wouldn't have been surprised if his hand hadn't left his sword during our entire walk through the city. Ever since he'd slain the liopleurodon, he'd been confidently waiting for his next chance to flex his sword skills. I didn't mind.

The Alaskans chatted thoughtlessly in the background, and I heard Neeri's small voice commenting on the tall trees, which were very different from those on Aolan. "They're so wide around," she mused, staring up into the branches.

Rhodes, no doubt, was looking Reed over to see if he could take him if it came down to a fight. There would be no clear winner in that match. Instead, I imagined they'd leave uprooted trees, trampled meadows, and upturned earth in their wake.

I was exhausted.

"Ah, I think she knows her way around." Reed's tone was smug, self-assured. I couldn't see his face, but I knew him well enough to imagine the expression that might be on it. He had a dimple on one side. I bet Earwyn was itching to smack it off his mug, but then again, maybe I was projecting.

I made my way back to the entrance of our lodging to give Earwyn a nod and let him know I would be alright. If anything, I was more worried about him being without me than the other way around. I jerked my chin toward Zara in an attempt to remind him to watch out for her, and he tapped the hilt of his sword with a half smile. The way he cared for our group warmed my heart, and I made a mental note to ensure he felt cared for, too, when we had a spare moment together. When that would be, however, I had no idea; everything felt tense and urgent and unknown.

I rubbed Maz's head, the familiar sensation of his feathers calming me, as I watched the group turn to leave. "Go with them, please."

Maz cocked his head at me, then flew through the doorway to land on Earwyn's shoulder. At least we'd have someone to sound the alarm if things went sideways…

I had just turned back into the building when I felt Reed's towering height behind me and stifled a sigh in response. He clucked his tongue, and every hair on my body stood on end. "Darlin' doe, welcome home."

"Ravenous wolf," I replied, not skipping a beat with our old nicknames. "It's been a while since I've heard that." I turned to face him, and without warning, he stepped toward me, urging me back into the dwelling. I wanted to fight back at the way he overpowered me with his size, but I knew that he'd win easily or take it as the type of challenge that he seemed to like; Reed didn't need further egging on. The early sunset of winter had crept in without warning, and the sun was beginning to set in the forest, with only trickling rays of sunset streaming in through the building's windows. Inside, however, the room was dimly lit by flickering bugs who came and went as they pleased, but managed to maintain a sense of ambience. If not for the overwhelming sense of dread in the air, the setting would've felt cozy and nostalgic… even a little romantic. I might've imagined snuggling up under the mound of blankets with Earwyn or enjoying a hot cup of tea by the window. Yes, when the world wasn't actively falling apart, I might make time for those small comforts.

Instead, I folded my arms over my chest. "Though it hardly seems appropriate to use those terms anymore," I scolded him, furrowing my brow. "I'm married… and pregnant."

Reed grunted, looking me up and down with little regard for how blatantly forward he was being. "Mhmm, suits you. Being pregnant, at least."

"Is that so?"

"You've always been the… bringer of life, ya know," he purred, his tongue flicking out over his shapely lips as he surveyed my body without warning. The filtered light of the forest, fall's last hurrah, reflected off of the gray peppered throughout his hair and beard; it had been there for almost as long as I'd known him. I recalled the sensation of his hair against my fingers; it was coarse, rough, like everything about Reed was, and I'd spent many a night with it gripped tightly between my fingers. "Bountiful, supple," he commented, musing aloud. His gaze trailed down to my chest, which had grown significantly during my pregnancy. Heat surged through my body, much to my dismay. The needs of the body and its involuntary reactions didn't escape me, nor did Reed's inability to control his own.

"And where is your filter, Reed?" I was torn between wanting to address his blatant flirtation and the fact that I did not see myself as the bringer of life. The last time he'd seen me, in fact, I'd been responsible for much destruction and death. It might be the same this time, though of course I hoped for a different outcome. "Besides, have you forgotten that—"

His next words were clipped. "I don't forget. You know that…" Then, he softened again. "And I'm s'posed to have a filter just because you're married? Say the word, and I'll stop, but as far as I'm concerned, ya can't be owned, Mycel."

I was already irritated with him. "It's not about being owned—"

"Good—"

"Besides," I continued harshly, insistent on claiming my space in our interaction. Reed was maddening, and the way he bulldozed his way into a conversation had me gritting my teeth. I considered for a moment putting my hand over his mouth, but knew he'd likely bite me in response, which would send him spiraling into a whole different argument. He had the ability to challenge me when it came to who was in charge, and it had been so long since we'd seen each other that I felt off my game when it came to dueling him. "I distinctly remember your attempt at owning me."

His gaze softened immediately, and he looked pleased with my admission. "So you do remember our time together… based on your reaction to seein' me… I wasn't so sure."

"Would I have used your nickname if I hadn't? Look, Reed—"

"Wolf," Reed corrected. His gaze was predatory as if to drive the point home, though as much as we'd played the game of prey and predator, Reed was as much of a fierce protector as he was a hunter. The only danger he'd ever put me in was purely for fun. I wouldn't lie to myself, we had had fun together, but this wasn't the time for a walk down memory lane.

"Reed," I forced out, overwhelmed by his directness. When I met his gaze again – deep and dark like the richest soil – I confessed with a sigh, "I need you."

"Well, good of you to finally admit it," he replied without missing a beat, as if he'd been expecting me to bend to his will.

Before he could carry on with his teasing, I'd pulled the knife from my boot and had it pointed at his throat. It took me a second longer to maneuver than it would've had I not been heavily pregnant, but I hoped I was still getting my point across. This wasn't the time or place for rekindling an old flame; not when I was pregnant with my husband only steps away, not when I was here to start a rebellion, not when I had no clue what was going on with my people or my aunts. Where the fuck were my aunts? Reed was starting to feel like a very intentional distraction. Had they sent him? What was his angle?

Much to my dismay, however, Reed looked down to the weapon in my hand, then promptly stepped forward so that the blade was against his skin. If I had truly wanted to injure him, I wouldn't have resorted to regular weaponry, especially when I had so much magick at my disposal; he knew that.

I groaned. "You know full well that's not what I mean. Something is not right—"

Reed moved closer again, so that the tip of the blade pressed into his flesh. A droplet of blood trickled down his throat and vanished into his shirt. The wound healed almost instantly, then Reed wrapped his hand around mine and forced me to lower my blade. "Maybe, but when you finally admit to yourself that you still need me in other ways." He leaned down to kiss my cheek, then whispered dangerously into my ear, "I'll be around." The moment his breath, warm and penetrating, hit the flesh of my neck, my eyes fluttered closed.

I was immediately plunged into a memory. I'd been out foraging, as I often was before life became so serious and complicated. I was on my knees, crouched low in the dirt to look between the blades of grass when I spotted my prize: a group of small mushrooms that reminded me of an acorn cap on a stick. Later in my life I'd learned that they were called "psilocybe azurescens" by humans, but back then all I knew was that they had extremely strong hallucinogenic properties, even with terrafolk. Young Mycel was not averse to experimenting with all sorts of plants and fungus for the sake of recreation. I plucked the little fungi from the ground, pocketed a few, then popped one into my mouth.

"Bitter," I grumbled, wiping my dirty hands on the front of my skirt. I pocketed a few more anyway; bitter or not, they were exactly what I'd been looking for. The Yannavi people were expert foragers and acutely aware of the way nature worked within the forest. We were able to sustain ourselves on plants, fungus, and animals from our surroundings alone; this included using these resources for food, but also for creating shelter, clothing, and, if you were like me, recreational opportunities. Unlike the Aolani, we didn't typically smoke any of the plants, but consuming mushrooms for the purpose of enjoyment wasn't out of the question. I wouldn't say it was common practice for everyone, but it certainly had been for me before my life in Yannava had taken a serious turn. Ever since my departure, however, I'd avoided those substances knowing that they had a tumultuous association in my brain.

"That won't stop ya, will it?" Reed was there, in the memory, just as he'd been ever since I stepped foot in Yannava again. He was ever present in both his physical form and his knowledge of the happenings inside of our society.

"Never." I grinned and looked up into the trees above me, where a thick branch was bowing under Reed's weight. When he hopped off, the earth trembled beneath us. The sensation made my body feel like it was vibrating; it was too soon for the mushrooms to be taking effect, that was just how I used to feel around Reed. He was big, overpowering, and self-assured. In many ways, he was the opposite of the man I'd ended up marrying, and while I had appreciated those traits of his back when we'd been together, I didn't necessarily find myself longing for them now. The version of me that was present in the memory, however, had been enamored by those traits.

Nevertheless, sometime later found us both lying in the grass on our backs as the trees swayed in the breeze above us, having both eaten our share of little brown hat mushrooms. I turned to Reed, whose laughter drifted in and out of my ears with the wind. His deep, dark eyes sparkled like precious gems; glimmering and bright, with facets that gave away only glimpses of his innermost feelings and thoughts. Before I could even recall what we'd been laughing about, he pulled me into him and crushed our lips together. The sweetness of his mouth – flavored with berries and mint leaves he'd been snacking on before he found me – masked any bitterness of our woodland treat, and I melted into him as I always did in those days: carefree and thoughtless. I smiled against his lips. I rolled on top of him and kissed him through the wild curtain of my hair, then gripped his muscled arms tightly in exploration as he reached around me to grab my ass.

In true Reed fashion, he broke the childishness of our giggling with his commentary when he pulled away and met my gaze. "Sit on my face." He'd always gotten to the point rather quickly.

"How eloquent of you," I commented with a smirk. It wasn't a "no." With him, it never was.

Reed laughed again, and the booming sound echoed through the trees, then he cleared his throat to test his phrasing again. "M'lady, would you please bless my mouth with your divine cunt?"

"Divine, huh?" My vision swam, and I laughed so hard I snorted, then rolled onto my back in the grass again. Heat bloomed in my belly. "If I can get up!" Whereas some lovers I'd experienced were all intense, all the time, Reed was the opposite; sex with him was fun, playful, and easy. He was generous in both the way he performed and the way he was able to keep me at ease even if things elsewhere felt heavy and serious.

"No need for that." It took him only a few seconds to fold me in half effortlessly, tossing my skirt practically over my head as he surveyed my naked flesh. "No panties?" He squeezed my hips and belly lovingly, like a big cat kneading with his paws.

I flung the fabric off my face just in time to meet his gaze before he dove between my thighs. He licked me from front to back, even going so far as to bury his face in my rear. If I hadn't been pinned and immobile, I would've arched my back into the ground, but all I could manage was a breathless whimper. He manipulated my body like I was a plaything, and back then, I loved it.

"Catch your breath, doe," he told me, looking down at me as his beard glistened with my dampness. The look in his eyes was mischievous. "I'm gonna make you come over and over…"

"Yes," I agreed with a sigh, submitting fully to what was sure to be an onslaught of pleasure.

"Then I'm going to fuck you into the earth."

I nodded.

"Good girl."

He kept his word; each and every time he sent me over the edge, I cried out his name, and blooms exploded from the ground around us until the grass could hardly be seen anymore.

Reed had been gifted with an extraordinary memory, which he occasionally shared with others through touch. Yannava leveraged this gift by positioning Reed as the society's historian just like his father and his father's father before him; they passed down the civilization's memories over time, each new historian the bearer of a richer and richer past. Sometimes, unfortunately, "richer" meant more tumultuous, as was the case with my initial ruling over Yannava. I wondered how often Reed replayed the carnage that had been caused by my misguidance. Did he hold it against me? How could he flirt with me when he knew what I was responsible for? Despite the immense pressure this must have put on him, Reed remained lighthearted. Perhaps it was a necessity, a coping skill, to not be dragged down by the darkness of some of his acquired memories. I wondered if part of him hated seeing me pregnant because there had been a point in time where we'd been so much closer, and perhaps he'd imagined that I'd give him the son that would take over his job one day. I remembered the look of relief on his father, Linden's, face when he had finally passed the torch on to Reed; it was as though years and years of weight and aging had been lifted from the older man's shoulders.

Reed, on the other hand, immediately looked older. I think that was when his hair had started to gray. It almost seemed cruel to be forced into such a position by birth and to know that you'd be burdening your offspring with the same wearying existence lest you carry on with the weight yourself. When I'd asked him his plans for passing the torch, he always dodged the question. I knew he'd eventually need relief, though. Besides Yannava, I hadn't heard of another terrafolk society preserving its history in the way we did. It seemed cruel, but then again, many cruel things were perpetuated for the sake of tradition.

But there were times he'd done this to me in the past, this sharing of memories. In fact, he'd used it as a sort of foreplay, positioning the two of us voyeurs in our previous intimate exploits. I hated that it worked so well. Sometimes, even in the throes of passion, he'd give me glimpses into his fondest, most intimate memories of me. It could be magical to see myself through his eyes, in a way that was so pure and loving. I was breathless, malleable, when his hand began to slip from mine, but then something else flashed before my mind's eye…

The view was from outside of a dwelling, one that I recognized very well in fact. I could see my aunts inside, arguing. Hyssop sat with her arms folded across her chest in defiance, her ashy brown hair piled high upon her head like the shape of her namesake flower. Her wife, Clove, stood above her, clearly frustrated. She was quite the contrast, with a straitlaced and tidy appearance and a permanently stern expression. The pair looked like a parent scolding their defiant toddler.

"It's the right thing to do, Hyssop."

"And are you willing to let our people die for the right thing? For the sake of morality? So you can say we did 'the right thing'?"

Clove set her jaw hard. "Yes."

"It can't be. I won't let it happen. Call me what you will, but when Mycel returns, we will turn her—"

"Wait, what was that?"

The look on Reed's face was stern, his gaze locked on to mine as if he hoped to deliver a message through eye contact alone. His tone, however, was as playful and flirty as it had been since our arrival. "Don't tell me you've forgotten about our fun. If you need a refresher, all you need to do is meet me in our special place again. Tonight." Before he left, his gaze flicked to the window of our temporary dwelling, where a small sparrow sat watching me intently; the hard thing about being surrounded by animals was the good chance that they were reporting back to someone else. Reed pressed the back of my hand to his lips, then left.

I didn't move, but the hair on the back of my neck stood on end when I heard him address the person who had apparently been standing by the entryway. "Mermaid," he grunted.

CHAPTER TWENTY-FOUR
MYCEL

"*L*ook, Wyn, I need you to trust me even though—"

"I do," my husband told me without hesitation, his blue-green eyes set intently on mine.

"That was… quick," I mused aloud, not even attempting to hide my surprise. I wasn't sure I would have been as quick to agree to things if the roles had been reversed. But did I trust him? Without a doubt.

"Why wouldn't it be? You know I trust you," he assured me again, taking one of my hands in his. When I looked down at them, I realized that he was running his thumb over my wedding ring. It was simply a tangible reminder of the promise we'd made to each other, but it was important to me; I'd held on to it so dearly ever since it was given to me and vowed never to take it off again. The puffiness of late pregnancy had practically cemented it to my finger anyway. He kissed the back of my hand almost as if he meant to wipe away the sensation of Reed's lips. "I'd never try to keep you against your will, Mycel. But if you're here, with me, I know that's where you want to be. I'll believe that unless you tell me otherwise. It's that simple with us."

All I could do was stare at him in awe. Of all the uncertainties in the world, in life, we were certain of each other. It gave us an unbreakable bond, a power no outsider could shake, not even a handsome ex-flame from my homeland. He knew when to fight, and he knew when to give me space. He trusted me, and that alone was invaluable. When I didn't respond, my husband continued his musing. "But if he puts a hand on you again… I have a new sword I wouldn't mind testing out." He also knew when to push, when to fight back, when to flex his strength. I liked that, too.

I didn't think as I blurted out, "As much as the damsel inside of me would love to see that—"

Earwyn didn't miss a beat. "Oh, would she?"

My mouth immediately went dry as I caught Earwyn's smoldering gaze. My comment had been an off-handed joke, but he was looking at me as if I were something to eat. I barely managed to choke out a breathless "yes" in response. This conversation, which I'd expected to involve me tactfully explaining why I needed to go into the woods, alone, later that night, had suddenly been derailed. I'd already been formulating the best way to explain it all, but that quickly left my brain. I couldn't complain about this delay, though, with the roller coaster my mind and body had been on over the past few hours. When in doubt, time with my husband set me straight again.

When Earwyn leaned down to bury his face in my neck, I felt the hilt of his sword brush against my hip and imagined him fully armed, heading into battle. The idea of him being injured was unpleasant, but the thought of him covered in sweat and grit and blood had me feeling flushed… Even without magick, I knew he would be a force to be reckoned with when it came to the fight. He had decades of training and pent-up rage that he wanted to unleash on those who had wronged him. I only hoped I had a way to restore his magick in time for the war because without it came the type of mortality I hadn't come to terms with yet. I'd kept a constant eye on the wound on his forearm, agonizing over the snail's pace at which it was healing. If I thought too long about his run in with the liopleurodon, too, I could see his demise very clearly.

"Does he know you're mine?" he asked as he brushed my hair aside so he could kiss my neck. When I didn't reply quickly enough, he asked, "Goddess?"

"How could he not?" I closed my eyes and leaned into his touch. He smelled like the woods and the sea and his sweat. I'd never get enough of that smell. It trumped every expensive cologne and left me wanting to lick his entire body. Would he let me, I wondered, lick the sweat from his underarms? "I've got your ring on my finger and your baby in my belly."

"And yet..." Earwyn mused aloud, placing a hand on the back of my neck. "He still touched you. I don't like that, Mycel." He tangled his fingers in my hair and used the hold to guide my head back so that he could look straight into my eyes. The act itself sent a chill through my body, and I found myself immediately pulled into the depth of his gaze. He radiated intensity, both in his distaste for Reed's pursuit of me and in the way he loved and claimed me so entirely. He knew that I was his, and yet, he didn't take it for granted; instead, he was determined to show just how passionately he loved me. That desire kept me feeling feminine and powerful. He pressed his lips to mine before pulling back again to look at me with his commanding gaze. "Would he dare to do so if your lips were raw and your flesh weak and tender from our lovemaking?"

Suddenly my body was alight with sensation, and I realized that, despite how inconvenient it was for us to be in this position right now, I needed it. I needed my husband. In fact, I was ravenous for him. The way he handled me so confidently only made my head spin with desire. He blurred the line between gentle and imperious so perfectly and always had despite the horrors he'd witnessed behind closed doors. "I… would imagine not," I finally choked out, completely under his spell. How sweet it was to be so utterly head over heels for my person. "But here? Now?"

Earwyn was unfazed. "Why not?"

"Someone might hear us, and I've only just returned and—" I was frantic in my explanation, but more than anything I wanted him to tell me it didn't matter.

Earwyn's voice was smooth and deep. "Who, besides you, is to say when and where I can delight in your body? And what better demonstration of your power than for someone to hear you being worshiped, goddess?"

Before I could protest, not that I wanted to, I was left speechless as Earwyn lifted me, pregnant belly and all, into his arms. He carried me to the bed within our temporary dwelling. It was a beautiful piece of furniture that looked like it had grown into the shape; its gnarled vines and roots came together to form the intricate structure of a bedframe. Atop the frame was a plush mattress layered with blankets to shield against the inevitable cold and wet of a forest winter. Meanwhile, I felt like I was burning up in my layered clothing. He stopped only to undo his belt and toss his weapon to the floor, though he kept it within arm's reach, then undressed me as if I were an exquisite dessert in fine packaging. "Stunning," he mused aloud as he peeled my pants from my body. I watched his gaze, which was intense and loving, before pulling him up to kiss me again.

He kissed me sweetly at first, then with more vigor until he had me pinned to the mattress. I wrapped my arms around his neck and savored the way the weight of his body felt against mine as he pushed me deep into the soft blankets of the bed. He was careful not to lay on me too heavily and traced one hand down my side, grazing the side of my breast, then ribs and hip, while the other stroked my cheek. When I realized that he was still fully clothed, I squirmed beneath him.

"What is it?"

"You're still dressed…"

"I want to focus on you," he told me seriously, brushing a stray lock of hair from my face before kissing me again. When he pulled away, he kissed down my neck and to my chest, where he took one breast into his mouth and sucked deeply. I attempted to clench my thighs together, but found his leg planted between them. If I thought too long about our situation, I could see how Earwyn was trying to reclaim his space as the masculine force in my life by leading our interaction. I was okay with that. "Now, now," he mock-scolded me before running a finger along my damp slit. "Let me take care of you."

"Please," I said while panting, finally relenting and letting my eyes flutter shut. I arched my back when he plunged one, then two fingers inside of me and rocked them between my thighs as he expertly brushed his thumb against my clit. The juxtaposition of him being clothed while I was bare had me feeling dominated in an entirely new way.

"This," he began, withdrawing his fingers from me and waiting until I was looking at him to continue. He licked his fingers clean, never breaking eye contact. "Better be because of me, not him."

"Only you," I promised him aloud, suddenly aching at the loss of contact. I needed him to fill me, stretch me, wear me out. I wanted to get lost in him and forget the predicament I'd gotten all of us into.

He replaced his fingers in one smooth movement, then brought me to the edge again with his expert massaging. He leaned over to kiss me softly as he kept me dangerously close to coming, and I loved the way I tasted on his lips.

"Wyn…" I whined.

"I hope you aren't meeting up with him for a while yet," my husband told me through kisses, which increased in intensity with each few words. "I need to make sure you're satisfied before I send you out there."

"I'll go only when you're done with me," I promised him, shamelessly grinding my hips into his hand as if I couldn't control my own body. "Not a moment sooner."

Earwyn let out a grunt of acceptance, flicking his fingers so perfectly that a shuddering storm of pleasure rolled through my entire body. I rode out my first orgasm against his hand, unable to stifle the whimpers and cries that burst from my lips. He lovingly stayed with me until my trembling had calmed a little, then buried his face between my legs without warning.

"Wyn, I need you," I begged, droplets of sweat beading on my forehead despite the chilled temperature of the forest. "Need you…"

"You're not ready yet, goddess." He pulled away to kiss my inner thighs as he spoke to me. "I'm so thick and hard for you, I need you to be primed and open." I'd never heard him speak so bluntly, so primally before, and it ignited something new with me that made me want him even more. Even when we'd been through so much together and perhaps thought we knew every facet of the other person, our relationship was still so new… which meant there was so much left to explore.

When he returned to eating me out, soft and deep, I came again and squeezed his handsome face with my thighs as I did so. "Ah, God, Earwyn!" I was boneless when he rolled me onto my side and undid his pants, his heavy length landing on my ass as he unleashed it. He was hot and hard, and my already tender tissue begged for him to stretch me. All around us, the room was in bloom with wintering flowers, like the moody reddish purple of hellebores that were sprouting from every living surface in the room. With how potent my magick was and how intensely I felt everything, I wouldn't have been surprised if I'd conjured an entire winter storm within the room at the crux of my next orgasm.

"You're mine," he told me as he finally plunged into me, reading each twitch of muscle and curl of my toes to even better position himself. "Mine to protect, mine to love, mine to satisfy."

"Yours," I panted, my eyes threatening to roll back into my head as the broad head of his cock rubbed against the tenderest parts of my insides. "Always." Somehow he found the perfect rhythm and hammered away at me, his gaze smoldering as he brushed my hair from my face and watched me unravel. Heat radiated off of us in the cool winter air, and I was on fire, burning with need, desire, passion for the love of my life. He brought me to the edge again and then sent me over at the same time as he nipped at my bare shoulder. He held me close as I came down and stroked my cheek gently before withdrawing from me. Apparently, he knew my look before I could even say another word.

"Later," he told me, slipping himself, still hard, back into his slacks and buttoning them again. "This was for you alone."

Catching my breath proved more difficult than usual, and as I struggled to do so, Earwyn rose from the bed only to return with a damp washcloth that he'd retrieved from a basin in the dwelling. He lovingly cleaned me where I was dripping from our lovemaking, then lay down next to me again. As we lay on the bed, my clothes and the bedding strewn haphazardly across our room, our sweat-slicked bodies cooling in the late autumn, the world crumbling around us, I ran a hand down my husband's chest. "I've loved a lot of people, Wyn." My husband had always known that. "But remember our vows."

"You're my first love," he recited dutifully, his stormy gaze set on mine. In it I saw the depths of the ocean the way it was meant to be: vast and layered, not cold and hollow like it had become for both of us.

I could've stared into those eyes forever, but instead I pressed my forehead to his with a soft smile. I breathed him in. "And you'll be my last," I finished, those vows permanently ingrained in my mind. I'd recited them to myself daily when we were apart. "No one have I loved in the way I love you, so fiercely or truly."

"Is that so?"

I nodded, then took his face in my hands and pressed our lips together. It took a moment, but he melted into my touch and in turn, I felt comforted. If we couldn't be a safe place for each other, regardless of the circumstances, it would be impossible for us to scale the mountains of our upcoming challenges. It was then, in our long-awaited closeness, that I was reminded just how well we fit together. Being around Reed had reminded me of the past, familiarity that was comfortable and curious, but Earwyn... he was right for me... a gust of fresh air in my lungs, exciting, interesting, hopeful, pure... strong and soft at the same time. I smiled against his mouth.

"I know you love me," he murmured.

"Always," I told him. "Here, in the quiet moments in between... on the battlefield, in the throne room... in the depths of the sea. I love you."

I PRACTICALLY STUMBLED INTO THE WOODS THAT EVENING, FEELING WELL-fucked and a bit more disoriented than was ideal for such an important meeting. My husband had ensured that I'd be so satisfied I could hardly walk and seeing Reed, whatever his attempts at digging up old memories might be like, would have no effect on me. If there had been even a hint or whisper of nostalgic longing there before, it had been effectively pounded out of me moments prior. I liked that. I hoped I could focus on my conversation with Reed, but even if I couldn't, that was a sacrifice I'd be willing to make a million times over if it meant being with Earwyn like that.

As was customary for our relationship, Reed spotted me before I noticed him. "My, my, Earwyn of Ulmos making a statement, yeah?"

He gestured to my hair, which was no doubt a casualty of our romp.

I snorted and blew a gust of air up into my hair to move it from my face. "Feel free to keep taunting him. I could use this kind of statement multiple times a day…" It wasn't as if the ring and the pregnant belly hadn't been enough, but I enjoyed any claim Earwyn wanted to make on me. I had to stifle a lovesick sigh.

A glint of mischief flashed in Reed's eyes. "*That* I remember. If he doesn't have the stamina, though, I could always step in, ya—"

"Reed, shut up." I rolled my eyes and pulled my coat a bit tighter around me, feeling the sensitivity of exhaustion finally setting in. We had a conversation to have, and that was it. The quicker we could get through it, the quicker I could come up with a plan – with or without Reed, but preferably back in bed with my husband. I was nervous to leave him alone for longer than necessary and had, once again, left Maz to keep an eye on him. Who knew when something more dangerous than Reed the wolf would attempt to close in on us.

The night air around us glowed with the dim light of thousands of fireflies, and they clustered together in our meeting place, illuminating our faces while we spoke.

"Tell me about that memory," I instructed Reed in an attempt to get down to business. I wasn't sure how long of a conversation we were in for, so I planted myself on the ground and gestured for him to do the same. I sunk my fingers into the frosted earth on either side of me with a sigh. Despite the obvious social strain, this forest still felt like home. The air was quieter than in other months, with many creatures hibernating or going otherwise dormant, and part of me wished we could be doing the same instead of preparing for continued strenuous work. Perhaps it was my tired, overworked body speaking. "When was it?"

"Not long ago, when they got word that you were gathering allies in Alaska," Reed mused aloud, his gaze distant as if he were viewing the memory again in his mind. I wondered if he knew what giant creature had been stalking us to gather that information for the Ulmosi. Had he seen the horrors of the ancient beast that had nearly bludgeoned itself to death on the ice? A chill ran through my body. He took my hands in his, not seeming to mind their frigid dirtiness, and shared more of his mind with me. The warmth of his own hands took me by surprise, but not as much as the imagery he filtered into my mind:

"...when Mycel returns, we will turn her over. That's our only choice."

Clove threw up her hands in frustration. "This isn't like you! You know this isn't right. We'd turn her over, and for what? So that we can slave away under Ulmosi rule, a rule that goes against everything we've stood for for so long?"

Hyssop shook her head as her wife spoke. "We're powerless here. Without a rightful queen, our own magick will dwindle away to nothing. You know that."

"Then we return Mycel to the throne, where she belongs," Clove said simply.

"She'd lead us straight to ruin!"

Clove turned her back to her wife, obvious rage brewing within her at the accusations. I was impressed at her siding with me when we were only related by their marriage, but I had always known Clove's morals to be in line with mine. I hadn't, however, known about my aunt Hyssop's clear distaste for me. It almost seemed like something else was eating away at her. "Have some faith in her. She was young when the forest flooded; she did what she could with what she had."

Reed released my hands, and I could fill in the blanks of what the rest of the conversation had looked like without actually seeing my own flesh and blood disavow me so openly. "When will they turn me over? Is that why everyone is avoiding us? Is that why I haven't seen them?" I rubbed my face in frustration, consequently spreading dirt over my skin.

"Whenever the Ulmosi arrive," he replied, and I saw a glimmer of pain on his face. I could infer the answers to the rest of my questions.

"You're worried," I said as I studied him, then followed his gaze to somewhere deep in the darkness of the woods. "You're never worried." Part of me ached to reach out and comfort him even though it wasn't my place. It's hard when you've known someone for hundreds of years and the context of your relationship changes drastically from one encounter to another; if there was anything I'd learned about human relationships, it was that they thought physical comfort and affection was only for romantic relationships. But we weren't human, and I didn't want to reserve my kindness only for the person I was in love with, so I reached out and took one of Reed's hands in both of mine. I squeezed it a little, hoping to transfer some speck of strength through my touch.

"No, I'm just good at hiding it. Mycel, when they come… and they will come… if your aunts don't hand you over and submit, they'll wage war. Hyssop has convinced the whole of Yannava that submitting is safer for everyone and that it's worth the sacrifice of your group to protect the rest of us." Reed's voice was laced with concern, his eyebrows knitted together as he spoke. He looked at me again, then down to our hands, and offered me a small smile that I took as an indication of solidarity. "Even if that means our lives will be miserable, she thinks it's worth it just so we continue living."

We were silent for a moment. Still, I asked, "And you? What do you think?"

"Ya know I'm supposed to be impartial, doe."

"When have you ever been?"

Reed's sly smile was enough to give me a bit of hope. "You know what I think… Yannava is aching, in its heart, for a true leader. But convincing Hyssop and the rest of our people that you're the one to soothe that ache, it's a huge task… nearly impossible."

I sighed. "It wouldn't be the first I've tackled this year. I'll need you to back me, though."

"Already there," Reed said with a nod. Then he flexed an arm at me with a wink. "And I've got one more contact that might be able to help us in that department as well. I sent for her when I heard your group was returning to the forest."

I had been about to ask about his connection when another thought popped into my mind. "I know you get memories from other historians, but… can you transfer them from anyone else?"

CHAPTER TWENTY-FIVE
MYCEL

I was flanked by both Earwyn and Reed – much to Earwyn's dismay – when I approached the home of my aunts. Maz could sense the discomfort between the two men and shifted on my shoulder, peering at them through my hair as we walked.

Earwyn's glaring. Reed's smiling. Is this normal male behavior? His tone in my mind almost sounded like embarrassment, which was an emotion I'd never really identified in my familiar before. Thank goodness, too, because we both knew I had an affinity for embarrassing myself.

"Yes, it's normal." I rolled my eyes. Perhaps the frivolity of their rivalry was a welcome distraction from the conversation we were about to have. The distraction faded, though, as he got closer to the treehouse that my aunts had lived in for as long as I could remember. Even more disconcerting was the fact that the Yannavi people we passed on the way seemed to scatter; it was as if they knew that the impending conversation – or fight – between myself and my aunts was not something to get in the middle of. It was a fair assumption to make, and we'd told the rest of our party to hunker down in their accommodations to wait for further information. If all hell broke loose, they needed to be ready. Again, I feared for Neeri. So many young lives had been lost at my hands – and would continue to be lost if war broke out – that I was clinging tightly to the young lives I could hopefully protect.

Soon we approached a treehouse on the outskirts of the city. It was high up in a towering cedar tree and accessible only by a wooden bridge that led from the edge of the land over to the patio of the tree-house. I stood at the entrance of the bridge and tried to steady my breathing. The roof of the house was thatched and covered with decades of frosty green moss. From the windows, the yellowish light that shone radiated warmth and if I thought hard enough, I could recall a time that I had associated that building with comfort, too. When I had been a small child, just a little sapling in the woods, my aunts had practically raised me. I didn't remember much about life before them. My parents had died, and so, I'd become the charge of my aunts; Hyssop was my mother's sister, and she'd been married to Clove since "the beginning of time, basically" they'd always said. There wasn't much else to it. I'd never longed for my parents because Hyssop and Clove had filled that hole in my heart so easily. But I'd also never let myself long for them once I left because I felt that my betrayal of my people had made me unworthy of their love, a love that had sustained me for so long. Reed must've sensed my reverie because he put a hand on my shoulder and sent a reminder into my brain:

"Mycel, Hyssop, come eat, my darlings!" Aunt Clove called from the open front door of the treehouse.

Little me, no bigger than a human eight-year-old, ran across the bridge laughing. It was much sturdier looking then, and the slats made a satisfying clicking sound as my bare feet pounded across it. I had the front of my dress pulled up so that I could use it to carry berries, and Hyssop followed behind with her own containers of them: a variety of bright, delicious colors.

"Aunt Clove, we're gonna paint with berries after dinner!" I looked so proud. I remembered mashing berries between my fingers and smearing them everywhere in a magnificent display of my artistic skills. That was what my aunts had called it at least.

"Only if you don't eat them all first, little one!" Clove had teased me, pointing out the smears of reddish raspberry juice all over my face.

I looked up at her with such admiration, such love in my eyes, that I couldn't fathom ever growing apart from her. I laughed. She laughed. I wiped my face with the back of my hand and followed her inside, where she set out bowls of soup for us.

"Seems like only yesterday and centuries ago at the same time," I mused aloud before stepping onto the bridge, slipping from Reed's grasp. It trembled under my new increased weight, and I let out an unsteady breath. Maz looked through my hair again at the front door of the house; the dwelling was small, and there would be no surprising them with our arrival. They had to know we were coming.

Reed stayed behind, at the far end of the bridge, while Earwyn walked behind me. He was so close, in fact, that I could hear every breath, every clink of his sword against his hip. As much as I loved his protection and devotion, I was glad he'd agreed to let me go first; the last thing we needed was for an Ulmosi royal to confront my aunts in their home and try to somehow convince them we were on their side. Of all the terrors I'd faced in the previous months, from dinosaurs to blood-thirsty ocean kingdoms, none of them scared me quite as much as confronting my family. The feeling was amplified when I lifted a hand to knock on the door, and it swung open before my knuckles hit the wood.

"Nice of you to stop by, Mycel." Her thin, graceful neck was adorned with layers of necklaces. Hyssop had a commanding presence. The people of Yannava listened to her – which had always been a point of pride for her – whereas Clove prioritized listening to the people.

"Aunt Hyssop." I nodded, biting my tongue as my brain told me to call her the nickname I'd used for decades – Aunt Hissy. "Can we come in?"

"No, I don't think that's a good idea." When Hyssop spoke again, her voice was thunderous and echoed through the entire forest. "Don't you want to speak in front of your people?"

Trees shook, and leaves fell. The wooden slats of the bridge trembled. Earwyn grabbed the back of my arm as if to steady me from an impending earthquake, but none came; instead, it was Hyssop calling the attention of the whole of Yannava. I looked back at Reed, who seemed irritated but unsurprised by this decision. When I turned back to my aunt, I could already hear the muttering of the Yannavi people who were leaving their homes to congregate in the central gathering space of the city. "Fine. Where is Clove?" But my attempts to peer behind Hyssop were thwarted when she shut the door behind her and with a flick of her wrist, sent the bridge rolling so that it shoved us unceremoniously back toward Reed.

"Don't worry about her. Let's talk."

CHAPTER TWENTY-SIX

EARWYN

I hadn't been expecting to find myself flying backward across the bridge at the hands of my wife's aunt, so when Reed cushioned my fall with a tactfully placed pile of leaves, I lay in stunned silence for a moment. For magickal folk, that would've been child's play, but as I'd recently learned our child's play was a one-way ticket to murdering mortals. I sat up and groaned a little, the hardness of the forest floor, even with Reed's buffer, sending a jolt of pain through my sad human body. There were many reasons for me to wish for resolution in Yannava, but the most pressing at the moment was how pitiful being without magick made me feel… especially when it resulted in my wife's ex-lover helping me. I resigned to swallowing my pride from then on out.

"What are you doing?!" Mycel screamed. I looked up in time to see her racing back toward me with her aunt close behind her.

"I'm okay," I assured her, putting up a hand to ask her to slow her pace and stay calm. Reed was already reaching out to get me off the ground. I gave him a thankful nod that hopefully also said "I don't wanna hear a word about this."

He smirked.

Mycel was by my side in an instant, but her aunt was close behind her. "I'm just escorting you all out for our talk!" Her voice was cruel and sharp.

Soon we were backing our way into the center of the city, where the majority of Mycel's people were gathering; they'd either ventured out from their homes into the open or, if they lived nearby, were standing in their doorways watching. It was hard to say exactly what they'd been told by their temporary rulers. Despite my lack of resources, I put myself between Hyssop and Mycel, with Reed nearby if we needed him. I'd rather go down as a human than put my pregnant wife front and center. When we arrived in the clearing, I was shocked at the population for the forest civilization; many of them must have lived in carefully camouflaged homes because the amount of terrafolk gathered to watch didn't match the dwellings I thought I'd seen. Nevertheless, I looked them over and then returned my gaze to Hyssop, who seemed to be our primary danger at the moment. It was with great sadness that I realized both Mycel and myself had been cast out by our flesh and blood. We'd never do that to our own families, especially not the child we were fighting so hard to protect.

"Well, go on then, Mycel," Hyssop said. "Tell the people what you've been wanting to say. I'm sure they're eager to hear." It was clear then that she'd already filled their minds with her own opinions.

I reached behind me and grabbed Mycel's hand, then gave it a firm squeeze. "Stay strong." But when had she not?

CHAPTER TWENTY-SEVEN
MYCEL

"People of Yannava… um, my people," I began, a bit unsteady in my address to the group. After all, I hadn't expected to be speaking to an entire community right off the bat and had hoped that communing with my aunts first would've given me steadier footing. Nevertheless, I moved on, drawing strength from the feisty speech I'd given in the throne room of Ulmos not so long ago. If I could tell an entire room of royals to go fuck themselves, I could talk to people from my homeland about my earnest desire to serve them. "Yes, you are still my people, regardless of my title… because the spirit of our land runs through my veins like it does yours. In turn, it unites all of us."

Reed offered me a small smile.

I continued. "In the past, I made decisions that led us astray."

Hyssop let out a sound that clearly meant "no shit." I told myself to ignore her, but couldn't help wondering what the Ulmosi had promised her to turn so cruelly on one of her own.

I gritted my teeth when I spoke again. "Despite the horrific outcomes of those decisions, however, I assure you they were made with your best interest in mind. I stand before you today to ask for another chance as your leader." I turned in my spot so that I could take time to look at each and every terrafolk who was watching me. It was hard to meet their judging gazes, even those of the youngest Yannavi. My chest burned with fear, rage, and likely the heartburn of third-trimester pregnancy, an experience I hadn't yet found the joy in. "Though I've spent time away from our home, not a moment has gone by where I haven't thought of it, thought of bettering myself to return, and thought of all of you. I've spent months searching for allies in this fight against Ulmos, a people who you know live in direct conflict with our own way of life; they are violent, materialistic, and self-centered. They want nothing but destruction. I know our people, though, and know that above all else, we value community and growth. It's not in our nature to demolish. It may be easiest to relent, to submit, to give in, but that is also not like us. And I know that with our allies by our side, we can win this fight. In doing so we would be limiting further harm to not only the humans, but other terrafolk. I think that's worth fighting for." I swallowed hard and steadied myself as I delivered my next vow. "Either way, win or lose, I promise to lay my own life on the line in pursuit of that end goal."

"Why should they believe you?" Hyssop asked, unsurprisingly. I wished she knew how to shut up. The people of Yannava were smart enough to gather information and make their own decisions. Could they see her blatant infantilization of their entire community? "You've brought the Prince of Ulmos directly to us, and you expect our people to believe that you know what's best?"

The crowd gasped, their gaze shifting to Earwyn, who kept his expression neutral.

I gave Earwyn a sympathetic glance before I spoke again, knowing that I was about to stir up old aches from the past. "Despite your attempt at delivering a shock to the group, everyone here knows that

Earwyn of Ulmos has been labeled a traitor to their kingdom; he's not with them. If he was, I don't think he would have walked into Yannava, without magick, and married to me." I held up my hand, wedding ring in full view. "His wish has been to join us in the fight against the horrors Ulmos wishes to wage on the human world. He's not like them. He's like us… at least the 'us' I remember. What more proof do you need?" I felt more separate from my people than I ever had before. Despite being surrounded by a handful of loved ones, those that had my back no matter what, I felt isolated. Even if we could convince the Yannavi to side with me again, would it be despite their reservation? Despite their resentment? Would they look at me through a cloud of anger? At this point in the game, it was difficult to say.

I looked around in questioning, still shocked at the number of people who refused to meet my gaze or worse, stood in silent judgment with their arms folded across their chests. Had they been threatened, or did they truly not find it possible for me to be committed to protecting them? I found Nora and Owen standing stoically in the group, their heads held high as our eyes met; they gave me a nod of support. Thatcher stood alongside Zahir, who had a firm grip on Neeri's shoulder. Zara and Rhodes, ever confident in my decision making and abilities, showed no sign of doubt. Even Genny, cuddled in Zara's arms, was intently watching the situation unfold; she knew firsthand the horrors that her people had put Earwyn through. If only she could talk to the group; she'd be able to tell them just what happened behind closed doors in Ulmos. I had to assume that those who would not face me did so out of fear for their own safety, not disbelief or rejection. But still, it felt like a losing battle.

"Who else will vouch for you, Mycel, when our last memories of you were the image of you fleeing and leaving nothing but destruction in your wake?" Hyssop argued, looking smug in her decisiveness. Those around her didn't seem quite so malicious and instead, looked fearful, concerned, and unsure of what to believe. I couldn't blame them; what ideas had Hyssop planted in their minds during my leave? And how many people needed to vouch for me before I was allowed to fight for my redemption? Why did I have to beg to lay my life on the line?

Maz chittered in my ear. *How many people does she want to vouch for you? You have folk from four different nations!* He was silent for a second. *Look, up there!*

I followed his gaze to the balcony my aunts' home, where I saw Clove bound, her mouth covered. She strained against her bonds and looked as though she needed to speak, to have some part in this conversation, but it was useless. At least I knew she was relatively safe, and part of me admired the fact that she'd fought hard enough that her wife felt the need to tie her up.

My stomach turned at Hyssop's accusation: one we all knew to be true, but that didn't make it any less painful to hear recounted. One of the pitfalls of being nearly immortal was that you had a very, very long life during which to be reminded of your mistakes; the people reminding you are also alive for a very long time, so you can't even hope that they'll die and drop it. At least humans only had to live with the shame of their mistakes for like, eighty or ninety years.

"Memories…" I said through a deep breath. They needed proof, something beyond just my words to indicate that I was serious. Even the rest of my group could fabricate an argument, but they couldn't modify the past. I looked at Reed, who seemed prepared for my statement, "They need to know I'm telling the truth."

He nodded and held out a hand to both myself and my aunt, who eyed it with suspicion in her gaze. We'd spent the entire night practicing this after we'd finished our conversation in the woods; it had worked with Earwyn, at least, and I hoped we could replicate it. Somewhere in our late-night practice, despite our shared exhaustion, the men had grown to understand each other more; it seemed they had the same shared goal, and that was enough to stifle at least some of their competitiveness. Reed had been particularly impressive in the level of effort he put into our pursuits, especially considering I had asked him to try something no other historian had ever done. The night had been sleepless for the most part, with me taking occasional breaks due to my exacerbated fatigue, and the men continuing to practice even without me. I was surprised and relieved to find that they didn't use the activity to taunt each other with memories of their time with me, though I hoped there would be plenty of time for teasing and jokes in the future. By the end of the night, both of them looked drained, especially Reed who had channeled every ounce of memory magick he could muster in order to develop an experience that would hopefully serve us well in convincing everyone else.

"What are you doing?" she asked with a sneer, eying Reed's hand as if it were part of some obvious trap.

"Showing you what has happened since I left," I said plainly, steadying myself to dig through memories that I knew would be painful at best. "I'm an open book; I'll show you anything you want. If you want proof that I will be a deceitful leader, that I have plans to ruin the land and people that I love, here is where you would find it. There's no way for me to modify my memories."

Hyssop hesitated, then took one of Reed's hands, seemingly only relenting because she didn't have to touch me directly. Was it disgust, I wondered, or the fear of dropping her facade of carelessness that kept her at arm's length? Nevertheless, I took Reed's other hand and with a deep breath, closed my eyes. The forest went quiet despite the density of our observers, and I let Reed, and consequently Hyssop, into my mind. The only thing keeping me centered was my husband behind me and my child happily rolling inside of me. Together, their presence said "show them." The resulting share of memories came by like a stream of consciousness, with important clips projecting from me, through Reed, and to everyone who was linked between us:

The projector inside my mind brought our entire audience into my apartment's bedroom, where I was stark naked and Earwyn and I were talking after we'd broken down some serious walls with each other. It felt so intimate, so private, that I almost resisted sharing it, but the people needed to see these vulnerable moments of truth.

"I can't fully understand why they are set on destroying everything we have with the humans, but it's clear it's been in the works for a long time… longer than I've been alive… I think it's my relationship with them that has the Ulmosi set on their plan, though." Earwyn lay in my bed still, a thickly muscled arm behind his head as he watched me pace around the room.

"You really don't feel like you're one of them," I murmured, noting how he referred to his people as a group that didn't seem to include him.

His gaze followed me, but he seemed elsewhere mentally, at least for that moment. "No… I mean, I suppose I understand it all to an extent; the humans have abused the ocean since the beginning of time. They're destroying it. Little conservation efforts aren't enough to make a difference. The only real way to heal the ocean is to—"

"Get rid of humans altogether," I interjected, not shocked by that conclusion but not pleased with it either. I crawled back into the bed next to him, feeling cold and empty at the thought of destroying an entire race of beings.

"Precisely… and this partnership is the perfect way to lull the humans into thinking they're in with the Ulmosi before using their position to leverage the situation. I can't fathom what that will actually look like when the time comes, but it won't be pretty."

"But you don't want to follow through with their plan," I tested out, trying to make sense of the situation.

My brain shuffled through memory after memory until I was standing in the Ulmosi throne room, gills still raw, having swam deep into the ocean to save my husband.

I pulled out the weapon I'd only realized I'd had moments before. Why had my body been rebelling against me? Why hadn't I bled in months? The chaos of my time with Earwyn had been so distracting that I didn't realize I'd believed us to be biologically incompatible until that moment, when I felt the flutter of life in my womb. "Because I'm carrying the heir to your throne."

The court gasped.

Then we were in Aolan, where I fiercely argued my case again in front of Tana and Ossian.

"Then tell us what happened," Tana suggested with a shrug, then turned to walk back toward her husband. "Clear the air if you're so certain we shouldn't be judging you."

"No. I don't owe you – or anyone – that information. All you need to know is that now I am willing to sacrifice everything for them and for this child, who is the rightful heir to whatever is left of Yannava and Ulmos when all is said and done. They deserve a world where we can coexist with the humans – and each other – peacefully. Wouldn't you want that for any child of yours?"

I was deep in the trenches of my own mind, trying to tactfully guide these onlookers who now felt like strangers through memories that seemed relevant to our cause when I felt a small hand on my shoulder. Reed's reinforcement arrived just in the nick of time, and boy, was it a relief to see another familiar face. My eyes flickered up to find Elan before me once again, her hair as bright and wild as I recalled, her glasses perched precariously on her nose. I wondered for a moment if she actually needed those glasses to see; they weren't a tool in the terrafolk world, but they certainly fit the image of a human therapist. She looked out of place there, in the forest, with her human clothing; it seemed she was more human than anyone there, except for Zara, due to how much time she'd spent away from our world. Yet, in the depth of her soulful gaze, I saw reflected the wisdom and connection of a Yannavi elder.

"I might be breaking doctor-patient confidentiality here, but I think they deserve to see this, don't you?" Elan asked calmly, a twinkle in her eye.

I gave her a wordless nod of consent and hoped that the others would be able to glean a crumb of context from the memories, considering that therapy was a human activity and not something terrafolk would have experience with:

We plunged into memory again, soaring deep into one that I felt I had long forgotten. To be living in Seattle as a human – so human that I was attending therapy – felt like it was a million years ago. But at the same time, Dr. Eline Jansen's office was as familiar as ever.

"I was in a position of power, but I failed. I felt powerless, unable to protect or guide them, so I left. I turned Yannava over to my stewardesses, and I left them… and now I really am powerless, Doctor. I have nothing. No magick, no connections, nothing."

"What happens after you get him back, Michelle? Will you return home?"

"If I get him back…" I pondered aloud, "and I return alive, I'll have to. I've left too much unfinished." And then I told Dr. Jansen something I only realized as I was saying it. "I don't know the extent of it, but my visit back home made clear that Yannava is in danger. They're being controlled by threats… making decisions that are very unlike them, unlike us, as a people."

"And yet you feel powerless…"

"I am powerless. If I go back, all I'll have to work with are my words. Hell, the last time I tried to return, they made it clear I'm no longer welcome."

"I don't think you're looking at this clearly, Michelle," Dr. Jansen commented, narrowing her eyes as she leaned forward to look at me closely. I must have looked confused because she continued speaking. "You may feel powerless… you may not have the magick that you think defines you, but prior to you being powerless, you would have never considered going back to help your people. You know that it's going to be a fight for them to let you in and yet... you're willing to return, now, with fewer resources than ever, to help them. I don't think that could ever be called powerless. I think it's stepping into your power. It sounds like you're fulfilling your destiny."

Somehow, I didn't think we were still talking in metaphors. Dr. Jansen continued, looking at me seriously as she did so. "When you return," she said with such certainty that I knew my return was inevitable, "tell them I sent you."

When the memory ended and we were all pulled back to reality again, we stood in silence. I couldn't bring myself to look at the people of my town, the people who'd known me since I was a little sprout, but instead kept my gaze set on my aunt. She looked unfazed. Unimpressed. Unwavering in her relentless judgment and rejection of my return. Before I could speak, Reed did.

"You don't want to believe her," Reed said with a grunt of indignation, eyeing Hyssop as we withdrew from Elan's memory and back to the forest. "No matter what she shows you, no matter how hard she fights, you'll keep the people trapped in these lies. I can't help you with that anymore. I had hoped that with enough show of her faith and willpower, you'd let her through, but you've proven otherwise. You don't want what's best for Yannava. Only she does."

I looked at Reed in confusion, unsure of what he was suggesting, but knowing that as the keeper of our culture's memories he had access to a lot more information than I did. Much of that information, until now, had seemed to be none of my damn business.

But still, he continued. "I don't care what the repercussions are, Hyssop. The people deserve to know the truth, and they deserve the leader they were meant to have." Before I could ask what he was talking about, Reed shook Hyssop's hand free and grabbed that of another Yannavi, closing the loop of our people with Hyssop standing outside it. Then, he showed us all a memory of his that I'd never heard of or seen before by almost everyone there.

I recognized the forest in our minds, but I would recognize Yannava anywhere. It was spring; plants were blooming, birds were chirping, and the fresh air was just beginning to tease at the idea of warmth. In a clearing much like the one that Reed and I had often gathered, the ground was bursting with an array of flowering buds of pink and white. I could almost smell them.

And there, in the midst of the clearing, near a long-fallen tree, was a massive bolete mushroom the size of a car tire. Its cap shimmered in the midday light of the clearing, dewdrops gathering atop it and causing it to all but sparkle. I couldn't see much beyond that, but soon the soft coos and burbles of a very young child filled the air along with the chirping of birds and rustling of frogs. Another person entered our sight and knelt near the giant mushroom.

"What do we have here?" a soothing, familiar voice asked. She reached beneath the mushroom, toward the sound, and withdrew the source: a small, red-haired baby who was naked aside from a generous layer of dirt. She had forest-green eyes that sparkled in the daylight and let out a small giggle as she looked up at the person holding her: Clove. The baby gripped her finger, an earthworm slipping from her grasp as she did so, and laughed again.

When Reed released us, I found myself breathless and confused. In turn, the look in his eyes was soft and loving, as if he'd felt the sacrifice to be worth it. I wondered what Hyssop had threatened him with for his silence, and I swore to myself that he would face no harm for what he'd done. In fact, I owed him my gratitude. I could piece together enough to guess what all of this meant: my parents hadn't died when I was younger. I was born from the earth, and there was something very important about that.

I turned to look at my husband, who was already staring at me in wide-eyed wonder. What was there to say, though?

"You're the daughter of the forest," came a voice I'd been longing to hear since my arrival, the voice from the memory. I whirled and came face-to-face with Clove, who gave an appreciative nod to Thatcher and Zahir; they'd left the group in search of her once I'd made clear that someone was missing. Maz had left my side after spotting her in the distance and had undoubtedly guided the two men straight to my imprisoned aunt. She looked at Hyssop, who seemed appalled at her blatant rejection of her ideas, tossed the thin green rope that had been binding her onto the forest floor, and then looked back to me once more. I hoped that no one aside from her wife had to see Clove's fury after things were all said and done. Oh, how I'd missed the sight of my other aunt, who radiated warmth, understanding, and equanimity. I knew now why she had fought so hard for me when her wife had preferred the easy and certain way; she had faith in me that others could not imagine. I couldn't help but smile through my bleary gaze at her, and it took everything in me not to fall into her arms as if I were a child again. Perhaps that was why we had always felt so close; how could I feel anything but attached to the person who had nurtured me from a bud? "There's no doubting that. I pulled you from the ground myself, covered in dirt and worms and thinking every living creature was your friend. You may have stumbled along the way, but Yannava knows its rightful leader because that's what you are to us: a leader, not a ruler."

Elan spoke again, looking between Clove and myself as if we were in family counseling. In a way, the whole group was, weren't we? We were one huge family trying to move forward despite adversity. "When I said this was your destiny, Mycel, I meant it. It's no accident that you have returned to take your rightful place with your people, nor is it a coincidence that you're carrying the heir to two terrafolk thrones; it's never happened before. You have the power, the ability, to change the course of the future and steer both of our kingdoms in the right direction."

Earwyn grabbed my hand from behind me and gave it a squeeze. He didn't let go as I turned to face my people, still wanting more than anything to prove myself but now feeling like I could, "Folk of Yannava – my people. Now is the time for reclamation, for redemption, and for resolution. Will you fight by my side?"

The resounding roar of agreement was deafening.

CHAPTER TWENTY-EIGHT

EARWYN

With the people of Yannava reunited with their true leader, I felt both a weight lifted from our shoulders and also the buzzing anxiety of the impending fight. On one hand, it was a relief to know that we actually had a chance to defend what we believed in, to protect those who deserved it, and to maybe live our lives the way we hoped. On the other, it was war… and that war would likely put me face-to-face with what I'd spent so much time running from.

When Mycel excused herself to spend a bit of time with her aunts – one of whom I was unsure of her view of – I took the chance to learn more about the weaponry we had at our disposal; I was still without magick and would likely have to rely on armor and other tools to make me an effective addition to our team. I took Zahir with me.

The armory of Yannava was better equipped than I had envisioned, and the variety of weaponry along with its discreet location gave me some hope in the coming fight. Now all that mattered was ensuring everyone could use the weapons they were given. That seemed a different story. In the early morning dark of the forest, I found myself pursuing the blades of my wife's people; they were intricate, sure, but functional. Unlike Ulmos, it seemed that their beauty came second to their practicality, but neither were skimped on. My people would've equipped their security and soldiers with clunky, heavy armor and weaponry to save the real craftsmanship for the upper class while Yannava clearly valued the safety and comfort of those protecting its borders. Even though all terrafolk – with the exception of us unique banished individuals – had magick of varying degrees of power, weaponry gave them all an additional edge. After all, it could be tricky to summon a wave to knock someone out on short notice.

I ran my finger over the blade of a particularly impressive sword and winced when it cut me, quickly being reminded that I might be fighting as a mortal. It was a heavy thought to carry and in a battlefield of mostly terrafolk, it would be a difficult fight to last in. I could stab and cut and slice and tackle with little impact but the same would have me dead in a heartbeat. Then what? There was no glory in hiding, but was there glory to be found in a five-minute fight? I was snapped from my blood-streaked daydream when the entryway to the armory – an impenetrable wall of vines and roots that undid themselves only for select individuals – unwound to allow Zahir to join me.

My forced smile must've betrayed me because Zahir looked dubious. "That confident in our fighting abilities, huh?" Before I could even reply, he continued in frantic, Zahir fashion, "Yeah, I'm having doubts too, you know, I'm not sure if I can do this, Earwyn, and—"

I felt his panic seep into my bones and my heart immediately began to race. "Hey, hey, hey, you don't have to—"

"No, look, I want to, I want to, I just…"

"You want to fight."

Zahir took a deep breath, but his voice was still bubbling over with untamable energy. It seemed that he might burst into flames at any moment. "Yeah, I do. I need to."

"Then you'll fight," I told him, placing a firm hand on the young man's shoulder. "It's that simple. Don't get into your own head. You'll fight for Neeri; you'll fight for redemption."

He set his jaw firmly, not daring to look away from my gaze. Out of the corner of my eye, however, I could see him flexing his hands; the look in his eyes betrayed his confident stance and I could see that he was stifling a wince of pain.

"Is it bad today?" I wasn't sure how else to ask.

Zahir looked down at his hands. "Did Mycel tell you?"

"No," I told him. "Mycel wouldn't tell me anything she thought you wanted to keep to yourself. But children, on the other hand, don't have the same filters." I offered him a sympathetic smile, not wanting him to feel like he owed me an explanation.

"That sounds right," Zahir chuckled a little at the mention of his daughter's oversharing. "She's an open book… and I never want her to feel like she needs to keep secrets. It's not like I'm ashamed."

"I wouldn't think so. Bodies work differently. Sometimes we need to adjust to accommodate their eccentricities." I thought about the young Alaskan girl whom Mycel had filled me in on. She'd told me about her passion and playfulness, her adept skill with magick, but also her recovery time; this was different, she'd felt the need to tell me because I would be responsible for helping her if I was nearby during the fight. It wasn't my information to share, but I hoped that Zahir knew he wasn't alone.

Zahir gave me a half smile and nod of understanding. When he looked at his hands again, flexing them impatiently, he answered my question, "But yeah, it's bad today, but I… I can do it. I've dealt with this for decades now. Today isn't any different."

I raised an eyebrow and held out a sword to him, the one that had left its mark on my fingertip. If I hadn't been so attached to my Aolani blade for making a dinosaur extinct again, I likely would've chosen a piece from Yannava. Last on the list would've been Ulmosi weaponry, which looked good at the expense of their efficiency and ease of handling. "Hold this. Let's see what it's looking like." We both knew that armor and weaponry would be necessary during the fight; if the Ulmosi were set on extinguishing his flames, he would need alternate ways to protect himself and those around him. Yannava's armor and weaponry were among the lightest I'd encountered, but they were still made of hefty material that would require strength to wield.

Zahir gripped the hilt of the sword and tested out the weight in his hand. He rotated it, getting his hand familiar with the feel of it. Swords were heavy, no doubt, and wielding one with agonizing joint pain was not something I could imagine. He had only been holding it for a few seconds when his fingers flexed against the leather wrapping and he let out a hiss of pain in response, then dropped the sword to the ground. "It doesn't matter," he said in frustration. "You can't reschedule a war for a flare up, Earwyn. This is happening."

"Sure. But that doesn't mean you have to push through pain to make it happen. There are ways to make it work for you, so you can focus on the task at hand." When I returned to our space in the armory, I carried leather straps that I'd found being used to assemble shields. There were plenty. Zahir eyed me curiously as I picked the fallen sword up off the ground, then pressed the hilt against his forearm, where I strapped it to him with the leather belts. "How is that? Show me how it moves."

When he looked a little unsure of what to do with it, I picked up my own sword. "Like this," I instructed, giving a little stab and chop at the air. I felt silly – what did I know about war? About killing people? I only knew what I'd been taught in private lessons since I was a child… I understood how to fight in theory, against trainers and siblings and inanimate objects, but lacked the practical knowledge as much as this young man did.

As if he could read my mind, Zahir said, "You're good."

I scoffed at his attempt at flattery. "Go on then, kid. Show me what you've got."

Zahir tried, relying on his feet to do most of the movement for him, but the strap and being unable to use his fingers limited him greatly. I could tell it was discouraging when he stopped to shove his dark hair out of his face in frustration and let the tip of the blade rest on the ground of the armory.

"Don't give up," I assured him, sheathing my sword before I reached out to unstrap the sword from his arm. "Maybe this just isn't the right weapon." I could see him preparing to argue again, so I put up a hand to silence him. "Let me try one more, okay? Then you can give up if I get it wrong."

Zahir watched me in silence as I surveyed the armory, looking over the selection of long and short blades, maces, bows, and other weapons that must have been so unique to Yannava that I'd never seen or heard of them before. Then, I found it. It was almost as if the air in the room shifted to guide me to it and a small ray of light shone just right to make it shimmer.

"An ax?"

"Can you imagine?" I asked, nearly breathless at the wonder of the weapon. I pulled it from its spot on the wall. "You don't even have to grip it, you can just..." I imitated a shallow swinging motion with the ax. "...swing."

And that was how Zahir got his ax.

CHAPTER TWENTY-NINE

MYCEL

When I took the throne of Yannava, winter had taken its frosty grip on the forest. Still, we celebrated despite the cold, despite me being heavily pregnant, and despite the impending war because Yannava deserved some joy, as did all of our group. Very few little Yannavi could recall the last time our community had a living ruler, let alone a formal coronation ceremony. We relied on Reed's memories to determine what the process was supposed to look like and how one actually took the throne in Yannava; most of us didn't even know what it looked like. We went to the clearing of what had always been referred to as "the throne room," though there were no visible thrones to be seen and stood in silence, the rest of the Yannavi waiting for us back at the center of the city. I thought it silly to have everyone trekking through the woods if we didn't know where we were good.

Again, Earwyn and Reed were behind me. Clove and Elan had joined as well. Because I had been given a second chance, I gave Hyssop the same kindness; she could join us in fighting for what was right, or she could leave Yannava for good. Until she decided, she remained in her home, guarded by several Yannavi soldiers. With Maz on my shoulder and Zara by my side, I felt like my own little family was finally in one place and safe, at least for the time being. The others, who had traveled so far just to back me, waited with the rest of my people, who had welcomed them with open arms once they were allowed. I couldn't have been more grateful.

There was little in the air of the clearing aside from the fog of our breath, but then it was as if a veil had been lifted and my prize was presented to me. The throne itself was simple: a stump in the ground. "That's it," I said, barely above a whisper.

"Sprout… that's a log. I know you all are forest people, but the throne of your queen has to be something a little cooler than that," Zara chimed in, clearly not concerned with offending a society with traditions as old as the earth itself. She had a point.

I couldn't help but laugh. Reed was sent to fetch the rest of the city. When our people joined us, I took a leap of faith and seated myself on the stump. The earth extended its gnarled roots that interlaced into the arms and back of an elegant seat. Each bit of bark and twig fastened to another. I looked up, just in time to see the branches of a mighty tree lean down and weave themselves into a crown. The snap of the crown separating from its maker echoed through the forest as the headpiece landed on my head. There was silence again, and then I stood, crowned as the new leader of Yannava: the rightful leader.

My people erupted in applause and cheers, and I felt a cloud lift from the forest town, despite what was yet to come for us. I looked out amongst them and saw the bright smiles of my husband, my friends, and those who had believed in me from the start. My child rolled happily inside of me, as if to show his own applause. It was time to celebrate. If these were our last moments as free people, we would let them be moments of joy.

Thanks to Zahir, we were able to warm ourselves by little hovering fires he'd placed along the lengthy dining table in our forest. The table was lined with a bounty of food that our people had foraged or hunted. This included a whole deer, the non-meat remains of which would be used for tools and clothing after we ate, as well as bread made from acorn flour; cranberry jam from wild cranberries; chanterelle, turkey tail, and oyster mushrooms; and a stunning array of nuts and seeds. To top it all off, Reed shared conifer-infused vodka, birch wine, and rosehip whiskey, all of which he'd concocted himself. The table was brimming with food, a sign of warmth, community, and abundance that I hoped would continue for Yannava.

We ate, drank, laughed, and sang. We danced. I danced with Earwyn, even though my feet ached, and then I danced with Zara, giggling until late in the night.

Evren Firth, prince of the forest and sea, was born the next day.

As he let his first fierce cry out into the biting cold air, the forest began to flood.

We braced ourselves for battle.

COMING NEXT

Will the fight for mankind be fruitful or foundering? Find out in Woman King, the final installment in the Terrafolk Trilogy.

ABOUT THE AUTHOR

Francesca Crispo is a fantasy romance author living near Seattle, WA. She received her B.A. in English Literature from Arizona State University in 2016 and her M.Ed. from Arizona State University in 2018. When she isn't writing or running a business full-time, she enjoys spending time with her family and dogs!

facebook.com/francesca.crispo.author
instagram.com/francesca.crispo.author
tiktok.com/@francesca.crispo.author

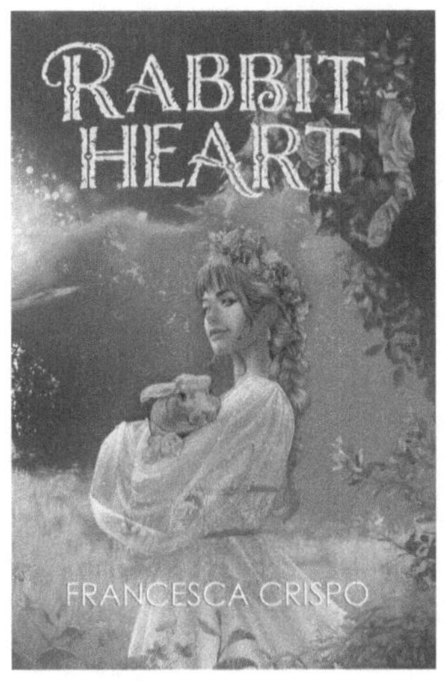

Rabbit Heart: Book 1 of the Terrafolk Trilogy

Beholden - Coming Soon!

www.ingramcontent.com/pod-product-compliance
Lightning Source LLC
Chambersburg PA
CBHW061242310726
48971CB00007B/2175